I WON'T BE HOME FOR CHRISTMAS

by

Amanda Prowse

Magna Large Print Books
Long Preston, North Yorkshire,
BD23 4ND, England.

British Library Cataloguing in Publication Data.

A catalogue record of this book is
available from the British Library

ISBN   978-0-7505-4528-0

First published in Great Britain in 2016 by Head of Zeus Ltd.

Copyright © Amanda Prowse, 2016

Cover illustration © OJO Images by arrangement with
iStock by Getty Images

The moral right of Amanda Prowse to be identified as the author of
this work has been asserted in accordance with the Copyright,
Designs and Patents Act, 1988

Published in Large Print 2017 by arrangement with
Head of Zeus

Magna Large Print is an imprint of Library Magna Books Ltd.

Printed and bound in Great Britain by
T.J. (International) Ltd., Cornwall, PL28 8RW

This book is for Jennifer Haggerty and Anne Ward, who became Jennifer Lee and Anne Smith.

Through thick and thin, and through the highs and lows – and God only knows, there have been a few! Nearly seven decades on and still laughing inappropriately.

Best friends then. Best friends now. Best friends forever. X

Prologue

As the breeze took the last of the heat out of the long, hot, July day, the two friends made their way up the steep grassy bank and slumped down on the slope of hard-baked ground that flanked the River Malago in the heart of Bedminster, Bristol. There they lay, side by side in their sleeveless floral shifts, catching their breath with their arms raised above their heads. Their white ankle socks and tan leather T-bar school sandals sat neatly alongside each other in the grass, removed so they could wade in the shallow water. Slipping off the flat rocks, they'd watched the sediment rise between their toes, then tried to cradle sticklebacks in their palms, but the fish had darted away. With neither jar nor net, the girls hadn't quite figured out what they would do if they did manage to catch one, not that this spoilt their trying, not a bit.

The sun-scorched skin of their shoulders stung as they moved. Their pale flesh, usually cloistered under cardigans, was unused to this exposure, but as her nan always said, 'The quicker you get through the burn, the sooner your skin'll be ready for summer.'

'I'd better be getting back soon, Elle. My mum'll have my tea on and it's a good few minutes' walk back to Mendip Road from here.'

'Yeah, mine too.'

Vivienne ignored her friend's fib. She had heard

9

her own mother talking and knew enough to figure out that Ellen's mum would more than likely be sloshed and dancing round the kitchen, and then it wouldn't be long before the laughter turned to tears and she'd slide down onto the lino and sit slumped in the corner. And there she would stay until one of the older kids gently guided her upstairs, where she would fall asleep, face down, in her clothes. She didn't like to think of her friend living in a house like that.

'Come to mine if you like?' Vivienne knew her mum would give her friend the warmest of welcomes. Everybody loved Ellen.

'No, you're all right. Reckon we might have egg and chips tonight.'

Vivienne watched her friend's mouth twitch at the prospect and it made her feel a bit sad. The girls loved each other, proper love, which meant that so long as they were side by side, all was right in their world. And that world was tiny: it consisted of school, this scrubby stretch of grass in the St John's Burial Ground, and their respective homes, which were a mere hop, skip and a jump from each other but just a little too far to be connected by tin-can phones on string. They knew this because they had tried.

It was 1971 and the eight-year-old girls were the very best of friends and had been ever since fate had sat them next to each other on their first day of school. Well, fate and an alphabetical system that saw them placed between John Payne and Lindsey Rathbone in the classroom and also on the register, where *Vivienne Peebles* hovered on the line above *Ellen Pinder.*

They were a comical pairing. Ellen was meaty, with a broad, flattened nose, eyes that were wide and hooded, and fingers that were square and masculine. Even her hair was thick and coarse, with a uniform kink to every strand. Vivienne was the opposite: slight and shorter, with fine hair, pale skin and narrow wrists.

They flopped back on the grass, breathing deeply and watching the clear blue sky overhead.

Ellen turned on her side, shook her short bobbed hairdo and propped her large head on her wide palm. 'I *have* to tell you what happened to me today, but you must not tell a single living soul, ever.'

Vivienne mirrored her friend's posture. 'Cross my heart.' She drew an X over her chest with her index finger. Her eyes were wide at the prospect of what Ellen might reveal. She'd learnt about so many things from her wise friend. Periods, illegitimacy, the music of the Jackson Five, and syphilis were just a few of the topics that she'd been enlightened on in the last few years. Ellen had explained that this was the benefit of having older siblings. They knew stuff.

Sometimes, as thunder cracked over Bristol and darkness cloaked the city, Vivienne would stare at the thick curtains of the box room where she slept and think about the tantalising information that her friend had shared. She felt waves of guilt and fascination for these snippets of wickedness, certain that neither her mum nor her grandma could know about such things. And the idea of mentioning them to either, oh my good Lord, she would die of shame!

Ellen tried her best to whisper, but for her this was a near impossible task. Her voice had a natural booming resonance that meant Vivienne always heard her before she saw her.

'It was just after break time and I was minding my own business and David Batchwood told me to look under the desk.'

'What did he do that for?' Vivienne was impatient.

'Well, I didn't know what for until I looked, did I?' Ellen tutted at her friend's stupidity.

'What did you see?'

Ellen sat up and looked left and right, scanning the riverbank, confirming what she already knew, that no one was within earshot, and making the most of the added suspense.

'I saw his thing!'

'His thing?' Vivienne also sat up at this revelation, her nose wrinkled in confusion.

'Yes, Vivienne Peebles, his dingle-dangle.' Ellen nodded her head, eyebrows raised, mouth fixed, her finger pointing downwards. 'He had it poking through the buttons of his shorts!'

'He never did!' Vivienne gasped, horrified and intrigued in equal measure.

'I swear on the Holy Bible he did!'

Vivienne placed her hand over her mouth, fighting the desire to laugh, scream and ask questions. But the temptation was too strong. 'What did it look like?' she whispered, scooting closer to her friend.

Ellen gave a little shudder and rubbed at her arms. 'Well, I only took a quick look. Naturally.'

'Naturally.' Vivienne nodded, chewing her bottom lip with nerves.

'As I said, it was only a glance.'

'Of course.' Vivienne understood. Completely. Just a glance.

'But it was kind of...' Ellen cocked her head to one side, moved her fingers in the air and considered how best to phrase it.

'Kind of what?' Vivienne prompted, hanging on her friend's every word, torn between wanting facts about this part of the male anatomy, the idea of which both fascinated and repelled her, and wishing she didn't have to listen.

Ellen flicked her head as though tossing the long, luscious locks she craved. 'It was like a snail,' she said, before falling back on the ground, covering her face and laughing loudly.

'A snail?' Vivienne repeated, confused and crestfallen. This was not what she'd expected. Not in the least.

Ellen nodded. 'Uh huh.'

'What, like a curly little shell?' She tried to picture it and failed.

'No, you idiot!' Ellen boomed. She laughed loudly until she wheezed. 'Not a curly little shell! Like a snail that's poking *out* of the curly little shell!'

'Oh! Oh, I see!' This made more sense. 'Yuk!' Vivienne joined her friend flat on the ground, both of them giggling hysterically.

'Yes, yuk! And I ain't never going to go near one of those. Oh my days.' Ellen gave a shiver of disgust as she borrowed one of her mum's favourite expressions.

'Me either,' Vivienne added for good measure,

13

picturing the slimy little mollusc with its tiny tentacles waving blindly in the air.

'I tell you this for nothing...' Ellen giggled. 'Ain't nothing as funny as a willy, Viv. I'm absolutely sure of that.'

Vivienne nodded in agreement. It sure sounded that way.

Both girls were silent, each picturing why and how such a thing could ever be considered attractive or desirable, before looking at each other and collapsing again into another fit of giggles.

After a couple of minutes they managed to contain themselves. They sat upright, restored their hair and tried to think sobering thoughts that might calm their hysteria. They were doing quite well until an innocent lad on a Raleigh Chopper cycled by on the path towards town. Both girls collapsed once again, laughing until their tears came. The poor boy sped up, red faced, wondering what on earth could be *that* funny.

One

As the boiler knocked loudly, doing its very best to pump heat into the chilly November morning, and the frost lingered on the inside of the single-glazed kitchen window, Vivienne rinsed her cup under the tap, preparing for her second cup of tea of the day. She'd already been for a quick march around the block and was dressed in her straight-leg jeans, walking boots and the blue micro fleece that she wore to death.

'Don't look at me like that. You've had your breakfast and you heard what the vet said: you need to lose weight.'

Bob stared at her, unblinking, his gaze occasionally wandering to the biscuits that sat on a little plate next to the kettle.

'I've told you, it's no use looking at me like that. It's for your own good.' She poured hot water onto the tea bag and did her best to ignore him. Which was relatively easy, until he started whining mournfully.

As ever, she felt her resolve weakening. As she snapped a digestive biscuit and lifted a crumbly shard to her mouth, his pleading eyes were more than she could bear. 'Oh, go on then.'

She threw the nibbled edge into the air. Quicker than you could shout 'Fetch!' the collie-cross sprang up and angled his head just so. It always amazed her how Bob, who was now in his middling years, could move with the agility and energy of a puppy whenever he was in sniffing distance of a treat. It was a trick she wished she could master.

The biscuit fragment landed in his open mouth. Vivienne laughed as he slunk back to his soft, sheepskin-lined bed in the corner and gave her a look of pure adoration. He ate his snack then placed his pretty head on his extended paws and closed his eyes, as if the exertion of biscuit catching had quite taken it out of him and another nap was required.

'I don't know, you live the life of a king. You've got me wrapped around your finger, or should that be paw?' She smiled at the dog she loved, then looked up at the sound of the letterbox snapping into place. 'That'll be the postman.'

She did this, gave a running commentary on her day, for whose benefit she wasn't sure – Bob certainly paid no attention. Maybe it was simply for the joy of talking, of filling the Victorian bay-fronted terrace with noise, trying to line the rooms that had once echoed with her daughter's music, her son's shouts, her mum's burbling and her grandma's tuneless singing, the noises of life. Now that it was just her and Bob, the idea of living in silence terrified her. Background noise helped keep any negative thoughts at bay.

She trod the intricately tiled floor to the solid wooden front door of the house her parents had bought back in the late fifties for the princely sum of two thousand pounds. Sixty years on and the area was now on a fast track to gentrification. The ornate wooden spindles of the staircase and the original fireplaces, mouldings and ceiling roses meant that her family home was now worth al-most three hundred thousand. Three hundred thousand pounds! The amount staggered and frightened her. Such a huge sum, and a wonderful return, of course, but it was all relative. Prices were rocketing right across her postcode. Not that she had any intention of selling, despite the numerous glossy flyers from estate agents trying their luck that were repeatedly poked through her door with the local paper.

The idea of selling the only house she had ever called home, where her memories and ghosts also lived, was unthinkable. Aaron, her son, had suggested that it might be wise to sell up and buy a small flat. 'Easier for you to manage, Mum, and great for future-proofing against any problems you might have getting up and down stairs.' She'd nodded, feigning interest, suspecting that the sale of their family home would be more about future-proofing his wife's Botox, holidaying and handbag habit. But rather than say this, she'd simply nodded, as if it was all going over her head; it was often easier that way.

Vivienne stooped low and gathered the pale grey envelope from the coir welcome mat embossed with doggy paws. The postmark revealed it was from New Zealand. A letter from Emma! Her heart leapt.

This was it, the big reveal.

Emma had told her three weeks ago on the phone that she had 'big news' and Vivienne had been mulling over the possibilities ever since. *Pregnant?* No, that didn't seem likely; she'd have told her there and then, far too excited to keep that a secret. *Moving on, changing both her job and her location?* Quite possible, as this was a regular occurrence and to Emma was always 'big news'. And then, a couple of days ago, as she was dusting off the advent candle ready to pop it on the mantelpiece on December the first, it struck her. *Emma's coming home for Christmas!* Her spirits soared at the prospect. Her daughter, back home for the first time in four years, with stories to tell and adventures to share. The thought of Emma asleep in her old room upstairs filled her with happiness.

She longed to hear the familiar creak of the

17

floorboards overhead while she pottered through her chores in the kitchen, and it would be a dream come true to have Emma on tap for a chat whenever she felt like it. Oh, that would be the finest Christmas present ever.

Her mind flitted to one of the best Christmases they had shared. The kids were eight and ten and Vivienne had pulled double shifts for three months to get them a Game Boy each. This was going to be a huge deal and certainly not what they were anticipating. Just for once, she wanted them to be the children who struck it big on Christmas morning, wanted hers to be the ones in the park that the other kids gathered around with their mouths forming envious O's, as they paraded their special presents from Father Christmas. The anticipation of seeing their faces on the day, as they ripped off the paper, was almost more than she could bear, but it made the long, long days and nights spent under the harsh strip light of the superstore, worth it. As she left work on Christmas Eve, she had grabbed a couple of flashing Santa hats from the bargain bin and these along with the usual and expected chocolate reindeer, warm socks and a Harry Potter book for them both, two different stories that they could then swap, meant their haul was complete.

She had watched, as each present was carefully taken from inside the pillow case in which the gifts were stashed, and smiled as they beamed their thanks at her, interested in the books, nibbling at the chocolate and putting the socks on their chilly feet. The three of them had laughed, as familiar Carols accompanied them on the radio.

'Ooh, just a couple more.' She had tried to sound nonchalant, as she first handed over the Santa hats. Aaron and Emma had immediately put them on their heads and with the lights flashing, laughed hysterically at each other. They then decided to put their heads under a duvet and in the darkness watch the other's flashing lights that bobbed this way and that, as they giggled and danced. The Game Boys had been much admired, but quickly discarded in favour of their new game, hide and seek in the dark, where they took it in turns to seek out the flashing lights of their hats in dark corners, the inside of the wardrobe and even behind the sofa. Their laughter filled the rooms, sweeping out the winter cold and creating Christmas joy.

She would never forget the sight of the Game Boys, nestling side by side on the swirly patterned carpet of the sitting room floor, representing hours and hours of extra work, while her kids laughed fit to burst and ran around the house, playing with the cheap hats she had grabbed as an afterthought.

Even now, the memory of it made her smile.

'Look, Bob, we've got a letter from Emma.' She nodded in his direction as she tore open the envelope and hastily pulled out a stiff, ornate card.

She stared at the lines of text and the fancy type, then wobbled backwards and sat down hard on the armchair by the kitchen fireplace. Resting her elbows on her knees, she studied the card again. Swallowing, she picked up her phone and called her best friend, who lived three streets away.

'Ellen, it's me. Meet me up the café. Be there

19

in ten.'

Vivienne reread the nine lines once more, before grabbing her shopping bag and purse.

'Shan't be long, Bob. I'll take you out again when I get back. Be good.'

Her sturdy walking boots barely touched the pavement as she sped up Mendip Road and rounded the corner into Cotswold Road, where Shaun Lewis was tinkering under the bonnet of his Fiesta.

'All right, Mrs Lane? Bit chilly, innit?' He clapped his hands together, summoning warmth and exhaling vapour with every word.

'"Tis, love.'

'I thought you were looking a bit thin, tell you the truth, Mrs Lane.' He sniffed.

'Really?' She ran her hand over her flat tum and wished, as ever, that she could put on a few pounds.

'Yeah, but then I realised it's cos you haven't got Mrs Nye with you. You two are usually joined at the hip and together you make a right hefty unit!'

'Shaun!' She tutted and laughed. He'd always been witty, that boy, even in primary school, when he and Emma had first become friends. 'I'm off to meet her now, in fact. I won't tell her that mind. How's your mum?' she added as she rushed past him, in too much of a hurry to stop and chat.

'She's all right, driving me mad, though. S'always the same, she gets in a right tizz over Christmas. I keep telling her, it's only one day, just a roast. A few extra spuds, an extended East-Enders and a bit of tinsel. How hard can it be?' He sighed, wiping the oil from the end of his fingers

20

with an already dirty rag.

'I'll tell her you said that.' Vivienne chuckled. 'Give her my love!' she shouted over her shoulder, waving in the air behind her head.

She had a sudden picture of a whimpering Emma coming home one afternoon with her shoes and socks wet and covered in mud; she could only have been about seven. Shaun had dared her to walk on the frozen Malago and of course she'd gone straight through the ice. Vivienne smiled at the memory. He was a cheeky boy, that Shaun Lewis. He was also a kind boy and one with a heart of gold, who on more than one occasion, had been there for Emma to lean on, guiding her, as she stumbled home in her teenage years with a broken heart and a face wet with tears, as her current, temporary heartbreak sent her spiralling into sadness. She would then retreat to the furthest recess of her bedroom, only to surface when her mood had lifted, which usually took about three days.

'Thanks Shaun for bringing her home,' Vivienne would coo, as the boy who lived down the road consoled Emma with a hug and a promise that it would all turn out right in the end.

Stamping her feet on the mat as was her habit, mindful of the muddy residue that might be clinging to her boots, Vivienne pushed on the door of Pedro's, their favourite café, and slid into her seat. The smell of bacon crisping and the lingering scent of cooking oil mixed with freshly brewed coffee was most comforting. This was where she and Ellen met to chat when she wasn't working her shifts in Asda and Ellen wasn't at home doing the books for Trev's painting and decorating business.

A couple of lads wearing paint-spattered white overalls over jeans and aged, holey sweatshirts were tucking into gargantuan fried breakfasts. Shiny fried eggs, fat sausages and mountains of beans fought for space among slices of black pudding, hash browns and strips of bacon. Their plates were so crowded, the requisite toast had to sit separately on side plates, next to their mugs of tea. The men ate with their heads down, staring doggedly at the plates and gripping their cutlery with silent determination, as if getting through the feast was a job in itself.

Vivienne sat with her back to them, in her usual spot, keeping her eyes on the large picture window. A peeling vinyl transfer dominated the far corner of the glass, depicting pizza, spaghetti and milkshakes spiked with stripy, colour-coordinated straws. She thought about the envelope nestling in her bag that had winged its way from the other side of the world. Her girl had drifted from job to job, acquiring friends and hobbies as she went: dog groomer, reiki healer, aromatherapist, life coach... The list was long. Although how she hoped to coach someone else when her own life was littered with unfinished jobs and so lacking in direction was quite beyond Vivienne. As usual, though, she'd chosen not to say anything.

Emma's unique way of looking at the world, her bouncy enthusiasm and disregard for convention, had thrilled Vivienne when she was younger and she'd convinced herself that this fearless free-spiritedness would lead to great things. But with every passing year she found herself hoping that her daughter might find a little stability, a routine, a way of life that Vivienne could relate to: a job, a permanent home, even children. She smiled at the idea but then quickly reminded herself that Emma was now thirty-one and unlikely to change her ways any time soon.

Aaron's wife of eight years had made her views on motherhood quite clear. With a small measure of sadness, Vivienne had long ago consigned the kids' stuffed toys, family heirlooms of a sort, to a box in the loft, not wanting to jinx her dreams of becoming a granny.

'How long are you going to be away for?' This was the question she had asked four years ago with false brightness to her voice. She often pictured that chilly November morning as Emma spoke of her plans to go and see the world. Vivienne could recall the detail: Emma, perched cross-legged on the chair like a yogi, wiggling her ringed toes while daintily eating yoghurt from the pot and licking the foil lid. To Vivienne, the idea of leaving the streets that contained everything and everyone she had ever known was quite alien. She felt a mixture of envy and fear at the prospect.

'Don't know,' had come the truthful if unnerving reply, followed by a shrug of Emma's tanned, tattooed shoulders.

Vivienne looked again at the rain-spattered window of the café and sighed; she finally knew the answer, confirmed via nine lines printed on a piece of fancy card. Forever. That was how long Emma was going to be away for. She was never coming home.

Vivienne swallowed the emotion that gathered in her throat and scanned the shoppers, who even at this early hour were weighed down with grocery bags in the grey gloom of the dark, winter morning. Their stooped forms cast grainy shadows up the graffitied walls, concrete lampposts and shabby shopfronts. She watched the procession of young women, without make-up, hair a little mussed and with scarves slung over worn coats, and thought back to herself at their age.

It was a lovely time in her life. On mornings like this, she used to drop Emma and Aaron at Parson Street Primary and then pop to the shops on the way home, stocking up on milk, bread for sandwiches and something for supper. That something was usually coated in breadcrumbs and accompanied by peas. Her repertoire might have been small, but she was unfailingly diligent; the kids never went without a cooked meal, come rain or shine. Just as her mum had done for her.

She would then meet up with Ellen and they'd while away the afternoon chatting over the laundry, tackling the tangle of weeds in their gardens or planting flowers and mowing grass. There were various hobbies, too, that consumed them for a bit – scrapbooking, crochet, Sudoku, aerobics – discovered, obsessed over and then discarded, the chief pleasure being in doing them together. It always made her chuckle when she stumbled across a box full of bits and bobs that had been her passion before being consigned to the attic where all her hobbies and fads went to die. It was the shadow of these shared memories, lurking on street corners and along every road she trod that made the place so special.

'What'll it be, Viv? Or are you waiting for her ladyship?' Pedro, the cook, waiter and proprietor interrupted her thoughts and wiped the already immaculate tabletop with a soft cloth before sliding it back into the pocket of his striped half-pinny.

'I'd better wait, love.' She smiled. It felt nice to share this little connection, this admission of Ellen's sometimes pushy nature, with the wonderfully scented Pedro. He always gave off a floral whiff. 'A gentleman should be well groomed. Expensive cologne, my one extravagance,' he'd trilled way back in the summer. She knew, however, that this was a lie. He had lots of extravagances.

'How's my friend Bob today?' He stepped back, hands on hips.

'Getting older, like me. But he's good company.'

'Also like you.' Pedro gave a quick bow of his head. He was a flatterer, for sure.

'Don't know about that.' She felt her cheeks flush, as unaccustomed to and suspicious of compliments now as she had always been.

'They are the best friends though. I still miss my Sheba.'

'How long is it now?' She kept her voice low, knowing that losing a pet was as hard as losing a family member; the fact that they had four legs instead of two didn't make it any less painful.

'Nearly two years.' He blinked.

Vivienne shook her head and gave a sympathetic smile. She couldn't bear to think about losing Bob.

'Talking of best friends...' He nodded towards the door and headed back to the counter as Ellen

25

tumbled in like a rowdy mob, banging the door against its frame and filling the room with her loud sigh.

'This better be important. I was bleaching my moustache and I only had it on half the time – means I'll have to do it again in a fortnight.'

'I don't think it works like that,' she pointed out.

Pedro waved from behind the faux-wood laminate counter where the till sat. Alongside him was a three-tiered glass display cabinet that held a plump array of delicious-looking fare. There was always a wide variety of cakes to choose from, as long as what you desired was vanilla in colour, stuffed with sultanas or raisins and sprinkled with sugar.

'What'll it be with your coffees, ladies? Scones, teacakes, Chelsea buns?'

'I think teacake today?' Vivienne looked at her friend.

Ellen shrugged her arms from her padded anorak and nodded. 'Yep, we'll split one. And one from the front, mind! None of the rubbish you keep at the back.' She pointed to the shelf, aware that yesterday's cakes were hidden from view; the fresh ones were always propped up at the front, the better to tempt less savvy customers.

Vivienne's shoulders tensed with a familiar mix of embarrassment and envy. She frequently cringed at her friend's outspoken demands but at the same time wished she had the confidence to speak up herself. Her life might have been very different if she had. Ellen had always been the mouthpiece for them both. Even all those years ago at school she would call out any injustice, whether the perpetrator was a pupil or a member of staff. She was fearless.

Pedro smiled. 'Would I dream of giving you anything but the best, Lady Ellen?'

Ellen ignored him and took her seat at the narrow table opposite her friend.

'Trev all right?' Vivienne was fond of Ellen's quiet husband.

'He's fine, but we haven't got time for small talk. Come on, let's have it...' Ellen laid her hands flat on the table, as if about to start a séance, and stared at her friend.

Vivienne took a deep breath. 'I got a letter from Emma.'

'Up the duff?' Ellen fired back.

'No!'

'Lesbian?' She tried again.

'What? No!' Vivienne shook her head.

'Well that's me down a fiver,' Ellen huffed. 'I made a bet with Trev.'

Vivienne ignored her friend's crass admission. 'She's getting married.' It felt strange to say it out loud.

'Your Emma, getting married?' Ellen shrieked.

'Course "my Emma"! What other Emma would I be talking to you about?'

'Good point.' Ellen considered this. 'So *this* is the "big news"? Did she phone?'

'No, I got a letter. An invite, to be more exact.'

'Well I never, that's a bit out of the blue.' Ellen looked skywards.

'Tell me about it. I feel quite shocked, a bit upset,' Vivienne admitted.

'I'll bet. I thought she was travelling or whatever, seeing the world with nothing more than a knapsack, a flower for her hair and a change of pants?'

Vivienne shook her head at her friend's all-too-accurate assessment.

Ellen wasn't done. 'I thought she wanted to be a free spirit, go about eating toffee...'

'It's tofu,' Vivienne corrected her.

Ellen carried on as if she hadn't spoken. 'Roaming mountains and swimming oceans, becoming one with Mother Nature. That was about the nub of it, right?'

Vivienne wished she didn't remember it quite so clearly. 'That's right.'

'Well, getting married doesn't exactly fit the bill. I mean, she could have stayed here and married whats'is face.'

'Fergus.'

'Yes, him. We liked him, didn't we?'

Vivienne nodded. They had indeed liked the arty, bespectacled Fergus, a strict vegan with a passion for hill-walking and tattoos. He ran a website, something to do with graffiti art.

'She said she turned him down because she was keen to see the world and escape the shackles of domesticity, escape the ordinary!' Ellen scoffed.

Vivienne thought about this. 'Yes, but maybe the shackles are a little easier to bear and the world a little less ordinary when you've got glorious sunshine for half the year and good New Zealand air to breathe.'

A delivery lorry tooted its horn, applied its wheezy brakes and fired thick black smoke out of its exhaust pipe, as if to emphasise her point.

'Ah, so it wasn't domesticity she was raging against, just domesticity here in Bedminster.'

'Apparently so.'

Both women looked out at the grey day. Drizzle slid down the window and pooled against the soft, blackened wood of the frame.

'Who's she marrying then?' Ellen slapped the table impatiently.

Vivienne pulled the envelope from her bag, slid the stiff card out of its hiding place, then slowly pushed it across the tabletop. She watched as her friend took it into her fingers and held it at arm's length, mouthing the words as she read them in her head.

'Well I never. It's a fancy invite.' She flexed the card against her palm, speaking at a volume a little louder than Vivienne was comfortable with. 'Quality.'

She nodded. It was.

'So who is this man?' Ellen scanned the ornate lettering again.

'As it says...' Vivienne pointed at the invite. 'Mr Michael McKinley, apparently.'

'Here we are, ladies.' Pedro interrupted them, placing two tall glass mugs on little saucers in front of them. Then he hurried back to the counter to retrieve two side plates with half a toasted teacake and a little rectangular foil-packed pat of butter on each, and a couple of knives rolled inside white paper napkins.

'Thank you, Pedro.'

'Thanks.'

They waited for him to retreat, sipping their

29

drinks before their fingers fiddled with the foil flaps of the butter pats and they took the knives in their palms.

'She's never mentioned him?' Ellen asked.

'No. Not a word. Last I heard she was with the Vietnamese chap she'd met in Auckland.'

'Hai.'

'Yep, that was it. Hai. And she was with him only nine months ago, so this latest development all feels very sudden.'

'I should cocoa,' Ellen agreed, tucking her chin against her chest to reveal a sag to her jaw.

Vivienne cut the butter into little blobs, which she then placed at uniform intervals across the surface of the teacake, as if each blob had an area to mark. She waited for them to melt a little before spreading the butter thinly all over.

'So who is this Michael McKinley?' Ellen asked before taking a huge bite.

'I don't know! You can keep asking, but you know as much as I do. I opened the envelope and called you, that's it.' Vivienne stirred her coffee. The two had always bickered in this way.

'Must admit, I'm a little worried, Viv. You know what she's like!'

'Oh God, don't.'

They laughed, both recalling Fergus's replacement and the way Emma had gushed about him one morning as they were drinking coffee in her kitchen.

'I've met a man! He's lovely,' Emma had enthused, wriggling excitedly in her chair.

'So tell us all about him. Where did you meet, what does he do?' Vivienne had asked, ignoring

Ellen's sly smile.

'Well, we met online, he lives in Croatia, he's a writer, not published or anything, but he has this great idea for a book, he's been researching it for years, it's going to be massive!'

Again, Vivienne had studiously avoided catching her friend's eye.

'He's a bit older than me – fifty – but age is just a number, right?'

Vivienne sighed, remembering her relief when the Croatian bestseller had stopped calling.

Ellen picked up the invite once again. 'December twelfth. Bit close to Christmas, isn't it?'

'Yes, but it's different over there, isn't it? They're all topsy-turvy with the seasons, so they can't have proper Christmas, can they? It'll be hot, more like summer holidays than Christmas. I can't imagine having a bit of turkey and my roasties while in a bikini.'

'Oh please, Viv, I don't think any of us wants to imagine that!' Ellen pulled a face.

'Charming.' Vivienne smiled at her friend, who had always been of a bigger build. Her own body hadn't really changed over the years; she was still slender and straight, and even if her skin now sat more loosely on her muscles and those muscles were a little slack in places, she was still in good shape.

She continued, 'I think you need snow and dark nights, a real fire and fat Santas for it to feel like Christmas. And all our little traditions, like queuing up in Marks and Sparks for your special tea-time bits, digging out the grotty tinsel from the loft and keeping the tin of Quality Street on your lap

31

while you watch the Queen's speech.' She looked into the middle distance, as if picturing just that. 'That's Christmas for me, always has been.'

'I hear what you're saying, but maybe we need a change. Are we going to go then, or what?' Ellen took another bite of her teacake.

Vivienne gave a small smile at her friend's correct assumption that if she went anywhere it would be with Ellen in tow. It had always been that way. God only knew what her family would make of being abandoned so close to Christmas. 'How can we? It's not like it's up the road – it's a plane ride, a long plane ride.'

'Probably two or three plane rides.' Ellen asserted her superior geographical knowledge. 'Might be fun though. I once read that the water goes down the plughole the wrong way in New Zealand.'

'Oh, you should have said! I'll give Thomas Cook a quick call; I wouldn't want to miss that. And while we're there checking out the plugholes, we may as well watch Emma get married.' She tutted.

There was a beat of silence while both of them sipped their hot drinks, savouring their frothy beverages.

'Reckon it'll be pricey too,' Ellen sighed. 'Mind you, I've got my savings.'

'Thought you had plans for that? Weren't you going to ditch Trev, have plastic surgery and then go to Vegas to woo Barry Manilow?'

'I was, but I'm not so sure now. Firstly, I don't think I'm Barry's type.' Ellen winked. 'And secondly, Trev is starting to grow on me.'

'Ah, that's good to hear. How long is it you've been married now?'

'Thirty-three years,' Ellen offered with a dead-pan expression.

Vivienne laughed.

'And thirdly, I'm beginning to doubt the wisdom of having the boobs of a twenty-four-year-old stuck onto my fifty-three-year-old body. It'd be like putting fancy headlights on an old banger – they might dazzle in the dark, but in the cold light of day you couldn't hide the rust or the fact that it won't start in the mornings.'

'Don't forget the leaky radiator.' Vivienne smiled over the rim of the tall glass, held in both hands, up to her mouth.

'You're right. I think I might be better off waiting for a head transplant and going the whole hog.'

'Whose body would you like?'

'Don't know, maybe something like Pedro's, he's in good shape for an older man.'

'You'd be a man?' Vivienne asked, a little shocked.

'I reckon. Yes, why not? As we both know, there ain't nothing as funny as a willy, Vivienne Peebles.'

They both snorted their laughter and choked on their mouthfuls of coffee.

'I don't know, Elle, I feel a bit thrown by the whole thing, if I'm being honest. I thought she was going to say she was coming home for Christmas, and I was over the moon. I'm a little bit disappointed. I'd never tell her that, wouldn't want to shackle her dreams in any way, but I want her home so badly. I miss her.'

'Course you do.'

33

'I don't feel the joy I should, as mother of the bride. It just feels odd because it's so far away and I'm so uninvolved.'

'It's probably because it's all a bit rushed and you haven't met him. That's hard, it must be. Say what we like, but in an ideal world we'd have a say in who our kids ended up with.' Ellen raised one eyebrow. 'I mean, you hardly would have picked Miss Weston-Super-Mare 2005 for your Aaron, would you?'

Vivienne hid her smile; it felt mean to be talking about her daughter-in-law in that way, even if Ellen's words did hold more than the ring of truth. She sighed and placed her coffee glass back on its little saucer. 'Maybe. I don't know. Aaron seems happy, most of the time, and that's all I ask. But with Emma, I suppose I thought she'd get the travel bug out of her system, see the world, have adventures, but then come home and settle down, have babies, see her school friends. That's what she said she wanted, said she always wanted to end up here and that she only broke up with Fergus because she wasn't quite ready to settle down yet and he wasn't quite the one. I never thought she'd choose to make a permanent life on the other side of the world.'

'We can all change our minds, Viv.'

'True.'

'But I thought she'd come home,' she rubbed her brow, 'maybe marry Shaun up the road. They've always been good mates, but I can't pick for her, can I?'

'No you can't, Viv. How old is she now? Thirty-one?'

'Nearly thirty-two.'

'Doesn't seem possible. I feel the same about Robbie. Our babies are getting older.'

'Thanks for reminding me. If Emma's getting on, what am I?'

'You are ancient, my girl.'

'And you are four months older than me,' Vivienne reminded her.

'Keep it down, ladies!' Pedro called from the counter. It was one of his favourite interjections, shouted out whenever their chatter or laughter rose above a hum.

Vivienne sighed and joined her hands at the knuckles on the tabletop.

'I suppose it's just that when she was little, I had a fixed idea of what her life might turn out like and I guess I thought it would be like mine but better.'

'We all want that.' Ellen nodded, clearly thinking of her own son, Robbie, who lived locally, worked up at Babcock's and lived with his second wife and new baby in Ashton, within spitting distance of the football ground and his first wife and baby, who, as a pair, looked remarkably similar to the new ones. Trev called them 2.0, joking that Robbie had got an upgrade, but this attempt at humour was only to mask the hurt they felt at their son's inconsistency.

'I was always a bit proud of Emma's ... defiance, if you like. That independent attitude that told her she could go anywhere, be anything, a wanderer. I encouraged her and it was easy too when I thought there would be an end to it. But...'

'But you thought she'd come home eventually and settle down, not be continually saving up for her next adventure, desperate to escape.'

Vivienne nodded, saddened by the idea that her child wanted to escape. 'Yes. I also worry that she's been a bad picker in the past, never with anyone too long, apart from Fergus, who we liked.'

'We did.' Ellen nodded. 'I think he might be shacked up with Mrs Haines' daughter,' she whispered.

'Fergus?' Vivienne squealed.

'Yes!'

'But he's got to be at least ten years older than her?'

'Well, I'm only saying what Robbie told me. He saw them out in town and said they were chewing the face off each other in the queue in Starbucks.'

Both tutted in unison.

'Well I never.' Vivienne pictured the man who had slept in her house for a year, until the engagement was called off and he was sent packing, the topaz ring he had placed on Emma's finger stuffed into his jeans pocket as he slammed the front door and jumped in his van, which was powered by old chip fat, apparently.

'You have to try not to worry. She's not you, Viv. She can spot a Ray at forty paces. You taught her that,' her friend offered comfortingly.

'Yes, well, it's not always that easy to tell. Especially when you're bowled over, dazzled.'

There was a moment of reflection when both women thought back to that time in their lives, nearly four decades earlier. The two friends, meeting two friends; it had seemed ideal.

'I didn't think I would be man-less at my age; it's not what I planned. Not that I want one, or need one, I really don't! And I know it sounds like I do, like I'm protesting too much. It's hard to explain. I don't *need* a man to be happy, I think I've proved that, but the fact that mine abandoned me still makes me feel awful. Like it reflects on me somehow. It was such a public rejection.'

'Well that's a load of rubbish. No one gives it a second thought. He was a tosser, Viv. No one had a good word to say about him once he'd gone.'

'That's as may be, but he was my tosser and he was the father of my children and for a while I imagined growing old with him, even if the idea left me a little cold at times. It wasn't the kind of marriage I had envisaged, true, but it was all I had to work with and I was prepared to do just that.'

'He was never good enough for you, Viv. Proof being in how it all ended. Everyone always said you could do much better.'

Vivienne gave a wry smile. The fact was, no one had told her she could do much better, not until it was over, then they all had plenty to say.

'I never liked him...'

'I never trusted him...'

'I said this would happen!'

No one, however, had dared to say these things to her face when she was in the first flush of romance, and if anyone had suggested that her man might not be all he seemed, she wouldn't have believed them anyway.

'And trust me, I know Trev didn't abandon me, but there's many an hour in the day when I look at his miserable face and wish he had. I tell you what, Viv, if Brad Pitt knocked on the door and suggested a swap, I'd bite his arm off.' She chomped at her teacake and spoke with her mouth full. 'Don't think it's likely though, do you? I've never seen him around here.'

'I don't, Elle.' She shook her head. 'And I don't need no Brad Pitt, in fact I don't fancy him at all, not with that long hair and him chewing gum all the time. No, I'd be better off with someone that likes the fresh air, is happy to potter in the garden and isn't afraid to peel a spud or two. Someone who'll pick me up from work and make me a cuppa while I put the shopping away. Or someone who owns a wool shop – save me a fortune in knitting wool!'

'Blimey, girl, you don't want much, do you?' Ellen chortled.

'No, I never have and look where that's got me.' She raised her palms.

'Up shit creek without a piddle.'

'The word is "paddle"! Why would it be "piddle"?' She laughed.

'I don't know. I always thought it was a bit nonsensical.'

The two collapsed on the tabletop again, weakened by their laughter.

'Thinking about it, Viv, I don't think Brad would be interested in me, even if I wasn't married. My courting days are over. I was working it out last night, how many people I've slept with.'

Vivienne leant forward, interested. She looked over her shoulder at Pedro and the two young men eating their breakfast, to make sure they weren't earwigging, before asking, 'How many?'

Ellen lowered her head. 'Four–'

'Four! Good Lord!' Vivienne sat back in her

chair with her hand at her chest. 'Well, I never. I knew about two, but four?'

Ellen looked up. 'You never let me finish.' She swallowed. 'It's fourteen.'

Vivienne stared at her in silence. 'Are you kidding me?'

'No.' Ellen sipped her coffee.

There was a beat or two of awkward silence.

'Fourteen?' her friend repeated.

'Yes.'

'Four*teen?*' Vivienne asked again, as if the fact simply wouldn't permeate.

'For goodness' sake, stop repeating it.' Ellen sighed.

'I can't. I'm in shock. That's a lot.' She nodded.

'Is it?' Ellen tipped her chair back.

'Yes! Well, I think so.' She took a deep breath. 'When did you manage that? I mean, you've been with Trev for ever.'

'Before Trev of course. Couple at school–'

'Couple at school?' she shrieked.

'Yes! For goodness' sake, are you going to yell out or repeat everything I say?'

'Quite possibly. I thought I knew everything about you – I'm shocked.'

Ellen continued, 'And then a few after school.'

'Good Lord.' Vivienne tutted, again.

'You have to stop saying that, sounds like you're praying for my poor deprived soul.'

'I think you mean depraved and you might be right. Carry on.' Vivienne wriggled in her seat.

'Then while Trev was working away and you were hitched and popping out kids–'

'But you were engaged!' she interrupted.

39

'Right, that's it. I am not going to give you any more details. You clearly can't handle the information if you're going to keep yelling at me. Shaming me.'

'Shaming you? Do you even know what that means?' she quizzed.

'No. But I read it in my magazine and thought it might be appropriate.'

The two stared out of the window without talking, each processing the last few sentences they had exchanged.

Ellen eventually broke the silence. 'So, come on then, how many have you slept with?'

'I don't want to say, now.' Vivienne looked at her lap and felt her cheeks flush.

'Oh go on, you have to, now I have.' She made it sound like it was the law. Just as she'd been doing since they were kids. *'If I jump in, you have to as well!'* Or, *'We have to both sign up for it, you can't have only one of us doing karaoke, it wouldn't be fair!'* Or, *'We should both leave school and get jobs together, we could start a business!'* And look how far that had got them...

Vivienne took a deep breath, knowing that her friend would pester her until she came clean. It was easier to get it over and done with. 'Okay,' she conceded, 'but you are not to go on about it.'

'Cross my heart.' Ellen drew the sign with her index finger on her chest.

'One,' she whispered.

'One?' Ellen yelled.

'Stop shouting!'

'You shouted! I am allowed at least one shout in return.' She paused. 'You mean to tell me you have

40

only ever slept with Ray?'

Vivienne nodded.

'But... But he buggered off in 1989.'

'Yes, thank you, Ellen, I am well aware of that fact.' She busied herself with the cutting of her teacake.

'So you haven't slept with anyone for nearly thirty years?'

'Well who did you think I'd slept with? You know everything about me. Although come to think of it, I *thought* I knew everything about you,' she retorted through a narrowed mouth.

Ellen considered this. 'I suppose I thought you might have had a thing with Tony from the fruit and veg shop.'

'Tony from the fruit and veg shop?' She was aware that her voice had gone very high; indignation did that to her sometimes.

'Yes.'

'Why on earth would you think that?' She shook her head at her friend.

'I don't know. I guess you two just always seemed to have a giggle and I know he gave you extra sprouts and those caulis that he said were going to spoil, but he never so much as tossed me a rejected grape.'

'I've known him for years!'

'So have I,' Ellen countered.

'Honestly. Sometimes you amaze me. Tony from the fruit and veg shop...' She rolled her eyes at the absurdity of her friend's suggestion. 'There's a world of difference between someone giving you an extra sprout and having S-E-X with them.'

'I was only saying,' Ellen spoke, as if affronted.

41

'I didn't think you knew fourteen men.' She looked up, as if trying to picture them.

'Don't have to know them, Viv.' Ellen winked.

'Oh just stop it!' She shivered.

'You are such a prude.'

'I'm not.'

'You are! It's only sex. It's good for you – life-affirming and funny.'

'Funny?'

''Tis the way I do it.' Ellen twisted her mouth.

'Everything okay, ladies?'

Neither of them had heard Pedro creep up behind them.

They both nodded into their hot drinks, waiting until he had left the table before squeaking their laughter behind their palms.

'Haven't you ever been curious? Or missed it?' Ellen whispered.

Vivienne cocked her head to one side. 'Haven't really thought about it too much. I just did it as and when necessary when I was married – truth is, it was more like putting the bins out or getting a spare key cut. You know, one of them jobs that you don't look forward to but sometimes are just unavoidable.' She looked up at her friend, who was staring at her with her mouth slightly agape. 'What?' she asked.

'We need to get you out there, girl. We need to get you a man.'

Vivienne laughed, loudly. 'Do give over. Some of us are quite happy not to have that many notches on our belt. Fourteen, oh my days...' She sighed, shaking her head.

'I mean it, Viv. You need to live a bit.' Ellen

winked at her for a second time.

'I must admit, I do feel very cosmopolitan.'

'Why, because you've discovered you can actually talk about S-E-X?'

'No, because I've just discovered that my best friend is a tart.'

Two

Ellen had, as ever been the distraction that helped, but as Vivienne put the key in her front door and petted the tail-wagging Bob, her smile slipped and she thought about Emma.

'Shall I give her a ring, Bob? What's the time over there now?' She glanced at the clock on the mantelpiece. It was 10 a.m. She did the maths in her head. 'That makes it eleven at night, might be a bit late. I'll wait until it's her morning.'

The phone on the hallstand rang. The caller failed to introduce herself, but simply launched into her topic of choice, as she always did.

'Okay, so it's one thousand and forty-one pounds including a fourteen-hour stopover in Hong Kong, which means we can explore a bit – apparently they've got a great knock-off market. I told Trev we're off and he says as long as I freeze him a big lasagne, stock up on KitKats and am home before Christmas, he doesn't mind. I'm already packing. Do you think my blue maxi frock is too over-the-top for a wedding?'

The two had been sharing thoughts, ideas and

plans since they were small, so for a conversation to begin in this way was perfectly normal for them.

Vivienne tried to assimilate her friend's points. 'How do you know that's what it costs?' She pulled the phone over to the stairs and sat on the bottom step.

'I got Robbie to look it up on the internet, but apparently the price will go up the nearer it gets, so if we are going to go, we need to book it a bit sharpish.'

'I thought I'd give Emma a ring when it's her morning time and just check that she wants us there and all the details, before you go packing your frock and fascinator.'

'Course she wants us there! We are her family. She can't get married without us being there!' Ellen tutted.

Vivienne closed her eyes; it was a little easier to talk with her eyes shut and with her friend at a distance. 'I just want to check she's not making a mistake, rushing into something she might regret. This isn't like dyeing her hair or ditching her job, this is getting married, it's serious and not something she should be taking lightly.'

'The invites are out, Viv. This is happening. And just because you got hurt, doesn't mean that she will.'

'Different when we got hitched though, wasn't it? It was so exciting, the planning, the buzz – we got right caught up in it, didn't we?' She remembered the excited bubble in her stomach that made sleep impossible.

'We did, love. But we didn't know what Ray was like, did we? Didn't know he was a player,

44

and a liar.'

'I sometimes wonder...' She paused.

'What?'

'I sometimes wonder what I'd have done if my mum *had* voiced her fears, told me that she didn't like the look of him, like she did after he'd left.'

'You wouldn't have believed her, Viv. You were smitten. For her to wade in with any opinion, either way, would have caused problems between you and your mum and she was wise enough to know that. I miss your mum.'

'Me too.' She smiled, looking at the picture on the wall of her parents in their finery on their wedding day. 'And I suppose you are right. But God knows who this Michael McKinley is, probably another musician waiting for his big break, or a writer halfway through the next great novel.'

'She has a type, that's for sure.' Ellen laughed.

'Yeah, but not a type that will give her stability or all the things I want her to have. That's my fear.'

'You old snob! Are you saying you want her to marry money?'

'No! Of course not. You know me better than that.' Vivienne sighed at the very suggestion and looked around the narrow hallway of their family home. It was hardly a palace. 'I would just like her to marry a man with a direction, a profession, something reliable, like a mechanic, so that her life can be steady. Is that too much to ask?'

'Oh, love, if only it was that easy. And what do you mean like a mechanic, we're not back on Shaun Lewis are we?'

'No!' she fired, 'I just want her to put down roots and have a more settled life and I think

45

there's no better place to put down roots than where you come from.'

'I know love, but look at Robbie, he had a good job up at Babcock's, cosy home, and a lovely kid and jacked it all in for a newer, shinier life with a Sharon lookalike! I told him the grass isn't always greener, sometimes you climb over the wall and land in a massive cowpat, but he wouldn't listen. Now, I can't say he's regretful exactly, and I only want things to work out for him of course, but I can tell the gloss has already lifted. A screaming new baby in a rented house gives you the same feeling at three in the morning no matter how much fun you had getting there. What'll he do? Move on again? I sincerely hope not. It worries the life out of me. But the point is we can't choose for our kids, we can only steer them out of harm's way, set them back on course if and when we need to.'

Both women were quiet, mulling over the truth of this. Then Ellen spoke calmly, 'Emma is carving her own path and all you can do is be there for her when she needs you. That's our job, remember? God knows, I wish Robbie had listened to me, but he didn't. Just like you wouldn't have listened to your mum, God rest her soul.'

'I don't know.' This was Vivienne's stock response when she needed to clarify her thoughts.

'See you in a bit,' Ellen sang.

'Yep.'

They never said goodbye. There was simply no point in being so final and formal, not when they knew they would chat or see each other again very soon.

Vivienne ran her hands over Bob's shiny flank, admiring his tawny, black and white markings. She smiled at him as her thoughts wandered to the enigmatic Michael McKinley and then inevitably to her own ill-fated marriage. Ellen was right really, she had no say when it came to Emma, but that didn't stop her worrying.

She didn't often think of Ray, not nowadays. The devastating hurt that followed the ending of their short union had all but healed over, or was at least buried under memories from the many intervening years. Today, however, with the topic now forced back to the surface, like a stubborn, spiky weed that grew through the cracks, she considered the way he had treated her, spoken to her and how she'd responded.

The pattern had been set in the first year of their marriage when she would tiptoe around her giant of a man, trying to please him, grateful for the crumbs of love that he tossed her way. Thinking, hoping, that if she loved him enough, he might one day feel the same. It was hard for her: she had always been treasured, had spent her childhood in a cocoon of care and protection, within the bosom of a close-knit family with her parents and gran at the heart, and it was as if her mind refused to understand that this man was different. He was her *husband* and yet he was not going to care for her in the way she was used to, was not going to love her unconditionally or treat her with absolute kindness, despite what he had promised. And by the time she did realise this, fully understanding just what she had got herself into, it was too late: Aaron was a baby and Emma was on the way.

47

She could pin down the moment her life had changed to a single moment – ten o'clock on a Saturday night in winter. It had been one of those evenings with a lot of build-up. She had bought a new top from Eastville Market, a royal-blue off-the-shoulder fitted sweater with three-quarter-length sleeves and a wide elasticated hem to show off her little waist and her pert bust. She spent an age putting on her make-up, applying the heavy black kohl that weighed down her eyelids but gave her a look that was pure Sheena Easton. Her fringe was backcombed and sprayed in an attempt to achieve some height.

When she left her parents' house in Mendip Road that evening, tottering along the uneven pavement in her red court shoes, she knew she looked as good as she could – not model perfect but good enough to boost her confidence, a rare thing for her.

'Where you off, Viv?' her dad called, sitting in the chair that used to be his dad's, while his wife and mum washed up the tea things.

'Oh, I'm going up to Clifton, meeting that David Bowie for me tea.'

'Well have a lovely evening, darlin', and be careful. Might turn cold later. Get Dave to drop you back to the front door.' Her dad winked, adjusting his pipe in the side of his mouth and crossing his slippered feet at the ankles.

'Where do you think I'm going?' she scoffed. 'Up the pub!'

'Might join you in a bit if I can drag your mum away from *Bergerac*.'

'Might see you later then.'

Her dad never made it to the Rising Sun on Windmill Hill, so instead she chatted to her cousin Ronnie, who worked behind the bar, his girlfriend Tina and of course Ellen, who was, as ever, on fine form, larking around with beer mats, balancing them on her head and dancing to Haircut One Hundred on the jukebox. The whole evening fell short of fabulous; apart from a wolf whistle from old Ted, who played the piano when he was sloshed, no one had paid her any attention.

Vivienne didn't know what she expected from these nights at their regular, but it was always more than she actually got. She'd routinely wander back home with Ellen on her arm, stopping for a bag of chips on the way, which she'd eat with her fingers, dipping them in ketchup and scoffing them quickly before reaching her front door. As she lay in the room she had slept in since she was a child, there'd be a new layer of disappointment sitting on top of the others, a tang of dissatisfaction in her mouth and a yearning she couldn't quite explain swirling in her stomach. Her eyes would wander to the heap of discarded clothes on her bedroom carpet and she would regret spending so much on a night out that had ended in this familiar fashion. She figured that if you cut her down the middle, she'd be like a trifle, with all her hopes, fears and dreams buffered by a big marshmallowy pillow of disillusionment, layered right there for all to see.

On this particular evening, Ronnie was collecting glasses and Tina and Ellen were mucking about, with Ellen trying to catch a glacé cherry in her mouth, lobbed over the back of Tina's head.

They didn't manage it, but Ellen screamed and squawked as if they had. Vivienne decided to call it a night. She gathered her bag and slid out of the sticky wooden booth that had been their home for the evening, and when she looked up, there he was.

He stared at her and didn't speak. Her eyes travelled up the hulk of a man, his stature only emphasised by the diminutive build of his mate, Trev. His oversized cotton jacket, rolled up at the sleeves over his white T-shirt, and his acid-washed jeans, turned up to above the ankle, made him look very *Miami Vice*. He was cocky, confident and good-looking, with the tan of a man who worked outside, and he was standing in such close proximity, it made her legs shake with a mixture of desire and something close to fear. His eyes were bright blue, piercing, as if they could see inside her, read her thoughts. And there he stayed, hovering inches from her, silent and staring.

It created an unbelievable, intoxicating tension. Vivienne felt her heart race and was about to walk out, make her way home, when he placed his hand around the top of her arm. His large fingers encircled her narrow bicep with ease, holding her fast. His face broke into a huge grin; his teeth were straight and very white. 'Film-star gnashers,' her nan would have said.

He had a Bristol accent like hers. 'Hello.' He smiled. 'Cat got your tongue?' he asked.

'No, some monster's got me arm though.' She held his eye with more confidence than she felt inside as her stomach jumped with nerves.

'Gobby for a little bird, aren't you?'

'You all right, Viv?' Ellen hollered, looking out for her friend, as ever. 'Want me to come over there?'

He ignored her, one of the only people Vivienne had ever met that did so.

She lifted her chin, trying to look taller than she was and braver than she felt.

He bent his head towards her and whispered in her ear, 'I've been waiting for you.'

'What do you mean, you've been waiting for me?' She screwed her face up as her heart pounded.

He smiled and studied her. 'I mean, I've been waiting for someone like you. And here you are.'

Her cheeks flushed red and her legs swayed. She felt as if she was drunk, and it certainly wasn't down to the two warm, flat Coca-Colas she'd sipped that evening. She didn't know exactly what was happening, but she knew it was something big.

Over the next two days, excitement bubbled in her blood, making sleeping or eating impossible. She planned every aspect of her clothes, make-up and accessories, in case their paths should cross, and by that time she knew, without a doubt, that it was love.

And when, a week later, after double-dating with Ellen and Trev, he lifted her clean off the pavement, held her up in the cold night air and told her he would love her until the day he died and that no one – no one – would ever lay a finger on her because he was her knight, her king, her lover, she believed him. It felt like a fairy tale. *It was a bloody fairy tale, if by fairy tale you mean a load of made-up rubbish.* She smiled to herself.

Bob barked, pulling her from her memories. 'What's up, mate? Fancy a drink of water?' She stood and patted his muzzle as they made their way into the kitchen. The ghosts of her past were strangely present today.

Hesitating in the doorway, she remembered the horrible morning when it had all come crashing to an end. She pictured trying to keep it together for the kids' sake, as she walked into this kitchen, which was then still very much her mum's domain. She had an icy feeling of rejection sitting in the pit of her stomach. The truth was, she had never felt truly warm since. Aaron had run into the front room and was playing with his toy car on the rug and Emma stood close to her mum with her small hand sitting trustingly in hers. The single suitcase, all Vivienne had been able to carry, was in the hallway, sitting forlornly on the cold tiles. It held the kids' clothes, a couple of toys, and the brush-and-comb set with the mother-of-pearl backs that had been her great-grandma's. He could have the rest, if and when he came back.

'He said he was going for Chinese food about sevenish, but he didn't come home.'

'Maybe there was a queue?' her mum had joked.

'No, Mum. He's left. He was never at the Chinese. I've asked all over. He's run off with a woman he knows from Eastville Market. Don't know much about her, apart from her name – Suzanne – and that's it, they've gone.'

'Are you hungry?'

'What?' She looked up at her mum.

'Just wondered if you were hungry, love, being

as he never came back with your tea and every-thing?'

Her mum's attempt at cheering her up had only made her cry even harder, until the tears rolled down her cheeks. 'I'm not hungry, Mum, but we could do with a place to stay. I can't pay the rent on the flat without Ray.' She sobbed; saying the words out loud had made it more real. 'And I don't want to be there when he comes to collect his stuff, don't want the row or the chat, none of it. It's been on the cards for a while.'

Her mum had swept her up into a warm embrace.

'You never have to ask – this is your home! Always has been, always will be.' She kissed her. 'How do you know he's run off with this Suzanne?'

Vivienne shrugged free of her grip. 'It was common knowledge, apparently. Everyone knew apart from me and Elle.'

'Did Trev not tell her?' her mum asked, know-ing that he and Ray were thick as thieves.

She shook her head. 'No, he was worried she'd kill him.' She managed a smile at the idea of her friend defending her to this degree.

Her mum straightened. 'Reckon he might be right.' She dusted down her pinny and turned to her child. 'Go hang your stuff up and wash your face while me and Emma put the kettle on and make Aaron some breakfast.' She winked.

'What do you fancy Little Em? Egg on toast?'

The little girl had nodded and slipped her hand from her mum's, eager to go and help her nan.

And, just like that, Vivienne had returned home.

She was back sleeping where she'd spent her whole life until Ray had carried her off with the lure of a two-bed flat and a view over St Mary Redcliffe church to the right and the docks to the left. He'd promised her an adventure and it had certainly felt like one, her heart regularly pounding with fear and expectation, until that last night when she'd realised the adventure was over and it was time to go home.

But even now, nearly thirty years later, Vivienne – who was in her fifties, had buried her parents, raised her children, worked hard and battled on, and hadn't seen Ray Lane since the night he walked out – still *felt* married, still sported the thin, worn, gold band on her left hand that she felt gave her status. That little ring had acted as a comfort and a deterrent over the years. Funny how something so small could retain so much power and meaning for her, when for the man who gave it to her it had absolutely none.

It was bed-linen day. She had got behind in her routine, owing to the distraction of the invitation. Vivienne stripped her bed and bundled the sheets and duvet cover into the machine before taking the dog-lead from the coat hook on the hallstand. At the sound of its familiar rattle, Bob duly left his comfy basket by the radiator and plodded into the hallway. There was none of the exuberance, darting about and heavy breathing of his earlier walk; he simply bowed his head ready to receive his harness. He knew the drill by now.

'Quick walk, eh, Bob? Then home to put the dryer on.' She smiled at her companion, wondering what she would do if he actually replied one day and what he might sound like.

The cold weather meant that clumps of snow remained around the edges of the pavement and sat in a dark sludge under the wheel arches of less frequently used cars. There was still a nip in the air and an almost invisible mist, as if the memory of the last flurry still lingered. Vivienne pulled Bob towards her calf and picked up the pace, as they made their way down the steep curve of Cotswold Road and took a sharp left into the green space of St John's Burial Ground. It was a cut-through to the main road, a patch of lush grass and mature trees with the narrow, meandering Malago trickling along its border and a cycle path bisecting it. Roughly a couple of acres in size, it was a little oasis in the middle of the city, a wasteland where drunks lolled, the homeless slept, kids loitered and lovers kissed fervently on the benches until shoved off or scared away by the regulars.

Vivienne unclipped the lead and let Bob explore. He sniffed at the undergrowth and rummaged in the long grass, hoping for a discovery despite knowing every inch of the space. There was never much variety in what he found: discarded cider tins, chip wrappers, the charcoal embers of measly fires and the waste of fellow canines whose humans were too lazy to bend down and scoop on their behalf. He kept her in view. She wasn't sure who was minding whom. He was a faithful friend.

'There you are!'

Ellen suddenly appeared behind her.

'Good Lord, you made me jump.' Vivienne placed her palm on her chest, trying to still her racing heart.

'I couldn't find you. I tried the house and you weren't there,' Ellen said accusingly. 'If you're going out, text me or leave a note, or at least take your phone – save me the walk. Do you think I want to run all over looking for you?'

'Sorry, Mum.' Vivienne shook her head.

Ellen linked her arm through her friend's and pulled her towards the wooden bench at the side of the path, the one with some slats missing and black felt-tipped love hearts with scrawled initials covering almost every inch of it. Their particular favourite was one that had appeared a couple of months ago. It read: *Marlon & Tracy 4 Ever.* But only weeks later, *Tracy* had been scored through and replaced with *Emily.* It made them laugh.

'Poor Tracy,' Vivienne had commented. 'In fact, poor Emily, if this is the rate he gets through his beloveds.'

Ellen marched her up the small incline to their seat.

'I *can* go out without checking with you first, you know,' Vivienne said.

Ellen laughed, and hugged her arm towards her, as if this wasn't true. 'So, I called the internet number I got from Robbie and spoke to a lovely man, who said he'd chuck in free car hire in Hong Kong.' She sat back on the damp wood and folded her hands into her lap.

'Have you heard yourself? Free car hire in Hong Kong? Who are you, Judith Chalmers? We don't even go up the mall without a lot of pre-planning and packing a flask just in case, and here you are talking about Hong Kong as if it's round the corner.'

'The man at the internet travel place made it sound so easy.'

'Maybe it is for him. I just can't see us driving a car around Hong Kong, can you? I've heard it's quite busy and neither of us are very good at driving in crowds, are we? Remember that time we were trying to find that garden centre and accidentally got stuck on the ring road? That was scary enough.' She shivered at the memory.

Ellen seemed to consider this. 'I don't know, Viv, I just think we are knocking on and maybe we should go and grab a bit of adventure. We said in our New Year's resolution last year we were going to be a bit more daring.'

'Yes, but I thought things like invest in a spiralizer or take up Zumba at the community centre, not jump on a plane and go to the other side of the world!'

'Your Emma is getting married. Are you telling me you would be happy to miss that?'

Vivienne shook her head. 'No, of course not, but...'

'But what?' Ellen asked as Bob lumbered over and sat down by their feet. He had clearly had enough of rooting around in the cold.

'It's such a long way.' She stared ahead. 'I honestly thought she might be coming home. I planned it in my head and I was looking forward to it. Getting married to a Kiwi means she might not be home for any Christmas, let alone this one.'

Ellen nudged her friend with her elbow. 'Don't think that far forward, Viv. Let's just plan as far ahead as we have to, but I do think you'll regret it if you don't go.'

Vivienne nodded. 'I know. Let me speak to her later and if it's a goer, we can book it tomorrow, how does that sound?'

'Sounds like we might be going on an adventure, Viv.' Ellen raised her shoulders in excitement, as she had been doing since she was a child. 'What side of the road do they drive on in Hong Kong and do they have English-speaking satnavs?'

Vivienne rolled her eyes. 'God help us.'

Having washed up her supper plate, and set aside the scarf she was knitting for Aaron's Christmas present, she looked again at the clock and did the maths. It was 7.30 p.m., which made it 8.30 a.m. in New Zealand. She pictured her daughter's previous boyfriends, all of them night owls, with whom Emma would sit up into the wee small hours, sipping tequila by candlelight, smoking and figuring out their own great adventures. So it was highly unlikely that Emma would be up and about at half eight in the morning, but she decided to try anyway.

'I'm nervous, Bob. Silly, really. She's my little girl.' She lifted her chin and carefully pressed the buttons of the number written on the Post-it note, not wanting the embarrassment or the expense of getting it wrong. She spoke the first digits aloud, as was her habit – '0064 9434...' – then got to the end and waited.

The alien ringtone made her sit up straight. She was unsure if it was ringing or engaged, until the call was answered and she gripped the phone in her palm.

'Hello?'

'Mum!' Emma's voice sounded bright and happy, instantly putting her at ease.

'Hello, love! Hope I haven't woken you up.'

'No, not at all. I've been up for an age – Michael always says it's the best part of the day; cool enough to get lots done and the sky is so beautiful. So I'm making a big effort to get up earlier and get going.'

Vivienne smiled; this was good to hear, if a little strange to her – it was the first time she had heard Emma flexing to fit someone else in this way. Maybe she was growing up.

'I got your invite. Well I never, darling, that *was* a big surprise!' Emma was too far away for her not to cut to the chase.

'Can you believe it!' Emma's accent had changed in the year she had been in New Zealand and the word 'it' sounded more like 'ut'. It saddened Vivienne how quickly the West Country was being erased from her daughter's life and her voice.

'I must admit, I wasn't expecting it. Is he nice?' She cringed at the question; what did she expect the answer to be? *'No, Mum, he's a proper waster, but I love him.'*

'Oh, Mum, he's...'

Vivienne noted the catch to her voice, the emotion, and it made her smile. She remembered when she had sat at the table in the kitchen and tried to explain to her own mum how Ray made her feel.

'He's brilliantly clever, a doctor! And even though he's so smart and could be arrogant, he isn't, he's kind and funny and very good-looking.'

'Wow!' This was not what Vivienne had expected – a doctor. That was a turn-up.

'I know, wow! I never knew someone like him existed and if I had known, then I never would have thought that he'd be interested in someone like me, but he is and I feel like the luckiest woman on the planet.'

'I've never heard you like this.'

'That's because I've never *felt* like this. God, I'm nearly thirty-two and I feel giddy, like a schoolgirl with a crush.'

'And you are certain? I mean, you haven't been with him for that long, I know you liked Hai...' Vivienne felt a little mean about bursting Emma's bubble, but with time and distance against them, it was vital she gleaned as much as she could.

'I know it seems quick, it is quick! But Hai was never a serious thing and Michael was with someone for four years, no kids, she was a doctor too, but that didn't work out and it's made him realise, made us both realise, that life is there to be lived. So we're going for it. We met on a night out and haven't really been apart since. We're moving from Auckland to stay with his dad up on the coast and Michael has a new job at Whangarei Hospital, which is commutable. He's already started and loves it. We are so happy, Mum, and it feels amazing to be choosing a new life. Michael says that time seems to go faster as you get older and you just don't know what's around the corner.'

Vivienne closed her eyes, marvelling at how mature and together her girl sounded. 'He's right about that,' she said.

'You are going to love him, Mum. I've told him

all about our little house in Bedminster and he thinks it sounds cute. I told him it's just crappy, but he is a real romantic. I won't shatter his illusions.'

Vivienne let her gaze sweep the rooms from her vantage point on the stairs: her parents' home, which had provided shelter when they'd needed it most. In her mind it was far, far from crappy.

She pictured her dad sitting in his sandy-coloured velour chair that he reclined when the fancy took him, usually every afternoon at about three o'clock, and on Sunday afternoons if the cricket wasn't on. He would nap, shielded from the street on which he liked to spy by the pristine white, net curtains that billowed lace into the room when the breeze took them. Her mum with her feet curled under her, always took up residence on the left-hand side of the sofa, where she turned the leather cushion regularly to make sure it didn't lose its shape; it never occurred to her to move to the other end of the sofa to even out the wear.

Vivienne had changed very little in the house over the years. She'd kept the clusters of her mother's ornaments and the corner display cabinet with its collection of crystal glass. Sometimes she felt like a caretaker, dusting and returning items to their proper place, a spot allocated by another hand, long dead. She rubbed waxy polish into the old pine units and buffed the terracotta floor tiles, as if she was watching over everything, just as her mum had. She wasn't sure what would become of it all; she certainly didn't see Aaron and Lizzie or indeed Emma ending up there, especially not now. What would happen to all the objects so lovingly cared for over the decades – the charity shop, possibly? That would certainly be the case if Lizzie had her way.

Above the fireplace sat a large gold frame around a bottle-green mount containing twelve different-sized shapes, from oval to square. From each shape poked a photo of Emma's face, taken at various ages. Toothy school photographs in the main, with a couple snapped in the back garden as she devoured an ice cream and turned a cart-wheel. An identical montage of Aaron sat next to it. Vivienne had seen the images so often that she didn't notice them any more; they were, like every-thing else in the house, simply part of the backdrop to her life, her history.

Cars, clothes, jewels – Vivienne had always known that this was not where her happiness lay; never in things. This she had learnt from her lovely mum, who had passed away when the kids were still little. Even a fleeting memory of her mum, of the way she used to smile, her scent, the image of her back at the sink as she busied herself in the kitchen, these were enough to bring a catch of longing into Vivienne's throat. Her grief felt as raw as it had on the day she died.

Emma continued to babble, talking animatedly about flower displays in terracotta pots and handmade bunting cut from vintage fabrics. Her excitement was infectious.

'You will come over, Mum, won't you?' she pleaded. 'You will come to the wedding? I know it's a long way and it's close to Christmas, but it goes without saying that I really, really want you there. You're my mum!'

'Do you think I'd miss my child's big day? Of course I'll be there, and Elle, of course.'

'Of course.' Emma laughed. 'Will Aaron and Lizzie come too, do you think?'

'I'm not sure, love. I will ask them. It is a very long way.' She felt stupid, as if Emma might be unaware of how many miles separated her and her brother. 'Did you send them an invite?'

'Yes, but it went in the second batch. I wasn't sure of their address, don't think it will have arrived yet. To be honest, I wanted to ask just Aaron and tell him to leave Lizzie at home – don't want that plastic face to melt in the sun.'

'Oh, Emma, you can't say that!' She shook her head in mock admonishment, secretly liking the shared indiscretion, a link across the miles.

'I'm only teasing, Mum. But I still haven't really forgiven her for how mean she was when I left Bristol, the way she huffed and spoke out of the side of her mouth, saying I'd probably only make it as far as Heathrow and would be back in a few days after a crisis, that was just horrible.'

'I know,' she had to agree, it *was* horrible, 'but maybe it was a bit of the green-eyed monster?'

'I don't care Mum, whatever it was, I don't choose to spend any time with her, which is a shame because I really miss Aaron, but one thing is for certain, nothing is going to spoil this wedding. I am so excited! Michael's dad is a sheep farmer and has a beautiful farm up here on the Tutukaka coast. We're having the ceremony outside, overlooking the water, on the cliff edge – in December, can you believe it? It's going to be amazing. You are going to love it.'

'I'm sure I will.' She tried to sound convincing, actually thinking that a tiny place on an island on the other side of the world didn't exactly sound like her cup of tea. Give her the hustle and bustle of North Street and a quick cuppa in Pedro's any day. She changed the subject.

'What should I wear?' The thought occurred to her for the first time.

'Anything you are comfy in – floaty frock, summer dress, nothing grand or special or new, it's going to be very casual.'

'Can I help with anything? Send some money? Organise something?' She felt a little awkward, knowing how little she would be able to do from this distance.

'No, it's all taken care of. But thank you, Mum. Tutukaka is like nowhere on earth, it's special, and you are going to be here and just to have you here will make it perfect!'

'I love you, Emma Lane.' Vivienne swallowed the unexpected tears that clogged her throat.

'I love you too. Just think, Mum, Christmas in the sunshine – what would Nanny say?'

'She'd be worried that her chocolate log would melt and her trifle might turn in the heat.' She smiled, picturing her dear old mum and knowing this was an accurate assessment.

'Mum, I have to go, Michael's giving me a lift into Whangarei and I need to pick up some bits – speak soon?'

'Yes, of course. I better go and book my flight.'

'Yep, fly to Auckland and we'll pick you up from there. Let me know what flight you are on.

I'm so excited!'

Vivienne again noted how 'excit-ed' had become 'excit-ud' and this time it made her smile. She sat for a little while after the call had ended, stroking Bob's head and letting the dark fill every space in the hallway.

'Looks like I'm going to New Zealand, Bob, can you believe it? Question is, what am I going to do with you for a fortnight?'

He lifted his face to gaze at her and gave what she could only describe as a look of disdain.

'You are too clever by half.' She smiled and patted his head as she yawned. It was nearly bed-time.

Three

'A doctor!' Ellen banged the table, alerting the woman and her child on the table next to them, who briefly abandoned their toasted bagels and gave them a look of interest. 'Well, I never. That's a turn-up for the books. What kind of doctor is he?'

'What do you mean?' Vivienne smiled apolo-getically at the woman for her friend's loudness, something she was rather practised at.

'Well, is he a medical doctor? A plastic surgeon rolling in dosh–'

'Oh God, you're not thinking about your new boobs again, are you?'

'No, but I am thinking about Emma's future. He

might be one of those medics who has bought his doctorship off the internet. I've read about it. There are millions of them all over the UK, people who set up as GPs but have no more skill than a Girl Guide with a first-aid badge and a bottle of aspirin. They could be advising you to have surgery when all you actually need is a glug of milk of magnesia and a quick lie down.'

Vivienne laughed out loud, accidentally snorting. 'I'm sure that's not true.'

'It is! I read it somewhere.'

This assertion only made her laugh harder.

'You can laugh, my girl, but it's the difference between her spending her days lounging by a pool with a pina colada in her hand or working behind a bar serving cocktails to women married to *real* doctors.'

'I don't think Emma likes pina colada.'

'That's not the point.' Ellen sighed.

'I know, you're saying that I know nothing about this man, and you're right, I don't, but there is very little I can do about it right now.' She spoke through gritted teeth.

'Here we are, ladies.' Pedro placed their coffees in front of them. 'How are we today?'

'We are planning our trip.' Ellen cocked her head, waiting for him to enquire further.

'Oh lovely. Where are you off to? Morecambe again? Might need a brolly.' He obviously recalled their last summer holiday.

'Not quite, Pedro. Actually we're off to New Zealand, via Hong Kong,' Ellen announced proudly.

'New Zealand? You lucky things. That's

somewhere that's definitely on my list. When do you go?' He placed his knuckles on his hips.

'In a couple of weeks. Viv's daughter is getting married.'

'Congratulations!' He smiled at Vivienne as she sipped her coffee. She was a little embarrassed to be the topic of discussion.

'Where's Bob off to?'

'Oh, I think Trev, Ellen's husband, might have him. Or my son, Aaron, not quite sure yet.' She had yet to firm up the plan.

'Ah, shame. I'd love to have had him for a bit. I could have nipped up to the flat during the quiet times and taken him round the block.' He looked wistful.

'I wouldn't want to put on you like that, Pedro.' She spoke softly.

'Put on me?' He shook his head. 'I would love it. You have no idea how much I miss that company of an evening, and just strolling the street with my little sidekick on a lead. I met some of my great friends, too, through owning a dog – like-minded people with dogs in the family.'

Vivienne noted the lump in his throat. 'I tell you what, Pedro, if you're serious, I'll bring Bob over for a visit, see how you like having him around and vice versa. Then, if you still want to, I think he'd be very lucky to come and stay chez Pedro while we're away.'

'Oh, really?' Pedro visibly jumped with excitement. 'I'd love that!' He scooted back to the counter with a definite spring in his step.

'Oi, and a teacake to share, if you don't mind,' Ellen called after him. 'And not one from the back neither!'

Vivienne pulled a face at her rude friend.

'What?' Ellen looked puzzled and sipped her coffee.

The two friends had hopped on the number 76 bus and were now wandering around the town centre. It was far easier somehow to tolerate the drizzle-slicked streets, where crowds jostled for space on the pavement when they knew they were heading for sunnier climes.

'What do you think, Viv?' Ellen called across the rails in Primark.

Vivienne craned her neck to see her friend holding up a neon-pink tie bikini with a sheer neon vest that would barely cover the bikini, let alone anything beneath it.

'I think I am not going near a beach with you in that.' She tried to sound decisive. 'I might crochet you a nice bikini that would offer more cover. Anyway, we don't even know if they're near a beach, do we?'

'Course they are. Emma said, didn't she? It's on the coast. It'll be like Spain but with more sheep, less paella and that Dame Kiri whats'er name singing up a storm.'

Vivienne ignored her and continued to peruse the pedal pushers that came in an array of colours. 'Weird, isn't it, buying for warm weather in the middle of winter. It makes it doubly special, some-how, going to the sun when it's so cold here.'

'I know what you mean. Every time Trev turns up the heating or rubs his hands together to ease his chilblains, I think about it.'

'He doesn't mind you going?' Vivienne felt a bit guilty about dragging Trev's wife halfway round the world.

'No! He doesn't mind much.' This was true. 'I think he's looking forward to the rest.'

'He'll think he's gone deaf!' She laughed.

It was Ellen's turn to ignore her. 'It's not long till we go, Viv, only a fortnight. What did Aaron say?'

'Haven't told him yet. I'm seeing him tonight.'

'You chicken,' Ellen clucked.

'I am not chicken; I just wanted to tell him in person, have a proper chat. I didn't want to tell him over the phone and I half hoped his invite might pitch up before I saw him.'

'If you say so, love.' Ellen smiled before making a squawking noise.

'I do. And what about this? This is perfect for you!' Vivienne held up a grey balaclava. 'I think this could only improve your look.' She giggled.

'I'll remember that, you know I will.' Ellen narrowed her eyes at her friend, who was still laughing.

The days were getting shorter and shorter. Vivienne tried to picture the spring, when things always felt brighter. She turned down the peas, which had just started to boil, and went to answer the front door, wiping her hands on her sweatshirt.

'God it's cold!' Aaron stamped his feet and pulled his fingers from the bulky leather gloves that encased them, as Lizzie sauntered in on impossibly high-heeled boots, letting the heat whoosh out of the door and up Mendip Road.

'Hello, love. Hi, Lizzie!' She added an injection

of enthusiasm that she didn't feel. 'I've made fish pie.'

'Told you,' Lizzie muttered under her breath, just loud enough to be heard.

'Oh, I can make you something else if you'd prefer? I've got a pizza in the freezer.' She felt her face colour.

'No, no, I just said that's what you'd make and I was right.' Lizzie gave a half smile.

Vivienne found it hard to guess at the point of her statement, but felt embarrassed nonetheless.

Aaron gave an awkward, embarrassed smile.

'Bob!' Lizzie beamed, before dropping down onto her knees and ruffling his fur and whispering close to his face. It always fascinated her how the warmest of welcomes was reserved for the dog; Lizzie had always been this way, as if he was the only member of the family, other than Aaron, she was comfortable with. Vivienne wished her daughter-in-law were able to lavish the same love and attention on Aaron's human relatives.

She watched as Lizzie stood and Aaron helped his wife out of her slim-fitting red coat and hung it on the hallstand before handing her her shiny, oversized handbag. He reminded her of an over-familiar cloakroom attendant, hoping for a tip. His shoulders were stooped, his stance subservient and the look he gave his wife, as she briefly raked his arm, was one of pure gratitude. It tore at her heart. She felt a spike of guilt, as she again considered the fact that his dad's bullish behaviour might have shaped her son in this way, wondering what more she could have done to give him the confidence he so clearly lacked.

Raymond Lane had been a big man, filling any room with his presence. A more aware character might have tried to counter this imposing physicality with humility, deference and a quieted tone, but not Ray. In fact, quite the opposite: he revelled in it.

Though not a criminal, exactly, he'd been a big shot in the area and there was always some kind of deal going on. She couldn't count the number of times he'd stepped over the threshold of an evening and offered her something she didn't need – seven pairs of identical sling-backed shoes in a size 4, three wheelbarrows, a Teasmade, a couple of frozen lambs. She always, laughingly, ignored the offers; better that than embroil herself in God knows what. Besides, Ray would do as he saw fit, with or without her approval.

Her mind flitted back to a morning not long before he left. It was a school day and six-year-old Aaron was sitting at the table swinging his skinny legs while Emma sang loudly from her bedroom along the hallway. Their flat was small but cosy.

'I was thinking, might be an idea to get Aaron up the boys' club, do a bit of boxing.' Ray eyed his son with a look of exasperation. 'My mate Den runs the place. He said he'd have him up there a couple of nights a week. Bit of sparring will do him good. What do you say, Aaron, boy?' Ray shuffled on his feet, jabbing his bunched left fist and then his right, breathing sharply through his nose.

'Don't mind.' Aaron shrugged his narrow shoulders and stared at the cereal in his bowl as he gripped the spoon. 'Can I have some more milk, Mum?' he whispered.

'What's boxing?' Emma asked loudly as she came into the kitchen and took a seat next to her brother. She too reached for her bowl of cereal, shovelling it into her mouth as she spoke.

'It's something I hate,' Vivienne said.

'D'you hear that, kids? No one is to do boxing. Your mother has spoken. I'll just phone up every boys' club in the country, and all them blokes who've been kept out of trouble through knocking about in a gym, and tell them Viv has decided: no one is to do any boxing!' He shook his head and made as if he was speaking on a phone, holding an imaginary handset to his ear. 'Is that you, Rocky? Listen, mate, sorry to have to tell you this, but Viv has spoken!'

She ignored him. 'I don't care what anyone else does, Ray. I only care about my kids and I don't like the idea of them boxing. It's violent. And Aaron is still so little.' She picked up the tea towel and started to dry the mugs.

He snorted. 'I tell you what's violent, is watching a boy get the you-know-what kicked out of him because he doesn't know how to box, standing there like a plank instead of putting up the dukes. Now that's violent.'

'Please, Ray!' She closed her eyes.

'I'm only having a laugh. She's on my case again, kids.' This he addressed to the table in a tone that sounded both jovial and threatening at the same time. 'I'm getting out of here. Time for Daddy to go to work.' Once again he jabbed his fists at his son.

Aaron smiled weakly at him.

'Might be late tonight.' This Ray said to his

cuffs as he folded back his leather jacket to reveal an inch of tanned wrist and the heavy faux-gold watch that graced his arm like a weighty Christmas bauble.

Vivienne nodded, knowing there was no 'might' about it. The smile that played around his mouth and the narrowing of his eyes told her all she needed to know. He and his shady associates were clearly up to no good, some grand plan that might just mean their ship had come in, but more likely would turn out to be a leaky dinghy that needed bailing. There was a time when this had caused her so much distress it made her gut churn and filled-her lungs with a cloud of misery, making it hard for her to breathe. She worried about his operations on the wrong side of the law and what that might mean for her and the kids. What if he got caught? What if her mum and dad found out? It had, however, been a little while since she'd felt like that. She now responded with silent acquiescence and nodding indifference, and the only thing that was bizarre to her about the situation was that Ray didn't seem to have noticed.

Vivienne waited for the sound of the front door closing before skipping to the table and placing her arm around Aaron's slight shoulders. 'Take no notice of your dad. He's only joking.' She beamed, just as she had practised, believing that if she smiled hard enough and laughed long enough she could erase the memory of the harsh tone and unpleasant atmosphere, smothering the flames of her husband's latent aggression under a blanket of beaming kindness.

'I don't want to do any boxing.' Aaron spoke to

his cereal, occasionally eyeing his sister for a re-action and embarrassed to be so fussed over by his mum.

'You don't have to, love. You can do whatever you want.' She ruffled his hair and filled the kettle ready for her second cup of tea of the day.

Bob's muffled whine drew her to the present. He wasn't happy that the petting had stopped, the spoilt thing. She felt his nose nuzzle her palm as she took him by the collar and led him towards his basket, as all three made their way into the kitchen. Remembering that episode with Ray had rattled her, she wondered not for the first time if this was one of the reasons Aaron seemed a little reluctant to become a dad, maybe he was scared of turning out like his father? She would have to find a way to reassure him, he was already a far, far nicer man.

'How's work, love?'

'Ah, you know, plodding on, Mum.' Aaron glanced at his wife, who leant against the counter-top and made a kind of 'tsk' sound, the noise suggesting that even Aaron's job was a source of dissatisfaction.

'You'll be breaking off for Christmas quite soon, won't you?' Vivienne searched for the positive.

Aaron nodded.

'Not that he's getting a rest, mind – I've got plans for him. I've decided we should decorate the hall, stairs and landing. I want to copy something I saw on one of my programmes.' For the first time since arriving, Lizzie looked quite happy. 'I'm going to have one feature wall with a printed mural, a theme, like the sea or a forest, I haven't decided yet, and then all the other walls will blend with it in a coordinating shade.' She smiled, moving her palm in an arc as if picturing the finished article.

'Sounds lovely.' Viv tried not to concentrate on the look of dread on Aaron's face, wishing her son could rest up for at least a day or two.

'Actually, I wanted to talk to you both about Christmas,' she began as she set the salt and pepper on the dining table.

'We only want vouchers, no pressies as such,' Lizzie announced.

'Oh, but I've already started knitting.' Vivienne pictured the half-finished, striped scarf that languished in her knitting bag.

'Well, your knitting doesn't really count,' Lizzie informed her, unaware of how her words cut her mother-in-law to the quick. 'We are asking for vouchers from everyone and we're putting them towards a beautiful multi-coloured, glass-droplet chandelier we've seen for the dining room, aren't we?' Lizzie glanced at Aaron, who nodded a little less than enthusiastically.

'Err, it wasn't about presents, exactly, more about the whole event, actually,' Vivienne tried again.

'It's *my* mum's turn, remember? We were here last year.' Lizzie stuck out her finger and made a circle in the air. Vivienne followed her finger, looking around the humble little room that was bursting with memories, and not a glass-droplet chandelier in sight. Lizzie's tone rather suggested that the whole experience had been something to be endured.

'Yes, I remember. What I wanted to say was that I'm going away beforehand but will be back in time for the twenty-fifth.' She turned off the stove and walked the saucepan of peas over to the sink, where she tipped them into the sieve, pulling her head back to avoid the steam.

'Where are you going, Mum?'

She turned and smiled at her son. 'Hong Kong and then New Zealand. Emma's getting married.'

'What? Never!' He looked a little taken aback. 'No way! Well, that's a turn-up for the books. Who's she getting married to?'

'His name is Michael McKinley and I don't know that much about him, to tell you the truth, but he's a Kiwi and she sounds absolutely over the moon, it's lovely. I spoke to her last night.' She beamed at her son, feeling joy in sharing this happy news.

'Ahh, that's great.' Aaron wrinkled his nose, pleased for his little sis.

'She has of course invited both of you, but I know it's a long way.' She let this hang, replaying Emma's comments about Lizzie in her head.

'It is a long way, Mum, and a bit pricey, but I would love to go, love to see her get married,' Aaron added. No one mentioned the extravagant decorating plans.

'I can't believe she's getting hitched.' Lizzie sat back in the chair. 'Wonder what her wedding will be like. I hope it's none of her hippy shit.' No doubt she was picturing her own extravagant nuptials, for which her parents had taken out a large loan. 'I always wondered who'd end up with Emma!' She let out a short giggle.

This angered Vivienne. She wanted to point out that whoever had managed to capture her lovely free spirit of a daughter was a lucky man indeed, but she didn't want to embarrass Aaron by arguing, so she swallowed and simply said, 'Well, you don't have to wonder any longer, Lizzie. She met a doctor. A tall, handsome Kiwi doctor and it's him that is going to end up with Emma.'

She noted the slight fall of Lizzie's lower jaw and knew Ellen would appreciate this in the retelling.

'A *doctor?*'

'That's right.' She nodded, avoiding eye contact, as if this snippet of news was incidental.

'Wow! How did they meet?' Aaron leant forward eagerly.

'I don't know, I'll ask her. But I think it was on a night out when she was probably up to her hippy shit.' She avoided the faces of her guests and set the plates on the counter top.

'That's ... that's great news, Mum. I hope she's happy. She really deserves it,' Aaron stuttered, clearly not wanting the tension to escalate.

'Right then, who's for fish pie?' Vivienne asked as she opened the oven door.

The phone on the wall rang.

'Oh Lord! Hang on a minute.' She placed the supper dish on the sideboard, its mashed-potato topping steaming away, and reached for the phone.

'What did Lady-Never-Dump make of your news?' Ellen boomed.

Vivienne felt her face go crimson as she prayed that her friend's words hadn't been as loudly delivered as she suspected.

'Not today, thank you!' She quickly hung up and reached for the serving spoon. 'Fish pie, Lizzie?' she asked.

'Why not.' Lizzie pushed her plate forward.

It was the middle of the evening when Vivienne waved them off. As she stood at the sink, washing up the plates and using the scourer on the remnants of mashed potato that were crusted round the sides of the casserole dish, she thought back to the many Christmases she'd spent in the house. She pictured her mum standing on that very spot, washing pots and swaying slightly after her mid-afternoon sherry with a frond of tinsel draped around her neck that made the most inadequate feather boa.

In the weeks leading up to the festive holiday, her dad would work extra shifts at the Wills factory, and her mum would always be in receipt of a lovely gift from him. It was often a fancy bottle of scent that she would use sparingly, making it last all year or, as she remembered one year, a beautiful pair of navy leather, hand-stitched Dent gloves.

Their little square house, built in the 1940s, sat within a mile of the Wills Tobacco factory. It was the beating heart of their community – a smoke-belching monster on which they all depended. That was what people in their postcode did: they grew up and went to work at Wills and spent the next four decades waving to their mums, dads, aunties and uncles across the canteen and courting and marrying people they met on the production line. Her mum and dad were no different.

But not Vivienne: she had been swayed by the

charms of Ray Lane, who promised her something more. She often wondered what might have happened if she had yawned a bit earlier, grabbed her bag and left the Rising Sun seconds before she did. Funny to think that for the want of a yawn she might have been someone quite different, living a different kind of life. Married to a steady man maybe, who worked opposite her in the factory, a man who wouldn't have left her behind. She stopped scrubbing and sighed, suddenly feeling quite tired.

The next morning, Vivienne smiled and lifted her chin as the pretty young salon assistant tied the plastic poncho around her neck and finished it with an extravagant bow that she patted down neatly. The girl stood behind her and smiled into the mirror. 'Would you like a magazine?'

'No, she wouldn't. If she gets her head in a magazine I'll have no one to chat to.' Ellen twisted her own poncho and craned her neck to loosen the tie.

'Coffee? Tea?' The young girl addressed them both, clearly unsure of the etiquette where these two were concerned and wary of the rather shouty, larger lady who answered on her friend's behalf.

'Two coffees, love, white without.'

'Do you know, Elle, it's a wonder my voice box doesn't give up altogether, what with you on hand to do all my talking for me.'

Ellen ignored the comment, as she routinely did with anything she didn't particularly want to hear, and twisted the chair to face her. 'So, what did she say when you told her he was a doctor?'

She picked up the conversation they had started as they made their way along North Street to their regular hair appointment.

'Not much really, but her mouth literally fell open! I could tell she was shocked and I'm sure there was plenty she *wanted* to say.'

'I bet.'

'And you know, it must have really meant stuff if even she deemed it too bad to be aired. Emma had said on the phone how Lizzie's attitude towards her upset her and I felt that last night, Emma gained a bit of ground. It's only right she gets the recognition she deserves. She's brilliant.'

'She is.'

Ellen agreed, while humphing her disapproval at Lizzie's antics.

'Aaron was pleased for his sister, though. Said as much, and I could tell by his manner.'

'He's a good boy.' Ellen smiled.

The two women still on occasion had difficulty seeing their children as the adults they had become. Vivienne would often find herself picturing her rosy-cheeked schoolboy when she thought of Aaron, and sometimes, when the stocky thirty-something man himself stepped into her home, she did a double-take, as if he were a stranger. This, and the fact that in a certain light he looked just like Ray.

'Morning, ladies!' Fatima stepped forward with her shiny mahogany mane draped over one shoulder, making Vivienne feel quite self-conscious about her own layered, greying hair that had thinned around the temples; she was convinced that, when she brushed it back, she could see straight through to her scalp.

'Do you like my Christmas decorations?' Fatima stood back and proudly pointed at the twisted loops of crêpe paper that crisscrossed the ceiling and framed a gold foil star that hung from a length of cotton in the middle.

'Not really, love. You need to either go for it or not. These are a bit half-hearted.' Ellen spoke directly.

'Say what you mean, why don't you!' Vivienne shook her head. 'Ignore her, Fatima, they look lovely.'

'Maybe she's right. Shall I get a tree?' Fatima looked concerned.

'Yes! A big tree with all the trimmings – now you're talking.' Ellen smiled. 'I haven't even thought about decorations yet. Viv and me are going away.'

'Away? At this time of year? Where are you two going?'

'Hong Kong then New Zealand.' The novelty of saying this clearly hadn't worn off, as Ellen beamed and then winked at Vivienne. 'Hard to imagine that in only a couple of weeks we will be wandering around in our string bikinis on a sun-soaked beach. Can you believe it?'

'How wonderful.' Fatima clapped.

'My daughter's getting married. Do you remember Emma?'

'Emma, yes of course I do! Congratulations, Viv, that's quite something.'

Vivienne nodded. It was.

'Well in that case, when I've finished your cut and blow dry, we shall pop you both upstairs to the beauty rooms. You'll be wanting to get your legs waxed and all your bits and pieces done before you go, especially as the mother of the bride.'

'Don't think anyone will be looking at her bits and pieces – they haven't for the last thirty years, have they, Viv?' Ellen chuckled.

Vivienne ignored her. 'I suppose it might be nice to get all summer-ready. Feels weird, though, when there's still leftover snow on the ground and I'm wearing my thermal underwear.' She felt the burst of excitement in her stomach, and then it spread, warming her limbs. She still couldn't quite believe she was going to travel to the other side of the world.

With their hair neatly coiffed, they trod the stairs to the rooms above the hairdresser's where Fatima's daughter Irena ran her beauty concession.

'Hello, ladies, what can I do for you both today?' Irena greeted them from behind the reception desk, looking as beautiful as ever, with her finely arched brows, perfect skin and blue/white teeth.

'Leg wax definitely for me and I'd like my tash bleached,' Ellen requested, running her fingertip over her top lip.

'Yes, leg wax would be great,' Vivienne agreed.

'Bikini wax too?' Irena suggested.

'I'm not sure that's necessary for me.' Ellen pulled a face. 'I can't see me parading around in anything shorter than a maxi dress.'

'I might wear shorts.' Vivienne thought aloud. 'But I haven't had it done in an age – does it hurt?' She grimaced, as if even enquiring caused her physical pain.

'Not really. It's very quick and so by the time

any discomfort registers, it's over. And it lasts for weeks, nice for your holidays. I could do you a Brazilian?' she suggested.

'What is a Brazilian, exactly?' Vivienne asked.

'We basically wax the entire area apart from a central strip.' Irena was most matter-of-fact; it was routine for her, after all.

'Ooh no, don't think I need a Brazilian.' Vivienne squirmed at the thought. 'I need something that, err, leaves a bigger area and is less painful, but just as quick.'

'Russia's bigger than Brazil,' Ellen piped up. 'Can she have a Russian instead? But not too Russian, not Cossack hat, maybe more Siberian hamster.'

Vivienne couldn't help the snort of laughter. 'For goodness' sake, Elle!' she managed, as they fell against each other and dissolved into giggles like the schoolgirls they had been a mere blink ago. Irena widened her eyes at the middle-aged ladies who were cluttering up her reception.

It was late afternoon when Trev pulled up to the kerb in his work van and leant across to open the passenger door. 'All right, Viv?' he said, shouting to be heard.

'Yep, good, Trev. You?'

'Can't complain.' He nodded.

Even after all these years there was a slight awkwardness between them. She had never been able to shake the feeling that he might have known more about Ray's whereabouts all those years ago than he claimed, that out of misguided loyalty to his friend he'd chosen to say nothing. And on

Trev's part, Ellen had told her that for quite a while afterwards he blamed Viv for chasing his best mate away. These two mindsets made for uneasy bedfellows.

'And I hear you're dragging my missus to bloody New Zealand!' he joked.

'More like she's dragging me.' She pulled her scarf around her neck. 'I never thought for a minute we'd actually go. But I mention Emma's getting married and the next thing I know she's got Robbie looking up flights and is planning to hire a car in Hong Kong.'

'Viv, you promise me you won't let her drive anywhere, let alone Hong bloody Kong. I've seen her trying to get the car in and out of our drive and that's hit and miss.' He laughed. 'And make sure she's back in time for Christmas. I don't fancy beans on toast for my Christmas dinner.'

'That and you'd miss her of course.'

'Yeah, of course.' He grimaced.

'I am here, you know.' Ellen elbowed past her friend and lowered herself into the passenger seat. 'You sure you don't want a lift, Viv?'

'No, I like to walk.'

'See you in a bit.' Ellen placed her bag on her lap.

'Yep.' She closed the van door and stood back on the kerb.

Ellen wound down the window as Trev pulled out. 'Keep your Siberian hamster warm!'

Vivienne looked up and down the street, thankful that no one seemed to be paying her friend any attention. Pulling her coat around her body and heading in the direction of Mendip Road, she decided she would go and grab Bob and give him a quick once around the block.

'Only me!' she called to the dog, as she pushed open the front door. There on the mat was a thin, square, white envelope with a post-it note stuck to the front.

'What on earth?' Having retrieved it, she pulled it to her face and read the messaged gummed to the side.

Mrs Lane – could you give this to Emma for me, cheers, Shaun.

Vivienne smiled at the black, greasy thumbprint on the top right corner where a stamp would normally lurk. 'Don't you worry, Shaun, I'll make sure she gets it.' She then popped the envelope on the sideboard, next to her sunglasses so she wouldn't forget it.

Four

She had finished the very early shift in Asda and was now back home, still in her uniform while most people were still in their pyjamas. The radio in the kitchen seemed to be playing Christmas carols on a loop and Vivienne hummed along, hardly noticing the interlude of chatter before another jaunty favourite blasted out. She pulled opened the curtains to let in the morning sun. It was a rare bright day among the winter gloom.

She was in the room that had been her parents' and then Aaron's and was now termed 'spare'. Her eyes drifted to the open suitcase that lay on the double bed. She had folded into it vest tops, shorts, summer sandals and a floaty floral frock that she'd worn only a handful of times. She had taken Emma's advice, going for something that was comfortable and not too grand. Ellen had insisted she buy two large orange flowers that she might or might not wear in her hair, depending on her confidence level; she would see how she felt on the day.

Balancing on an old dining chair that lived in the corner of the room, she reached around on top of the wardrobe for the shoebox where adaptors and electrical bits and bobs were kept. As she did so, her hand happened upon a flat wooden shape. The moment she pulled it into view, she remembered lobbing it there an age ago. It was the framed photo of her and Ray as they left St Aldhelm's Church, pausing in the arched doorway to pose for the snap. Their wide grins, eyes that sparkled with anticipation, and tightly clasped hands betrayed no sign that for one of them the vows they had just exchanged were not in fact as solemn or binding as intended, but had instead been spoken casually, to be discarded when a blonde bombshell called Suzanne wiped them from his mind.

Her tears were unexpected and unwelcome, building until they formed a sob that filled her nose and throat. Stepping down from the chair, she sat on the edge of the bed and held the picture to her chest. Oh, how she had loved him! Even during the bad times, before he went, there had been a glimmer of hope that he might come back to her, reformed. And just the sight of this image was enough to remind her of those emotions on that happy, happy day.

She remembered the afternoon she'd introduced Ray to her mum and dad. They had been excited, keen to meet the man who'd put a spring in their daughter's step and a smile on her face. They'd been quizzing her for weeks. 'So who are his people? Where did he go to school? Who does he support?' It was the usual interrogation. She had laughed, dizzy at the possibilities of this relationship and proud of the catch she had made. She couldn't wait to see her man sitting on their sofa, chewing the fat with her dad. She loved him and wanted her mum and dad to love him too.

'What does he do?' her dad had asked.

'This and that.' She'd been evasive, giving the answer Ray had given when she'd asked him the same question.

'It don't matter what he does, love, as long as he makes Vivienne happy. That's all I ask,' her sweet mum had said, believing this to be true. It wasn't until the coming months and years, when she got to know her son-in-law better, that she found herself asking for a whole lot more.

'I can see where she gets her looks from!' Ray had smiled, filling their narrow hallway and flashing those teeth.

Her mum had twisted coyly. 'Oh, behave!' She giggled, batting away the compliment with her tea towel.

He had then presented her with a boxed gift, the sort of present that might be given on a landmark occasion. From the scarlet tissue paper she lifted a garish glass creation edged in gold. It was a swan with its head turned backwards and its wings mid stretch. 'Oh my!' her mum had gasped. 'It's … it's beautiful!' She had been quite overcome by the gift and by Ray's generosity.

Everyone had loved him, or at least the image that he presented.

Vivienne let her head hang forward, remembering the night he went, the way she had paced the hall, staring out of the window, squinting at the street below, holding back the curtain, as she knelt on the sofa, trying to spot him in the encroaching darkness while Aaron and Emma, oblivious to what was happening, slept in the little room they shared down the hallway. And the next morning, arriving at Mendip Road with the kids and one crappy suitcase, on autopilot, numb and petrified in equal amounts. The way her mum had dusted down her pinny and turned to her. *'Go hang your stuff up and wash your face while me and Emma put the kettle on and make Aaron some breakfast.'*

That day had felt endless; the kids seemed extra noisy, extra clingy and her nerves had hung by a thread. Her parents tiptoed around with fixed, insincere smiles that did little to reassure. Not even Ellen's gentle coaxing or humour could shake the black cloud of melancholy that enveloped her. It had felt hopeless.

Night after night, she lay on the bed and thought about the phrase that got bandied about so casually, in the supermarket, on the bus, after a disturbed night of tossing and turning and waiting for the alarm – 'I didn't sleep a wink!' – and she wondered if any of those people truly knew what it felt like to lie there wide awake, listening to the deafening tick as every second seemed to pass more slowly than the last.

Before Ray left, she used to quite like the still of the night, the quiet solitude that gave her the chance to think, to plan. But that was before. Now the quiet pained her, taunted her, gave her too much time to think and to worry about what might happen to her fatherless children. Her brain whirred relentlessly and it was exhausting. She longed to escape into oblivion.

As the days turned to weeks and then months, there was a depressing sense of finality about her circumstances. She knew that this was it: she would live in her parents' house until the day she died, a rejected wife, caring for her kids and her parents as the years rolled into each other, and then one day she would look into the mirror and see that her life had slipped by. When she voiced these fears, Ellen had cuffed her about the head and then hugged her. 'Don't talk rubbish! You'll be swept off your feet by someone gorgeous, just you wait and see, and that'll teach Ray. And when he comes snivelling back, begging for forgiveness, you kick him up the arse and send him packing!' But that hadn't happened and even all these years later, she took no joy in having been proved right.

Vivienne placed the picture back on the wardrobe, then sniffed and wiped her tears on her sleeve. She stared at the old pine chest of drawers in the corner of the room, remembering how one rainy day, Emma had removed a drawer and made it into a bed for several of her dolls and teddies. 'My babies, Mummy,' she had lisped, while rocking them and placing them like sardines in the drawer, before covering them over with a baby blanket Vivienne had knitted for Aaron's pram. It had made her smile, the idea that one day, Emma would have her own children. And now, with her wedding day in the calendar, maybe that dream was getting closer to becoming a reality. What she hadn't banked on was how it might feel if those much longed-for grandchildren grew up on the other side of the world.

Bob loped up the stairs and sat on the floor next to her leg; just his presence gave her comfort. 'Look at me, eh? Sitting here all on my own having a good old cry.' She patted him. It occurred to her then that the reason for her tears might be that, in those early years, she'd always pictured Emma being walked up the aisle by Ray. Silly, really.

The front doorbell roused her. Blowing her nose, she scurried down the stairs and opened the door to a boy from D. R. Butt, the master butcher's on North Street. His wasn't a face she recognised. He looked very young in the white coat that was a little too big for him and with the D. R. Butt logo embroidered on the left breast. He had a clipboard resting on his crooked forearm and a pen in his other hand, which he flourished as he spoke.

'Good morning, Mrs Lane. I've come about your Christmas meat order. What shall we put you down for – the usual? Turkey, fresh sausage meat and a pound of streaky? We're doing a special on ham, lovely on Boxing Day with a bit of pickle and a lump of crusty bread...' Despite his youth and small stature, his confident tone and well-rehearsed patter soon eradicated any thoughts that he might be out of his comfort zone.

'Ah, it's lovely that you thought of me. Thing is, this year I don't have the family here...' She cursed the tears that gathered at the back of her throat. 'So I don't think I want a big turkey. Can I have a think about it?' She had more or less decided to buy something from work, ready to pop in the oven as and when she needed it, in the hope that Aaron and Lizzie might visit at some point on her return.

'Course.' He beamed at her, skilled at hiding any irritation or disappointment. 'You know where we are, Mrs Lane, and I hope you have a very merry Christmas.'

'Oh, you're the first one to say that to me this year.' She smiled. It wasn't even December, not quite. 'Bit early, though, isn't it?'

'That's D. R. Butt – always one step ahead!' He walked down the street with a wave of his clipboard.

Vivienne turned to Bob, who had followed her down the stairs. 'He's good.' She laughed and went into the kitchen.

It felt strange walking past the familiar café to the door alongside it and waiting there on the pavement with Bob. He whined. She suspected he could sense her apprehension.

'It's okay, mate, I've got you.' She patted his flank. 'If you don't feel comfy, you can go and stay with Uncle Trev, this is just a try-out. You know I wouldn't leave you anywhere you weren't happy, even if it is only for ten days.'

'Ah! There he is!' Pedro opened the door and greeted them. Dropping instantly to his knees, he took Bob's head in his hands and smoothed his fur, looking into his eyes and talking excitedly. 'Are you going to come and stay with me then, Bob? We will have a great time! I shall give you steak, but don't tell your mum, and we can walk all over town, a couple of bachelors together. What do you say?'

Bob wagged his tail and pushed his nose against Pedro's cheek.

'You are lovely, you are so lovely. Who's a handsome boy?' Pedro continued to address her dog, as though she wasn't standing on the pavement, attached to his lead. She felt like a spare part.

'Oh hello, Viv.' He finally looked up, seeming to notice her for the first time. 'Come in, please, and let's see how we all get on.' He held open the door.

Vivienne watched as Bob raced up the staircase with Pedro following and laughing. It seemed this was going to work out very well indeed.

'Cold, innit?' Ellen tutted, as she closed the front door, then headed straight to the sink to pop the kettle on. Vivienne followed her into the kitchen.

The home she and Trevor shared was very similar to Vivienne's in size and shape but entirely different inside. Where Vivienne's looked much as it had in the 1960s and was still cluttered with her mother's memorabilia, Ellen's was light and modern. She'd ripped the guts out of the building, tearing down walls to create space and choosing furnishings that were neutral and contemporary. It made the place feel very modern, the polar opposite of Mendip Road. One thing both homes had in common though: no sooner had a guest stepped over the threshold than they were always greeted with a cup of tea.

'Yep, it is a bit chilly.' Vivienne kicked off her walking boots and smiled. Her friend did this, commented on the weather all year round. As if, despite having lived on the planet for more than five decades, the seasons continually surprised her; as though she expected something other than a little bit of sunshine in July and a whole lot of cold in February. Vivienne had once seen a documentary about a group of explorers climbing Mount Everest in which, every so often, the heavily bearded, ice-studded, snow-spattered men would look into the camera and murmur, 'It's so c ... cold!' As if they had been miss-sold the adventure and the weather wasn't what they had expected at all. They reminded her of Ellen.

'How did Bob get on? Did he like the idea?' Ellen asked as she foraged in the cupboard for a packet of biscuits.

'He loved it, loved Pedro, loved the whole thing.'

'Well there's no need to look so glum about it. That face of yours could curdle milk.' Ellen shook her head.

'I know. It's just that I kind of hoped Bob might be a little resistant. I mean, I want him to be happy, to have a nice time, of course, but he barely gave me a second look. His tail was wagging, he nuzzled up to Pedro and when I said it was time to go home, I reached for his lead and he actually whined.' She sighed.

'Don't tell me you're jealous?' Ellen ripped open the packet of digestives and dumped them on the table.

'Yes, I am a bit.' She would only ever admit this to Ellen.

'Well, snap out of it. Far better that than to have him crying and fretting. How would you feel leaving him then?'

'You have a point. I guess I can't have it both ways.' She reached for a biscuit.

'All packed and ready?' Trevor asked as he ambled into the kitchen, freshly showered and in his stocking feet, his work clothes replaced by clean jeans and a jersey. 'Only a week to go.'

'Yep. Getting a bit nervous, actually,' she admitted.

'What is there to be nervous about?' He smiled. 'You've got Elle with you, Mrs Calm-in-a-Crisis, what could possibly go wrong?'

'Don't. You're making it worse.' She bit into her digestive.

'Personally, I'm looking forward to the break.' He winked, just before a tea towel came flying across the room and unfurled itself around his head.

It was at moments like this that Vivienne wondered what it might have felt like to be part of a foursome, to have Ray larking around, joining in the banter. He might have been a spineless loser, but he did know how to have fun and with him there she would have felt less like an interloper.

'Look at her face,' Ellen pointed at her friend. 'She's worried Bob might have feelings for another.' Ellen updated her husband.

'Oh, it's not that, I was just...'

'Just what?' Ellen pressed.

'You're right.' She gave a tight smile. 'I am

94

ridiculously jealous over Bob.'

'Do I have to throw a tea towel at you as well?' Ellen snapped.

Vivienne shook her head and finished her biscuit.

Having ironed the last of her T-shirts and put them all in the case, hoping they might arrive crease-free, she switched on the lamp and sank down on the sofa with Bob lying on her feet and the theme tune to *Corrie* playing in the background. It was only early evening but having worked her last shift before her holiday and said goodbye to her Asda colleagues, tiredness was now creeping up on her and she could quite easily have dozed off. At the sound of the doorbell, she sighed. 'Who's that then, Bob?' she asked, as if he might tell her, having not only magically acquired the ability to speak but also displaying hitherto undiscovered psychic powers. He was less than impressed at being shifted from his comfy position.

'Aaron! What a lovely surprise.' She gratefully accepted a kiss on the cheek. 'Lizzie not with you?' She looked over his shoulder before shutting out the cold winter's night.

'No, spin class.' He sighed. 'Are you not putting your decorations up?' he asked with an air of disappointment, casting his eyes over the walls and shelves where usually ceramic Santas would wobble on legs made of springs, dusty wreaths of dried holly with shrivelled berries would perch on top of the pictures and miniature tinsel Christmas trees would sparkle next to the lamps.

'Do you know, I didn't see the point, not with

me going away and Emma's big day. That's taken up all of my thoughts and planning. Besides, there's only going to be me here when I get back, so I thought I might get a tree last minute if I feel like it. I'll be at Elle's on Christmas Day.'

'You can come to Lizzie's mum's, you know that.' He looked a little sheepish and Vivienne, knowing her son's every expression, could tell that the invite must have been offered if not reluctantly then without any great enthusiasm on his wife's part.

'Oh, that's kind, love, but I don't really know them and there's nothing worse than those awkward silences with strangers at a time when everyone should be having fun. I'll still see you, though. Maybe Boxing Day? Or whenever.' She was careful not to apply any more pressure to his narrow shoulders.

'Fancy a cuppa?' she asked, walking towards the kitchen.

He nodded.

'It's not like you to pop in on a work night. Not that I'm complaining – it's lovely to see you,' she added.

'I was passing by.'

She registered the lie, a little saddened that he couldn't just say he wanted to chat.

'I try to do everything I can to make her happy, you know, Mum.'

His admission was a little random, but was obviously something that had been playing on his mind. She abandoned the kettle and turned towards her son. 'I know you do, love, and you are patient and hard-working. You're a good husband.'

'I'm not so sure.' He kicked at the floor and stuffed his hands in the pockets of his suit trousers, reminding her so powerfully of his twelve-year-old self that it brought a lump to her throat.

She considered how best to proceed. 'Are you happy, Aaron? Because, as I've always told you, that's the only thing that really counts. That's the goal and if you are happy, you're winning and if you are not...' she let this hang.

He looked up. 'Sometimes I am, very happy, yes. And I don't think anyone can be happy all of the time, can they?'

'Maybe not.' She drew breath. 'But you do have a right to happiness, as much as anyone else, certainly as much as Lizzie, and you shouldn't ever compromise that.'

'She doesn't mean it, Mum. It's just her way, she puts up a shield. I know she can seem off, but she's quite vulnerable underneath it all. I mean the fall-out with Emma, she has always wanted to travel and I think she let her jealousy get the better of her.'

'Well that's no excuse, love. Plenty of people feel a bit of envy for all sorts of reasons, but that's no reason for meanness, least of all to someone like Emma who doesn't deserve it.'

'I know, Mum.' He held up his palm, as if this might deflect her comments. 'I think it's more than that. She had a crappy childhood, her mum and dad weren't like you, they were forever putting her down, telling her that she wouldn't amount to anything and that's why she's so keen to have a nice house and all the trimmings. She wants people to see that she has succeeded where her parents told her she wouldn't.'

'I thought she and her parents were close?'

Aaron shook his head, 'No. She's still trying to get their approval. She'd do a somersault if they asked her to and even that wouldn't be good enough. As I say, she's not as tough as she makes out.'

'Are you both coming to the wedding?' she asked with a mixture of dread and hope.

'No.' He shook his head again. 'Things are still a little bit strained with Emma and it's not fair and I would be on edge and it's a lot of money.' He ran out of reasons and breath.

'It's okay. I understand and Emma will too. She loves you, you know, very much.' She didn't want him to think that Emma would be frosty over his decision.

'And me her.'

Vivienne nodded. 'The thing is, love, I only want you to be treated well, never taken for granted or dismissed, and sometimes...' She paused, wondering how open to be. 'Sometimes I think you try so hard to please her that what *you* want or need gets swallowed up, like you don't count as much. And if she is being forced by her parents to jump through hoops for their conditional love, she should know it's not the way to be. It doesn't make you feel special and it shouldn't be like that in a marriage. You should look after each other.'

'Did you and Dad look after each other?'

It was so rare for him to mention his father that this threw her a little. 'No.' She shook her head. 'No, we didn't. I looked after him and he treated me with indifference. It got to the point where I just stopped expecting to get anything in return, and that's why I'm able to say it to you. I don't want you to make the same mistakes. I think if I had fought my corner a bit more, stood up to him, even just once–'

'He wouldn't have gone?' Aaron jumped in.

'No.' She shook her head. 'Oh no, he would still have gone, but I think that the me he left behind might have been a bit more able to cope with it. Stronger. I might even have made a new life for myself, who knows, if I'd had the confidence.'

Aaron smiled at her, reading between the lines. 'I remember that first Christmas after he'd left, you were so sad and I didn't know how to make things better. I hated how useless I felt.'

'You were only little,' she said soothingly. 'That was never your job.'

'I know, but I still felt bad.'

'Oh, love.' She shook her head. 'I'm sorry you felt that way.'

'I don't remember much about him, in fact I seem to remember him less and less as time goes on.'

'You look like him, that's for sure, and he was funny, like you, but he was cocky and loud, un-like you.' She smiled. 'He had a way of making you feel like you were the most important person in the world.' *And the worst. When he turned his affection off, it left you bereft, lost, broken...*

'I'd like to be a dad,' he admitted. 'But I worry that I might be as rubbish as him and that scares me.'

Vivienne felt her heart swell at the admission. 'Well it is scary having kids, but it's scary having them no matter who your parents are, plus you are half me!' she joked. 'Have you talked to Lizzie about it?'

'Yes.' He laughed, looking to the ceiling. 'A lot. And she's worried she might be rubbish like her parents, I think we put each other off, planning for the worst case scenario.'

'I think you should both have more faith. Most of us parent differently to the way our mum and dad did it, so you can take consolation from that, you can set your own path. Plus, look how you and Emma have turned out, you are both fabulous, kind, funny people, great citizens of the world and your childhood was a bit rocky for a while back there.'

'I guess so.' He seemed to perk up at this thought. 'She's also worried that she will lose part of herself and that scares her.'

'And like I said, it is scary, and no less so now that you are in your thirties than it was when you were little. And you *do* lose part of yourself, that's true, but the part you lose grows up into a beautiful human that more than fills that gap and brings you more joy than you could ever have thought possible.'

'I love you, Mum.'

Vivienne walked over and took her boy in her arms. 'And I love you. I'm always here for you, you know that, don't you?'

She felt him nod against her neck.

Five

Vivienne leapt out of bed. Worried about sleeping through her alarm, she'd checked the clock many times through the night, making sure that her alarm was actually set and continually verifying the current time. Nerves and adrenalin now saw her firing on all cylinders, getting ready to leave the house.

It had been strange spending a night under her own roof without Bob's reassuring presence, but she'd decided it was best to drop him off at Pedro's the day before. She didn't want the panic of getting him settled at this ridiculously early hour.

Pedro had made a big fuss of Bob when they'd arrived, hugging him and letting him sniff around his immaculate apartment. 'Don't you worry about a thing,' he'd reassured her. 'I shall take great care of him and I'll drop you a text update every so often.'

She was more than grateful, deciding there and then that she'd bring Pedro back something nice by way of a thank you. But the sight of the kitchen floor without Bob's basket and bowl made her feel tearful. Even though she told herself it was only for a couple of weeks, she knew she would miss her faithful friend.

Trevor pulled up outside her house and opened the boot of his car. 'All set, Mrs?' he asked.

'Think so.' She pictured her passport, purse

and travel documents nestling in the front pocket of her handbag.

As she climbed into the back, Ellen was shuffling around in the front seat. 'Do you think I need to buy some Imodium? Don't want a dicky tummy on that long flight and I can get a bit that way if I eat fried chicken.' She pulled a face.

'Well, don't eat fried chicken!' Vivienne stared at her friend.

'But I always have fried chicken at an airport, it's a tradition,' Ellen replied.

'A tradition that might give you the trots and it's me that's got to sit next to you for goodness knows how long.'

'Thirteen hours to Kong Hong,' Ellen replied, wide-eyed.

Both Vivienne and Trevor snorted their laughter. 'You said "Kong Hong",' he snickered.

'I never did!' she yelled, convinced as always that if she shouted loudly enough, that made her right.

'God help me.' Vivienne settled down in the back seat. 'This is going to be the longest thirteen hours of my life.'

Trevor smiled at her in the mirror but offered no words of solace.

After a rushed decanting from car to terminal at Heathrow, Vivienne watched, as Ellen and Trevor exchanged a brief peck of farewell. She felt the blush of awkwardness, even after all these years that there was no one special to kiss her goodbye. She found herself smiling at the departures boards flashing up destinations like Amsterdam, Tokyo, Sydney, Cape Town, Berlin, Lagos, Saigon and

Kuala Lumpur. It was a wonderful feeling, standing there as planes ferried people around the planet with seemingly just as much ease as she might catch the bus to Patchway or Severn Beach.

Once they'd cleared security, both of them jittery and nervous of saying or doing the wrong thing, they were relieved to be sitting in a coffee shop, in uncharacteristic silence, watching businessmen in suits tapping away at phones or slender laptops, many of them with harried expressions. At the opposite end of the scale, tanned, elegant women with silk pashminas cast over their shoulders and decked out in perfectly pressed slacks and cool, breathable blouses walked at a leisurely pace, meandering in and out of designer stores with vast handbags on their arms, looking thoroughly bored by the routine of travel. Vivienne wondered how they managed to look so unruffled. Her own linen trousers were already creased and she felt in need of another shower and they hadn't taken off yet.

Ellen's stomach growled. 'Fancy splitting a tea-cake before we get on the plane?'

'Might as well.' Vivienne nodded.

She watched as her friend queued and heard her loudly direct the girl who was serving towards the teacake she fancied at the front of the display. 'None of that stale rubbish at the back, mind.'

Vivienne pulled her sunglasses from her hair and covered her eyes, trying to hide.

Finally installed in their seats on the plane, the two friends gripped each other's hands, grinning and excited, as they secured their seatbelts and wriggled back to get comfy. The seat closest to the aisle was empty.

'Hope no one sits there. We can have a gap between us for napping in. Take it in turns to flop over and doze on the other one.' Ellen nodded, pleased with her plan.

No sooner had she spoken than a man in a suit sat in the free seat. Vivienne tried to look the other way as Ellen turned to her with crossed eyes and pulled a face.

'Hello!' Ellen suddenly swivelled and waved at the man, despite sitting only inches from him.

'Hello.' He gave a tight smile and immediately looked away, running his hand through his neat hair and busying himself with the in-flight magazine; anything, other than chat to her.

'Where are you travelling to today, anywhere nice?' Ellen asked.

He turned his head sharply. 'Erm, Hong Kong – that's where the plane's going.' His expression was quizzical.

'Oh yes, of course. I do get in a muddle.'

He nodded and once again flipped the magazine open at a random page.

Ellen leant towards him. 'If you don't want your pudding off the little tray later, can I have it?' She blinked.

He shrugged his shoulders and gave a nervous titter. 'I … I suppose so.'

'I should apologise in advance,' she continued. 'I've had fried chicken. I've taken me Imodium, but you never can be too careful. Just wanted to warn you in case I have to jump over you when you're napping.'

Vivienne covered her mouth with her hand and

looked out of the window, making out she was unattached to her friend, but not before she saw the man's skin lose some of its colour. He gave a small nod.

With shaky hands he fiddled with his seatbelt then jumped up to go in search of a flight attendant. In less than no time, the attendant had moved him to another row entirely.

Vivienne laughed until her tears ran.

Ellen looked at her. 'What?' She smiled.

The friends held hands again as the plane made a wonky ascent and gave off the odd unidentifiable noise. They then watched the same two movies back to back, so that they could laugh and comment in the same spots. They giggled out loud, oblivious to the stares of the more sedate passengers around them. After eating the food that came in little square foil boxes and sipping their plastic tumblers of rather nice white wine, toasting each other as though they were in the finest restaurant, the two dozed.

Vivienne lay back with her arms beneath the thin blanket and her head on the inadequate pillow. She smiled, thinking of Emma, soon to be married and waiting for her, and pictured how wonderful it was going to be to take her girl in her arms again. *I'm coming, Emma. I'm on my way, my darling...*

By the final couple of hours of the flight she was beginning to feel a bit antsy. The excitement had all but disappeared and the seat, which had seemed okay for the first few hours, now seemed restrictive and small. The cabin was either too hot or too cold and she longed to breathe clean, unfiltered air and to stand up straight and have a proper walk around. She could tell by the way Ellen was fidgeting that she felt the same.

But pretty soon it was nearly time to land. She restored her table and seatbelt and scooped up their combined litter for the cool, smiling flight attendant with her hungry bin liner. As the plane began its descent, Ellen leant over her to look out of the window. 'God, we're a bit close to the sea – and those buildings!' She pointed across Vivienne at the long, low warehouse-type structures that skirted the edge of the water.

'I'm sure they've done this a million times before. Just sit back, it'll be okay.' Vivienne hid her own nervousness to try and keep her friend calm, unwilling to admit that her heart was also racing at the sight of the blocks of flats so close to the airport, and the mountains, which at one point had appeared to be within touching distance of the plane.

The landing, however, was faultless.

'Jesus H. Christ, that was a bit hairy!' Ellen clearly regretted having looked out of the window.

A surge of excitement saw them giggle their way off the plane, from where the travellator transported them to arrivals. Without bags to collect, they were unencumbered for their fourteen hours in Hong Kong. The airport was white, sparkling and dust-free; the place gleamed. It was busy, yet well laid out with big wide open lounges that meant it didn't feel crowded. It was quite something to see the airport signs written in Cantonese with English translations underneath, but in many other ways the inside of the airport looked remarkably similar to Heathrow, though Vivienne wasn't sure what she had expected. She felt a frisson of both excitement and fear at the prospect of leaving the safety of the airport and venturing out into this strange country that was halfway round the world from all that was familiar.

'Good Lord, Viv, look at them flats!' Ellen pointed. 'All piled together, so cramped, and the windows are tiny.' She gave a running commentary in her usual style on the apartment blocks they could see from inside the terminal.

'I'm sure they're lovely inside.' Vivienne didn't know what else to say to compensate for her friend's lack of tact, so she quickly changed the subject. 'Right, we have to be back here in fourteen hours ready to make our connection, so we need to keep an eye on how long it takes us to get to wherever we're going, then we'll know to leave that much time on the way back.'

'Good thinking.' Ellen nodded and hitched her large raffia beach bag up onto her shoulder. She smiled at her friend who looked ready for a day on the beach not a stint exploring Hong Kong.

The two joined the throng of people exiting the terminal and followed the signs for the bus station. They had no idea where they were going, but figured that if they followed the crowd they couldn't go far wrong. The first thing that struck them when they walked out onto the remarkably clean concourse was the temperature. It might only have been early morning in Hong Kong, but the sky was clear blue and the ground radiated heat.

'Flippin' 'eck!' Ellen pumped the front of her T-shirt. 'It's hot, Viv!'

She nodded. It was.

To the left of the exit was the surprisingly small ticket office. An elderly Chinese lady, her face a beautiful lattice of creases and wrinkles, sat behind a single glass screen wearing an expression that could best be described as sour. Her mouth puckered, as if she was already furious at the world. It did not bode well.

Vivienne had to prise her tongue from the roof of her mouth, nervous at having to try and engage, praying the woman spoke at least a little English. 'Hello.' She smiled, but there was no response. 'We need to get a bus into town?' She spoke slowly, using her hand to mimic a fish swimming along – why, she wasn't sure, but it was all she could think of at the time.

The old lady responded in a rapid fire of Cantonese, gesturing over Vivienne's head, clearly angry and frustrated at the foreign woman who was making fish signs at her while a queue of impatient passengers, all of whom had places to be, formed behind her.

'Probably thinks you want sushi. What's that all about?' Ellen mimicked her hand signal.

'I don't know! I just panicked a bit. I was trying to show her that we need to travel.'

'What, by river or log flume? Let me have a go.' Ellen elbowed her friend to one side and placed her raffia bag on the counter, staring at the old woman, deaf to the shouts of those behind her who were clutching coins in the heat and trying to board one of the many buses that sat in a chevron formation along the kerb.

Ellen held up two fingers. 'Two tickets,' she shouted, 'for...' She then made as if she was holding a cup and saucer and tipped the imaginary cup to her mouth. 'And...' She then mimed eating very quickly, as if her hands were gripping cutlery and shoving food into her mouth. 'In...' She drew a tall rectangle with her index fingers and made a pyramid with her hands to show a roof.

The woman yelled back, firing off a volley of incomprehensible sounds and unfathomable words, as if she was furious, waving her hand and angrily smacking her gums. However, she did also print off two cardboard tickets, which she pushed under the little grille at the bottom of the glass window. Ellen shoved the requisite Hong Kong dollars by way of return and the two friends made their way over to the buses, laughing and leaning against each other, as much out of relief as anything else.

'It's much easier when we go up the mall, isn't it?' Vivienne laughed as Ellen, buoyed by her ticket-purchase success, went ahead to figure out which was their bus.

'Thing is, Elle, we've managed to get two tickets, but we have no idea where we're heading. Could be anywhere!'

'Well, aren't you Little Miss Sunshine! I figure as long as lots of other people are on the bus, we can't go far wrong.'

'But they could be going anywhere. A family wedding, a funeral!' A wave of anxiety washed through her.

'This is our adventure, Viv. We shall just have to make the most of wherever we end up. Now let's get on a bloody bus. A funeral!' She tutted under her breath.

Taking seats at the back with a good view, Vivienne pressed her face against the slightly smeared glass on the less than pristine vehicle and marvelled at the sharp-peaked mountains on the horizon.

'Bit uncomfy, isn't it?' Ellen shifted on the barely sprung seats that gave the bus the feel of an old coach, the kind that had once taken them on school trips. She nudged Vivienne. 'Do you remember when we went to Bristol Zoo and you wet yourself?'

Vivienne glanced round to see if any English-speakers might have heard her gobby friend. 'I did not wet myself.'

'You did so! I remember it. You had to put on Nicola Brown's gym knickers that they found in a carrier bag.'

'Well that's you getting old and your memory playing tricks. You're right, I *did* have to put on Nicola Brown's gym knickers, but it was because I tipped my Ribena over my summer dress. I didn't wet myself.' She sat up straight in the seat.

'Ribena, wee, same difference.' Ellen shrugged.

'Not when you have to drink it, Elle.'

And just like that, they were back to snorting and giggling.

Vivienne pointed out of the window. 'This is quite something, isn't it – look at the tower blocks.'

Ellen leaned over until they were both staring out of the window, taking in the narrow, soaring high-rises in the distance, lined up in rows like monochrome dominoes, unappealing to look at, with tiny windows dotted uniformly all over them.

The matchstick buildings sat incongruously against a stunning backdrop of early-morning sun, the golden orb shimmering from behind the dark grey mountains.

The road twisted, climbed and dropped, until the landscape altered and they were driving alongside a port. But for the sunshine, it could almost have been Avonmouth, a vast, faceless tract of reclaimed land, busy with forklift trucks and cranes, where vast ships loaded and unloaded containers behind secure gates and checkpoints. Both women were quiet now, neither wanting to admit to the fear that their bus could indeed be heading anywhere. Vivienne felt her friend shift closer to her on the seat. Both were clutching their bags on their laps.

'Polo?' Ellen whispered as she reached into her bag, extracting the little foil-wrapped tube and peeling open the end. Vivienne nodded and both sucked on the sharp, hot mints; they were a little bit of home that brought a smidgen of comfort in the alien landscape.

Their trepidation eased, as the bus veered onto a multi-lane road, clearly aiming for the city that loomed in the distance.

'Hong Kong!' Vivienne raised her shoulders and beamed at her friend. Sighting the skyscrapers in the distance, the functional bridges over motorways, the throng of cars, lorries, buses and bicycles all carrying people and goods towards the city suddenly made it real. They had arrived.

Removing her camera from her handbag, Vivienne remembered the lesson hastily delivered by Aaron and switched it on, waiting for the little green light as instructed. It was then a simple case of pointing and shooting and this she did with enthusiasm. She snapped away, capturing the yellow overhead road signs that blazed the way to Central, North Point and Kowloon, and then turning her attention to the shops with their rooftop Coca-Cola signs and the beautiful script of Chinese characters below.

Her eye was drawn to a crocodile of approximately twenty schoolgirls, no older than six or seven, who were marching parallel to the road. Treading the dusty pavement in lilac-and-black tartan kilts, immaculate short-sleeved white shirts and matching tartan ribbons crossed under their collars, they held hands in pairs. They wore "Hello Kitty" backpacks between their shoulder blades and their neat, blunt bobs were either fastened with hairclips to create a fringe or tied into two chunky bunches either side of a neat parting. Two little girls at the back of the group whispered to each other and threw their heads back, laughing; finding themselves out of step with their classmates, they had to run to catch up. Vivienne turned to Ellen and smiled, her meaning clear. *Remind you of anyone?*

The roads were so congested that the bus snaked along slowly, giving her the perfect opportunity to peer down side streets, which were alive with activity even at this early hour. Men and women in grey overalls swept the streets with wide, wooden brooms. Battered trucks and lorries with heavy loads listed towards the kerb, as slight boys in grubby white vests, jeans rolled above the ankle and nothing more substantial than flip-flops on their feet wheeled heavily laden porters' trolleys back and forth. They transported everything – sealed cardboard boxes, crates of pop, stacks of raw materials – from the lorries and vans to the myriad of tiny shops and factories that were crammed inside the rabbit warren of alleyways. Everywhere she looked, people humped boxes on their shoulders or in outstretched arms. Stock was pushed along on rickety trolleys and everything from fresh produce to livestock disappeared into the corridors between the buildings and along the narrow hallways inside. She longed to glimpse the secret world behind the battered concrete facades.

Businessmen in suits emerged like film extras from hidden doors to hop onto buses and into cabs, and schoolchildren and siblings held hands as they made their way to the nearest underpass or Metro station. She looked up and gasped at the thirty or forty floors of apartments that sat atop the ground-floor buildings. Multiple flats and rooms were crammed in at all angles, their windows thrown open, some with prison-like bars, others with airers clipped to the frames and lines of clothes drying in the dusty morning heat. Elderly men propped themselves against the sills, cigarettes held between long fingernails, as they greeted the morning. Other windows revealed women in bubble-gum coloured overalls leaning far out, shouting exchanges to neighbours in the flats opposite, whose postures mirrored theirs. From a window high above, someone shook a duvet, sending tiny feathers fluttering down below; higher still, there was a cage with a pot inside it, fighting for space next to a clunking, rusted air-conditioning unit, and a plant grew up between and over the bars.

'Well I never, Viv.' Ellen stared and pointed at a window at their eye level, through which they could see metal bunk-beds jammed against a wall, clothes on hangers draped all around the window frame and narrow shelves on the wall holding all manner of toiletries and a couple of framed photos. It made Vivienne feel thankful for her three-bedroomed house in Mendip Road: more space than she would ever need, even if Emma thought it was crappy.

'Crowded, isn't it?' Ellen stated the obvious.

Vivienne nodded, wondering if it still felt crowded if it was all you knew or whether you simply shrank to fit your environment.

The bus pulled over and disgorged a third of the passengers, some of whom immediately placed paper surgical masks over their noses and mouths, securing them with thin elastic looped over their ears, before heading off on foot.

'Why do they wear them masks? Do you think they're sick?' Ellen asked.

'Not sure. I guess it's easier to catch things when you're living this close together, or it might be because of pollution.'

'Do you think we should get some?' Ellen sounded worried.

'Don't think we'll be here long enough for it to matter. Besides we breathe in diesel fumes in Bedminster twenty-four seven at home.' She gave a wry smile.

'When are we getting off?'

Vivienne noticed that her gobby friend was now

the one asking questions, not quite so keen to take the lead in this alien place. 'I reckon the next stop, then we should go and find a cup of coffee, what do you think?'

'I think yes. Wouldn't say no to one of Pedro's teacakes right now.' She smiled.

'Hope Bob's okay,' Vivienne said, thinking aloud.

'He'll be having the time of his life.' Ellen sounded certain. 'Feels like we've been gone forever already, doesn't it?'

Vivienne nodded. It did. Time was already out of kilter. Her body had no idea if it was noon or night. She pictured Emma passing through these streets and other places like it and for the first time she understood the fascination, the appeal of arriving somewhere you had never been before, somewhere that meant you had to keep your wits about you, where everything was a challenge, even just getting from A to B. And where you could be anything you wanted to be because no one knew who you were or where you had come from.

As the bus pulled into a more commercial part of town, Vivienne grabbed her friend's arm. 'Come on!'

They rattled down the aisle, thanked their driver, who acknowledged the universal wave of gratitude, and got off. They found themselves on a clean, white pavement without a dot of litter or stroke of graffiti, very different to their own city. Fancy shop windows with classy displays boasting names like Louis Vuitton, Chanel, Breitling and Jimmy Choo were just as intimidating to them in Hong Kong, as they were in any shopping centre back home. The shops seemed to have made minimal concessions to the Christmas season; there was just the odd sprig of fresh holly in a carefully positioned handbag, and a couple of champagne flutes with coils of shiny foil ribbon coming out of them – more general-purpose celebration than UK-style Christmas decorations.

As the two of them stood there, looking upwards and taking in the sights, they felt a bit lost in the sea of people, who all appeared to be walking with purpose. Vivienne clutched her handbag and stared admiringly at the shoppers strolling past them, slender women with diamond-cut cheekbones, geometric haircuts and pale, unblemished skin hidden behind oversized sunglasses and designer silk scarves tied at the neck in jaunty styles.

Ellen breathed in through her nose. 'It's funny, isn't it, if you closed your eyes and couldn't hear anything, just the smell would let you know you weren't in England.'

Vivienne inhaled. Ellen was right. The air was warm, of course, but it was also tinged with the woody scent of perfume, the tang of spicy food, cooking oil and diesel, and even the vaguest hint of sea salt.

'There are lots of Chinese people here, aren't there?' Ellen observed.

Vivienne ignored her, unable to think of an appropriate response that wouldn't involve sarcasm or invoke an even louder response.

But Ellen wasn't done. 'It's weird, because I am with all these foreigners and yet I am the foreigner! This must be what it felt like for Ying Soo for all those years at Parson Street Primary.'

'Yes, probably.' Vivienne recalled the shy girl, the only Chinese girl in their class, who liked to be left to her own devices.

'Do you think people are looking at us and thinking we look different?'

'I think they're looking at us and thinking, God, that blonde one has a loud voice.'

Ellen poked her tongue out at her friend. 'Right then, I won't talk to you at all.'

'Amen to that.' Vivienne raised her eyes skyward.

'You don't mean that – you'd miss my chat.'

'You see, you can't be quiet for five seconds!'

'I can,' she snapped.

There was a pause of a second or two before Ellen drew breath. 'I could do with the loo,' she whispered.

Vivienne laughed. 'I could do with a nap,' she confessed.

'You can cut that out – we've got a whole day to kill first. Let's get you coffee'd up, that'll give you some energy.'

'Hope so.' Turning sharply to look behind her, Vivienne saw the familiar Starbucks sign and pointed to it.

They made their way through the throng of people. Inside, rather disappointingly, it looked like any Starbucks anywhere. She didn't know what she had hoped for, but certainly not the homogeneous familiarity that took the edge off her adventure. She could get paper cups, Frappuccino mocha lattes, icing-coated buns and sticky table tops anywhere.

'Can I help you?' the young Chinese man behind the counter asked in perfect English.

'Two lattes, please, love.' She smiled.

'Of course. And your name?'

'Ellen.' He scrawled her name on a cup in black felt-tipped pen. 'You can wait for your coffee at the end of the counter.'

'Your English is very good.' Ellen nodded at him.

'Thank you, so is yours.' He smiled back.

'We're from Bristol, England.' She grinned. 'Bedminster, to be precise.'

'Ah well, that would explain it,' he said sincerely. 'I'm from Swindon, England. Toothill, to be precise.'

'Well I never!' Ellen gasped.

'Yes.' He nodded.

'Are your relatives here?' Ellen asked.

Vivienne shifted awkwardly on the spot.

'No, they're in Swindon. Why would you think my relatives are here?' he asked flatly.

'I ... just...'

The boy laughed loudly. 'I'm only teasing you. I have some second cousins here.'

'It's a bit different to Swindon,' Ellen added. 'Quite crowded. We were looking at the flats on the way in on the bus, all those little rooms squished together. People hanging out of windows, laundry being dried way up high.'

Vivienne felt her cheeks flame and wished Ellen would find something more complimentary to say.

'That's what happens when land is at a premium. My cousin's flat is less than one thousand square feet and it cost him about four and a half million Hong Kong dollars. That's about four hundred grand in pounds, and it's tiny.'

'You're kidding me.' Ellen was fascinated.

'I'm not. Imagine what that would buy in Swindon?' He winked at her.

'Can I ask you, if you were only in Hong Kong for a day, what would you go and see?'

'Oh, that's easy. I'd get the Star Ferry over to Hong Kong Island, just to see both parts of Hong Kong from the water, and then I'd jump on the bus to Stanley Market – they've got some great bargains there, if you like a market.'

'Oh, we do!'

'And then I'd probably take the funicular up Victoria Peak – you shouldn't miss that view. And if I was feeling flush, I'd have afternoon tea at the InterContinental on Tsim Sha Tsui Street; if you get there just as dusk falls, you'll see the lights come up on the other side. It's a sight you won't ever forget.'

'Thank you. You take care of yourself, love.' Ellen smiled at her newfound friend.

Feeling much refreshed after their coffee, and having used the facilities in Starbucks, the two women hit the streets with restored energy and a determined spring in their step. It was now mid morning in downtown Hong Kong and very hot. Vivienne fanned her face with the map she'd picked up from a streetside stand. Following the suggested route, they walked behind the Hong Kong Museum of Art, across the manicured grounds and pale paving stones, until they found themselves on the waterfront. Vivienne broke into spontaneous laughter. This was the scene she had always imagined. This was the Hong Kong that existed in her mind. The wide choppy channel was awash with boats. Pleasure cruisers, junks, harbour police and vintage green-and-white Star Ferry boats, distinctive with their two-tiered passenger decks, squat central funnels and tyre fenders hanging on either side, tootled back and forth across the water. There was even a paddle steamer, which she always associated with films set in America's Deep South, slowly making its way across.

'Look at this!' She turned to Ellen, who for once had nothing to say. She was simply leaning against the wall and letting her eyes sweep across the panorama on the other side of the harbour, taking in the vast skyscraper offices of huge companies, whose names – Philips, Samsung, Hitachi – were emblazoned across the horizon, their towers of shiny glass and distinctive rooflines all catching the light of the full sun, glittering against the porcelain blue of the Asian sky.

'Wow!' Vivienne fished in her bag for her camera and began snapping away.

The ferry trip across to Hong Kong Island was a highlight. The river breeze lifted their spirits, as they marvelled at the sights and sounds of the beautiful city. Ellen leant over to her mate, speaking extra loudly so as to be heard over the knock of the engine. 'Look at us, Viv, up the river without a piddle!' They both laughed.

Stanley Market, despite being chock full of tourists like themselves, also proved a hit. The bus ride there gave them the chance to take in the calm of the coastline and to marvel at the grand residences of Stanley sitting behind high gates that overlooked the crescent-shaped bay. They trod the narrow lanes of the covered marketplace. Ellen picked up pressies for Robbie and the kids, and Vivienne chose a beautiful leather purse for Lizzie and a matching wallet for Aaron. Even her fussy, label-chasing daughter-in-law couldn't scoff at these gifts, surely. She thought about Aaron's words that highlighted the girl's insecurities and resolved to try a bit harder with her.

Time was marching on. It was three o'clock in the afternoon and they had five hours left. 'What do you think? One quick trip up the funicular or take the train back to the airport for a freshen up and a quick snooze?' Vivienne gave Ellen the options.

'I think we can snooze all the way to Auckland, but this is our one time here, so let's do as much as we can.'

'You're right, Elle. Funicular it is.'

The bus dropped them at Garden Road, where they joined the end of a long queue; apparently the view from the top of Victoria Peak was so breath-taking that this jaunt was on every tourist's list. As the line snaked inside, Vivienne was glad of the shade, a welcome respite from the searing heat of the day. She wished she could shower and change before getting on the plane, but being a novice traveller, it hadn't occurred to her to put a change of clothes or any toiletries, bar her toothbrush, in her hand luggage.

'I'm a bit sweaty,' she confided in Ellen.

'Nothing a quick spritz with my bottle of Chan-nel No. 5 won't fix!' Ellen laughed, referring to the knock-off perfume she'd picked up at the market. It was only after she'd bought it and studied the label that she'd noticed the intentional typo.

The queue moved slowly through the darkened walkway and fatigue washed over them. 'Don't mind admitting, I'm almost done,' Vivienne whispered.

'Me too, but we'll sleep good on the plane. Quick drink, a bit of a natter and then eye mask and ear plugs all the way. Bonus.'

Vivienne laughed at her friend, who had now found her stride and sounded like a seasoned traveller.

Finally they reached the front of the queue and climbed into one of the tram-style carriages. Ellen sat by the window and Vivienne squashed up on the narrow wooden seat alongside her. The rows filled quickly and soon everyone was sitting with shoulders hunched up to their ears, breathing in, making as much space as they could. Still more people got on.

'Don't think it will be able to get up the mountain at this rate,' she whispered out of the side of her mouth. Tiredness overcame her and, even though the ascent only took five minutes, Vivienne knew she must have dozed off, as suddenly she was aware that people were disembarking onto the platform, some twelve hundred feet above the city. Her heart raced at the thought that she might be left behind.

'Oh, Elle! Quick! We're here!' She nudged her friend, who was leaning against the window. Pulling her handbag into her chest, she stood and was quickly engulfed by the crowd of passengers making their way to the exit. At one point, she felt her feet briefly lift from the ground, as she crowd-surfed for a yard or two. It was actually quite fun! She turned to tell Ellen, but she'd lost her in the crowd.

Trying to look behind her was tricky; she scanned to the left and right, hoping for sight of her friend's blonde hair. Still calm, she knew that they would wait for each other at the end of the platform before stepping out onto the viewing deck. Vivienne stood and waited, smiling like a greeter at everyone that walked past her, making their way to the highest point, with cameras in hand, the reason for their journey.

As the crowd thinned and she still hadn't spotted Ellen, her smile began to fade and she felt a twitch of nerves under her left eye. She reached into her bag for her phone and spied Ellen's nestling next to hers; remembering that Ellen had handed it to her when she'd visited the loo earlier. Vivienne swallowed and started to make her way back down the platform. As she did so, the carriage doors shut and the funicular, freshly packed to the gunnels with tourists eager to get back to ground level, started its return journey.

It was then that she spotted her friend, sound asleep just where she'd left her, squashed next to a complete stranger and sleeping like a baby.

'Elle!' she shouted. 'Elle!' She tried again, waving her hands above her head as her friend slept, eyes shut and jaw slack, head lolling on her chest, dead to the world in the deepest of slumbers. Vivienne jumped on the spot, unsure of what to do. The round trip on the funicular, with queuing, had taken an hour; she tried to do the maths to work out what would happen if she got the next shuttle down and Ellen, having woken, took the next one up. She pondered how many times they could miss each other before they missed their flight to Auckland and the horrible answer was, not many.

She felt her heart race and a dry-mouthed panic setting in.

Six

Vivienne fastened her seatbelt and as soon as she caught her friend's eye started laughing again. 'I can't believe you! I nearly lost you in Hong Kong! What would I have said to Trev and Robbie?'

'I wasn't lost, just napping.' Ellen shifted to get comfortable in her seat.

'Napping? I've seen bears in hibernation sleep less soundly. I stood there like a lemon waiting for you to come back around and, blow me, when you did, you were still snoring like a good 'un. I never even got to see the view! I queued for a bloody hour, went all the way up there and didn't get further than the platform.' She tittered.

'Funny thing is, Viv, it wasn't your shouting or the man nudging me that woke me up.'

'It wasn't?' Goodness knows, she'd tried her hardest to get Ellen's attention.

'No. Truth is, I farted, that's what did it.'

'Good God, no wonder everyone got off! You're

as bad as Bob.'

Ellen laughed to herself and patted the blanket around her legs as they prepared for take-off. 'Just think, next time we touch the ground, it's to see your Emma married.'

Vivienne nodded, feeling a wave of excitement at the fact that Emma was waiting for her and she was getting married! This excitement was tempered with a measure of nerves. Supposing Michael's family was hoity-toity? How would it feel staying with them, and how would Ellen fare? She shook her head, reminding herself that Emma was many things, but tolerant of rudeness was not one of them. So long as she felt comfortable, it would all be fine.

The two weary friends, with their Hong Kong adventure behind them, slept for the majority of the eleven-hour flight to Auckland, snoring through two meals and a couple of safety announcements. Having got on to the plane with little idea as to whether it was day or night, they both needed the rest furnished by their eye masks, blankets and bed socks.

When the cabin lights were switched on and the flight attendant announced that they would be landing in one hour, Vivienne sat up straight and ran her fingers through her hair. She then queued for the loo, keen to clean her teeth and wash her face, wanting to look her best before seeing Emma for the first time in four years.

She wobbled in the tiny cubicle, trying to find her footing, and practised her smile in the mirror. Rubbing her palm over her T-shirt, she tried in vain to remove the creases and then spritzed her underarms with deodorant and her décolletage with perfume. It was a poor substitute for a shower but made her feel a little better nonetheless.

Tiptoeing her way back up the aisle, she eyed the mess that surrounded Ellen: her blanket lay in a tangle on the floor, there were magazine wrappers and discarded cups in the seat pocket and she was sprawled rather inelegantly over Vivienne's seat as well as her own. Vivienne smiled fondly at her friend, who created this sort of homely chaos wherever she went.

As the plane began its descent, Ellen leant over, her voice no more than a whisper. 'You okay?'

She nodded. 'Yep.'

'We are already having quite an adventure, aren't we?'

'We are that, Elle.'

'Not bad for two girls from Bedminster.'

'Not bad at all.'

'We'll have lots to talk about when we're sitting in Pedro's – this will feel like a dream.' Ellen smiled.

'It already does.'

Ellen took her friend's hand inside hers, resting them together on the arm between the two seats, as they touched down on New Zealand soil.

The wait for the luggage seemed interminable. The thought that her daughter was standing in that very building while she was stuck in another part of it, unable to see her, was almost torturous. *Come on! Come on!* Vivienne chanted silently as the empty carousel squeaked around, waiting for its load.

'Excited?' Ellen grinned at her.

She could only nod, already feeling the lump of emotion gathering in her throat.

Her suitcase was one of the first.

'You go. Go!' Ellen ushered her on with her hand. 'I might be an age, just go see your girl. I'll catch you up in a bit.'

Vivienne smiled at her friend and practically ran towards the exit, dragging her large suitcase on wheels behind her, relieved that it had made it all the way there from London, despite the break in Hong Kong.

Once she'd cleared customs, her heart rate increased, as she rounded the walkway and found herself in an airy concourse a little smaller than the ones at Heathrow and Hong Kong. She bit her lip and scanned the crowd, spying Emma on her first sweep. Letting her case fall behind her, she rushed forwards. Emma did the same and mere seconds later her daughter was in her arms and just like that, it was as if they had never been apart. Vivienne inhaled the scent of her; no longer a disembodied voice on the end of a line, she was real, a solid thing beneath her trembling hands. They cried in unison.

'Oh, Emma!' she breathed, as her child locked her hands behind her neck and held her tight. 'I missed you so much!'

Vivienne ran her hand over Emma's slender back, recalling the countless times she'd palmed circles on it as Emma had heaved with a sickness bug or needed comforting; the times she'd laid her toddler daughter over her shoulder and carried her to her bed; the teenage years and

127

beyond, when she'd patted and soothed her broken heart, taking her into her arms as Shaun Lewis handed her over on the doorstep. It felt wonderful to be holding this beautiful human whose shape was as familiar to her as her own.

'I missed you too, Mum!' Emma coughed, her eyes wet with tears.

Vivienne pulled away and took in her child's dark tan, her hair, bleached blonde at the front by the sun, and her almost transparent white vest that showed off her inkings, now all the more striking against her bronzed skin. 'My beautiful girl,' she said, marvelling at their being there together.

'Mum, this is Michael, my fiancé.' Emma beamed, impatient to introduce them. Clearly the novelty of using the word hadn't remotely worn off.

The young man stepped forward. In her mind, Vivienne had envisaged someone slight, with a build similar to Fergus or Hai, but Michael turned out to be tall and broad, with large features and a ready smile. He dwarfed them both. She reached out to pull him to her for a hug, but he simply clasped her hand and shook it – warmly, none-theless. He was blonde with hazel eyes and Vivienne couldn't help but picture their beautiful Kiwi children.

'It's really lovely to meet you, Michael.' It felt odd that this man to whom she was about to be-come attached, related, was such a stranger, from a place where the landscape and customs were so different from what she knew.

'Likewise.' He smiled before going to retrieve

her luggage, which was still lying on the floor.

'What do you think?' Emma whispered, full of anticipation.

Vivienne was chuffed that she clearly wanted her approval. 'Gorgeous, Emma, really gorgeous.'

Her daughter threw her arms around her neck once again. 'I can't believe you are here.'

'Me either.' She beamed at her girl.

As Michael re-joined them, Ellen came into view, running along the concourse and shouting and waving. 'Emma! Oh, Emma, we're here!' Her large beach bag hung off her arm, as she crushed Emma to her. 'Look at you. Oh, love, you look wonderful! Fancy it being summer here while we're all freezing at home, isn't that funny?'

'It is.' Emma laughed.

'Now...' Ellen turned to Michael, who was eyeing her with trepidation. 'You must be the young man in question, and I wanted to ask, what kind of a doctor are you?'

'Elle!' Vivienne tutted at her friend.

'I'm just curious, that's all.' She turned back to the tall man. 'I was only saying to Viv a while back, some doctors aren't all they seem, they buy stertificates off the internet and aren't proper doctors at all.'

His eyes visibly widened. 'What? No... I am a proper doctor. An urologist. I specialise in kidney function.'

'So you did go to university?'

'Yes. For a long time, and I'm still learning, but now I do it in a hospital.'

'A bit like learning on the job?' Ellen pushed.

'Yes, exactly like that.' He shot a quizzical look

129

at Emma, clearly wary of her mother's strange friend.

Ellen nodded, convinced and happy, as she turned to Vivienne. 'Pina coladas for Emma it is then.'

'I don't like pina coladas,' Emma said, as if this might be relevant.

The first hour of the drive from the airport was spent in a chaotic, noisy bubble, with Vivienne, Ellen and Emma firing rapid questions at each other and often not even waiting for the answers. Emma's Bristolian twang became more and more pronounced as the words flowed and each of the three struggled to make themselves heard.

'Are the Morrisons still around?'

'They've moved, gone over to Winterbourne to be nearer her son.'

'Aaron okay?'

'Oh, you know, love, to be discussed.'

'I hear Shaun and Nat split up.'

'Yes, a little while ago, Shaun's mum told me. Shame, I like Shaun.'

'Me too. I sent him an invite. I knew he wouldn't come, but I wanted him to know that I wanted him here, if that makes any sense.'

'Ooh, that reminds me love.' Vivienne slipped her hand into the front pocket of her handbag and pulled out a slightly crumpled white envelope with a black thumbprint in the corner, and handed it to Emma.

'What the...?' She ran her finger over the mark.

'Engine oil,' she explained.

'Ah. I know who this'll be from then.'

She watched, as Emma slid her finger under the

flap and pulled out a lined sheet of paper, still with the little rounded holes on a tattered strip on the left hand side where it had been torn from a pad. Emma's eyes scanned the letter in her hand before her eyes crinkled and she smiled, 'Oh bless him!'

'Bless who?' Michael asked, keeping his eyes on the road, but twisting his head to the left to be heard.

'This is a note from my mate, Shaun, do you remember me telling you about him?'

'I don't.'

'Yes! You must. Shaun! I've mentioned him before; lives down the road from my mum. Our mums have been friends since we were babies, and we went right through school together.' She shook the letter in her hand, and read. 'He's saying he was chuffed to be invited to the wedding, but can't take time off, as he's opening his own garage, up on Sheene Road?' this she addressed to her mum and Elle.

'Ooh, get him with his own business!' Elle commented, 'he deserves it, works hard mind.'

'And plus,' she looked up and smiled, 'he says he wouldn't want to miss City's league match that's coming up and it would clash.'

'Well good to know where you sit in his priorities.' Michael shook his head, 'Some friend.'

Emma exchanged a look with her mum, knowing exactly where she sat in Shaun's priorities.

'Anyway, he says he hopes we have a lovely day and wishes us every happiness for the future and he hopes that the weather holds up.'

Again, Michael tutted, before pulling his sunglasses from the top of his head and putting them on. 'Think we might just be okay for the weather.' He laid his hand on her thigh and gave it a small squeeze.

'I must admit, it is lovely, isn't it? Not having to make a Plan B in case of snow.' Vivienne looked out of the window at the big, big blue sky.

'We do get rain, but it tends to be short and fierce, doesn't hang around and anyway, nothing matters, not even the weather, we have the space inside, but I'm keeping the wedding simple, don't want anything too fussy.'

'Oh, you have to have a bouquet, something to throw,' Elle added.

'I wish Aaron was coming.'

'I'm sure he does too and Lizzie in her own way.'

'Goodness, is that you defending her, Mum?' Emma asked with mock indignation.

Vivienne shrugged, 'I just think there's more to her behaviour than we probably know about and that we should probably cut her a bit of slack.'

'Bit of slack?' Elle squeaked, 'I think the girl would still rather get her hall decorated than come over here.'

Vivienne decided to change the topic, not wanting Michael's first interaction with them to be soaking up the more dysfunctional facts about their family

'Can't believe it's nearly Christmas and you're wearing flip-flops.'

'They call them jandals here.'

'Jandals. I wonder why?'

'In Australia they call them thongs.'

'Good Lord! In my mind, a thong is something

very different. I wouldn't fancy having one of them riding up my...' Ellen coughed.

The three laughed and carried on catching up, with Emma pausing only to place her hand in her mum's. Four years was a long time to have been apart.

'I missed you, Emma Lane.'

'Soon to be Emma McKinley!' She clapped.

'Emma McKinley,' Vivienne repeated. 'Sounds very grand. Where does that name come from, Michael?' She was doing her best to try and include him.

'It's from Cork, Ireland. My grandparents emigrated in the 1930s, looking for a better life.' He offered nothing else.

'That must have been a brave thing to do, to travel to the other side of the world with no idea of what life would be like there. It's not as if they had the internet to check it out, and it's too far to come for a look, I would think.'

Michael nodded at her in the rearview mirror. 'You're right; they were great pioneers, risk takers. They bought the land at Tutukaka for peanuts, really, and started the farm. My grandfather built it up, and my dad...' He paused. 'My dad never saw the need to expand. He seems content to simply enjoy it as it is, just him and Tessa and the sheep, so it's pretty much as my grandfather left it. It would drive me crazy, but that's how Dad likes it.' He splayed his fingers on the steering wheel before gripping it tightly.

Vivienne noted the slight edge of disapproval to his comments, as if he would have liked his dad to be a bit more of a go-getter. She and Ellen exchanged a knowing look.

Emma bounced on the seat. 'So, for the evening do...' And they were back to nattering and back to the wedding.

Her daughter had changed; there was no doubt about it. As well as the physical changes – a little weight loss, a sharpening of her bones under her reduced frame – there was something subtler and more significant. She seemed to have plastered this huge smile onto her face and wore it like a mask. Vivienne hoped that her girl's happiness was true and permanent and that she had found peace.

Michael drove the sturdy 4 x 4, concentrating on the road and occasionally smiling at the two women in the back and at his wife-to-be, who had twisted round in her seat, facing her mum so they could have a proper chat. With the heightened excitement and constant chatter, Vivienne's fatigue had faded; it was only when she sat back in her seat and looked out at the passing scenery that she yawned. Ellen had fallen asleep, caring little that she was in company, as she snored with her head thrown back. Michael chuckled at the sound.

'It's so lovely to see Elle, Mum,' Emma whispered over the sleeping form of the woman who had been a constant in her life too.

Vivienne nodded.

The scenery was unlike anything she had seen before. Rolling green hills sat in the foreground, a blanket of fields, bordered by vast tree lines, with mountains as their backdrop. Sheep were dotted across the slopes like little white punctuation marks to the pages and pages of emerald green that opened up before her.

'This is so beautiful! I've never seen anything like it.' She pressed against the window, a little reluctant to snap away with her camera, preferring to commit the views to memory instead of seeing it all through the veil of a lens.

'It's amazing, Mum, isn't it?'

Vivienne smiled; it really was. Emma's Kiwi accent sounded most pronounced when she spoke about the country that had become her home. The vast, majestic landscape was made all the more incredible because of its remoteness, as if it were a secret. With only an occasional car, barely a building for miles and just the big, big sky, it could not have been more different to the crowded streets of Bedminster where they'd both grown up.

'How lucky are you, Michael, growing up somewhere like this? It's incredible.'

'Not sure I always felt that lucky. Sometimes I wanted to be in the hub of things – I fancied New York or London. Thought there must be things going on, an amazing pace of life that I was missing out on.' He again sought out Emma's thigh with his hand. 'Still, that's the plan, eh, Em? New York for a few years or even China.'

'Oh, that sounds ... exciting.' Vivienne felt a swirl of embarrassment at being so unaware of her own child's plans, formulated with this stranger. It felt churlish to admit that she'd hoped they might come to Bristol; she had even considered taking a leaf out of Lizzie's book and redecorating the spare room, just in case. It was hard to explain why this made her feel tearful.

'You okay, Mum?' Emma didn't miss a trick.

135

'I think my tiredness might be catching up with me.' This was probably also true.

An hour later, Ellen roused herself, sat forward and peered out of the front window, restored by her nap. 'This is lovely!' she said as the car began winding its way up and down the Tutukaka cliff road, meandering down to sea level and then climbing again, skirting rocky bays and grassy banks where houses sat in glorious isolation with boats resting under carports, jet skis on trailers and pick-up trucks laden with diving paraphernalia.

'Not far now.' Emma rounded her shoulders excitedly and reached for her fiancé's hand.

With glimpses of the sea through the trees, it was hard for Vivienne to get her bearings. Suddenly Michael swung the vehicle to the left and drove through a narrow gap in the hedgerow, easy to miss were it not for the two vast blue hydrangea bushes that flanked it.

'Look at them beauties.' Ellen gasped at the flowers, which really were something. 'Don't think I've ever seen any so handsome. Not even in the garden centre.'

'They're everywhere on the farm.' Emma beamed.

The track instantly widened into a sweeping driveway that veered around in a sharp arc. A large wooden sign read *Aropari Farm*.

'Aerro-pahrie,' Vivienne tried to say it.

'It's Arrow-purri,' Michael helped her out, his pronunciation was punchy with heavy accentuation on the 'r'. 'It means clifftop.'

'That's beautiful.'

Emma wasn't lying. The drive was lined with more of the huge blue hydrangeas, which were at least five foot tall and beautifully full; it was quite magical. Either side of the driveway were lush, manicured lawns. The one to their right stretched all the way to the cliff edge.

Vivienne was quite taken aback; the size and setting of the place astonished her. At the top of the drive sat the house. She and Ellen exchanged a knowing look. No wonder Emma had described their little home in Mendip Road as crappy; compared to this, most things were.

Michael's family home was a sprawling, single-storey, ranch-style house that seemed to go on forever, with wings and outbuildings that looked as if they'd been added at a later date. It was clad in aged Douglas fir timber that had clearly been limed to give it a lighter look. Other sections were made entirely of glass, giving a view clean through to the other side.

'Wow! Oh my days!' Ellen said it for them both.

Michael pulled on the handbrake and he and Emma jumped down onto the gravel of the vast turning circle, which crunched underfoot as they opened the back doors for their guests.

The wide wooden front door was set back behind a deep portico with a grey shingle roof that matched the rest of the building. Two sturdy wooden pillars supported the structure, beautiful features in themselves. The theme was continued in a wraparound terrace; the section to the right of the front door was home to two large rocking chairs with saggy patchwork cushions nestling in the seats.

'Michael, this is really something. What an amazing home you have.' Vivienne was quite overwhelmed.

He nodded and flexed his arm from the elbow, as if directing traffic. 'The land goes way back, all the way up to the High Road, about four hundred and fifty acres. That's where the sheep graze.'

'Blimey, that's some back garden,' Ellen commented. 'Great for a game of hide and seek, but I wouldn't fancy mowing it.'

Michael lifted their heavy suitcases from the back of the car and wheeled them, one in each hand, towards the house.

'Come and see this, Mum, it's the best bit. And promise you'll be careful, Ellen – I don't want you falling off the edge.' Emma laughed.

'You trying to say I'm clumsy, Emma?' Ellen put her hands on her ample hips in mock indignation.

While Michael entered the house and disappeared to the left, Emma guided them into the cathedral-like glass-roofed hallway. Both women looked up and around, taking in the grand surroundings: the slate floors, exposed brick walls and inglenook fireplaces that were big enough to walk into; large wood-burners sat in readiness for the chill of winter. In pride of place hung a huge oil painting of the farm.

To the right of the hallway were three shallow steps that led to an open-plan dining area, and beyond that looked to be the kitchen. To the left was a vast sitting room divided by huge, aged nubuck sofas the neutral leather of which was brightened up by multi-coloured jute rugs that had been slung over the backs.

'I've never seen anything like it, Viv. It reminds me of the mall – you know, the glass bit by the fountain.'

'Ssshh...' Vivienne waved her hand at her friend and Emma visibly cringed.

'What?' Ellen was nonplussed. 'I mean it in a good way. I love the mall!'

Emma grabbed her hand and with her other hand on her mum's back pulled them to the other side of the hallway, through a large, sliding glass door and into the back garden.

The three stood in silence for a second. Emma looked from the view to the two women and back again, as if seeing it for the first time through their eyes and also keen to gauge their reaction.

Vivienne took a deep breath and let her eyes travel the length of the lush, close-cropped lawn that was bordered by yet more massive blue hydrangeas as well as clumps of tall, pretty grasses and spiky-tendrilled tropical plants with fiery orange centres. It was, however, neither the planting nor the dainty wood-lined path that wound its way across the lawn that had rendered her silent. A hundred feet from the back door was a huge raised deck. Unadorned planks of wood had been slotted together to form a sturdy platform at the edge of the grass and on it sat another pair of comfy-looking chairs and a wide wicker sofa. On the floor was a thin green quilt, resplendent with a Maori design of looping gold arcs and swirls that formed leaf-like patterns against a brown background. Matching pillows were scattered around. But even this impressive terrace wasn't what had stopped the words in Vivienne's throat and caused her to stand wide-eyed at the sight that greeted her.

The deck sat on the edge of a cliff. The women advanced cautiously, looking from left to right at what lay below. It was a bay, as beautiful as any Caribbean shoreline they had ever imagined. The sea was choppy, with sunlight highlighting the foaming crests that bobbed and swelled. To the right of the bay, grey, jagged rocks rose high out of the water, becoming smoother as they formed the cliff face on top of which Aropari sat. To the left of the bay were rolling hills covered in scrubby, wind-resistant bushes and long, lush grass that swept down to the edge of the water, and beyond the hills was another bay, where Tutukaka marina sat in a sheltered basin. Both sides of the inlet were peppered with gnarled, pale trees whose spiky foliage gave the place an almost arid feel, a striking contrast to the vivid green landscape and the dark, moving sea. It was as if two worlds had collided and they were at a vantage point, able to see both. The narrow beach had a jetty, entirely exposed at low tide, off which were moored two boats: a wooden clinker-built rower and a twin-engine speedboat.

'What do you think, Mum?' Emma asked eagerly, her hands clasped under her chin.

'I think this is the most beautiful place I have ever been.' She spoke the truth. She walked up onto the deck and closed her eyes, letting the sun kiss her face and the warm South Pacific breeze dance over her.

Ellen was uncharacteristically quiet, as if she too was quite overawed by the inspiring landscape in front of them.

'Just think, in four days I will be marrying Michael, right here on the deck and with this view!' She threw her arms wide and squealed.

'I tell you what, Emma, this might not be a church, but I reckon it's as close to heaven as you can get on earth.'

'You won't hear any arguments from me on that score.' The man's voice was deep, his speech slow, measured.

Vivienne turned to face him, but her eyes, dazzled from the sun, cast him in shadow. She placed her palm to her forehead and blinked a few times, until he came into focus. As her eyes adjusted, they fell upon a tall man in his mid fifties, wearing jeans and a pale blue T-shirt. He was unshaven, with close-cropped grey hair and the beginnings of a moustache and beard. She felt her face break into a smile; it wasn't forced or considered but was simply her natural reaction at seeing this person to whom she felt an instant, powerful connection. Her heart beat a little too fast and she was suddenly conscious of the fact that she had been travelling for what felt like days and was in dire need of a shower. She surreptitiously teased her fringe with her fingertips.

'Mum, this is Michael's dad, Gilbert. Gil. Gil, this is my mum, Vivienne, and her bonkers friend, my Auntie Ellen.'

'Oi, less of the bonkers if you don't mind.' Ellen stepped from the deck and took the hand Gil offered. 'Hello, love. This is one lovely house you have here and that view, oh my word.'

'Thank you.' He gave a small nod of his head

and then turned expectantly towards Vivienne.

She stepped from the deck and held out her hand, which Gil took into his.

'Vivienne.' He spoke her name slowly and this too made her smile.

Seven

The two women were delighted with the beautifully decorated, spacious room for their stay, tucked away to the south of the main hallway. It was light and airy with wide twin beds and a luxurious bathroom. French doors opened onto their own small terrace where there was a bistro table and two chairs.

'Reckon I could get used to this!' Ellen laughed as she removed items from her open suitcase and placed them in drawers or hung them up, hoping the creases might drop out of her dresses and skirts so that they wouldn't need ironing. 'Emma seems happy.'

'She does.' Vivienne was undecided, as to whether or not to mention her worry that Emma's happiness, her grin, had felt a little theatrical.

'Michael's not what I expected,' Ellen whispered.

'What, a real doctor, you mean? I can't believe you asked him that.' She gave a nervous laugh.

'I was only checking. You can't be too careful.'

They continued to unpack, until Vivienne broke the silence. 'And what do you mean, not what you were expecting?' She wanted Ellen to voice her thoughts first, which would make it easier for her to discuss her own concerns without feeling guilty or sounding as if she was gossiping.

Ellen shrugged and shook out a pair of white linen trousers. 'Don't know really, just a bit ... sober, I suppose is the word.'

She nodded. 'Yep, I know what you mean. Maybe he's shy?'

'Yes. Maybe.'

There was a beat of silence while they considered the man they'd only just met, both preferring to think that his slight standoffishness would disappear with time.

Ellen gathered her underwear from the corners of her case and folded the garments into the top drawer of the wooden dresser against the wall. 'Anyway, you can keep Dr McKinley – what about Gilbert, McKinley senior?' She sucked in her cheeks and pulled a face. 'He's a proper Christmas cracker!'

'Yes, he seems very nice,' Vivienne replied neutrally, concentrating on her own unpacking.

'Seems nice?' Ellen tutted. 'Are you kidding me? He's like a cowboy. A sexy, quiet cowboy.'

'He's a sheep-farmer!'

'Okay then, Miss Pernickety Pants, a sexy, quiet, sheep-farmer cowboy. All I can say is, lucky Tessa. Getting to wander the farm with him on a lonely night must be a good way to live.'

Vivienne laughed loudly. 'You are so nuts.'

Ellen placed her clean knickers on her head. 'Are you only just realising this now?'

'No, I've always known it. It was my bad luck to

be stuck next to you in the register. Why couldn't I have been called Vivienne Thomas and been sat next to Pamela Tindall. She seemed nice.' She giggled.

'Pamela Tindall? She was so weird and have you seen her recently – walks around town with her cats in a shopping trolley. Anyway, you don't mean it – you love me!' Ellen grabbed her friend and embraced her in a bear hug.

'Get off!' Vivienne shouted. Reaching up, she pulled Ellen's knicker hat down over her face and the two stumbled and fell into a heap by the door.

Suddenly Michael knocked and appeared in the doorway. He looked from his future mother-in-law to her friend, who peered back at him through the leg hole of the pants on her head.

'Hey, Michael!' Ellen yelled, making no attempt to remove the offending undergarments or release her friend.

'Oh!' His face visibly coloured. 'Sorry to inter-rupt. Emma sent me to say that supper is nearly ready.' He indicated the terrace with his thumb before retreating slowly, looking more than a little afraid.

Neither woman could speak for laughing. They snorted their amusement and clutched each other as they tried to stand.

'Bet Pamela Tindall wouldn't get me into so much trouble, cats or no cats,' Vivienne managed as she crawled on all fours to the bathroom. Laughing that hard at her age was never a good idea.

The table was set under the porch at the back of

the house. Candles in glass votive holders flickered at each place setting and wine glasses shone in the light thrown from the vast glass atrium, now illuminated from within. The crashing of the waves against the rocks below provided the background noise and with the hum of conversation and laughter it was perfect. It felt surreal to be sitting at this stunning table in this beautiful place, as if she'd been teleported there. The whole experience was quite magical.

Vivienne was careful not to give Ellen any more ammunition and did her best to avoid making eye contact with Gil, the sexy, quiet, sheep-farmer cowboy, who sat at the opposite end of the table. As she took a sip of wine, the thought of Michael finding them in a heap on the floor earlier made her smile against the rim of her glass.

She watched as Emma ate dainty mouthfuls and continually glanced at Michael, placing her fingers on his forearm and smiling when she caught his eye. Vivienne wished the affection was more readily and obviously reciprocated. It sent a quake of anxiety into her gut, reminding her very powerfully of how she had fawned over Ray, desperate for any crumb of affection. *Don't be silly, Viv,* she told herself. As Ellen had said, he was probably shy or maybe it was a cultural thing; she had, after all, only known him for a matter of hours.

Dinner was a great success: a hearty tomato and avocado salad with new potatoes and spicy lamb chops that had been blackened on the enormous outdoor grill. There was something about meat cooked on an open flame and eaten al fresco that gave it a taste like no other. She barely had room for the chocolate tart and Chantilly cream that appeared for pudding, but she did her best.

Michael had remained quiet throughout, apparently preferring to whisper to Emma rather than share what he wanted to say with the wider group, but that was fine too. It felt strange to see her daughter with her head cocked to one side, listening intently to the quiet words of her lover and laughing softly into her napkin. The Emma that Vivienne knew and loved had a loud, infectious, open-mouthed giggle and was more prone to dancing on the table than sitting demurely at the end of it. She tried to look at things from his perspective and decided he probably felt a little overwhelmed. She also reminded herself that she was looking at the world through the veil of fatigue, which was never that reliable.

The evening progressed, and the wine slipped down easily. The fuzzy stupor in which she found herself was quite lovely. She didn't even mind the sound of Ellen's booming voice asking Gil how he dared eat lamb when the poor wee thing's mum was his pet.

She liked his hearty laugh and the way he humoured her friend.

'You are right, they are all my pets!' He chuckled.

'Do you name them?' Ellen asked.

'Yes, of course,' he said dryly.

'How many do you have?'

'Two thousand, two hundred and twenty-seven.'

'Can you tell them apart?' Ellen pushed.

'Yes, it's easy.' He smiled.

'How?'

'Let me see... Daisy has a freckle on her nose, Ruby has beautiful eyes...'

'Are you teasing me?' Ellen banged the table.

'Not at all.' Gil gave another chuckle.

'Do you ever get lonely up here, Gil? I mean it's beautiful, but there's not much to do if sheep and boats aren't your thing,' Ellen asked in her typically frank manner.

'No. I like the peace and I like sheep and boats, plus I am only a short drive away from coffee shops, cinema, the market, there's plenty of life and bustle within reach. Truth is, Tessa and I are quite used to the pace of life here. It suits us.' He smiled, as if picturing Tessa with love.

'So do you and Tessa ever go away?'

Vivienne knew Ellen was trying to glean information. Nosey thing. She was, however, strangely interested in his responses.

'I take holidays. Well, I did, a few years back.'

'Where on earth would you go when you live somewhere this stunning?' Vivienne asked.

Gil turned towards her. 'I went to Bali, actually. I'd always wanted to see the temples.'

'Was it amazing?'

He nodded. 'It really was.'

Ellen suddenly bellowed. 'My cousin Gwen's boy lives there! You might have seen him, quite small build, beautiful dancer, has a fancy for foreign food. Went on a cruise ship and never came home. Loves it there.'

'I don't think I met him.' Gil looked at Vivienne and gave an almost imperceptible wink.

'Come on, Mum!' Emma leapt up and pulled

her arm, dragging her from the table.

Vivienne stood and followed Emma out onto the wide deck with its incredible view over the Tutukaka coast. In the far distance, the lights of the boats moored along the jetty of the marina bobbed against the darkness like captured stars. Even in the dark, the jagged shadows of the rocky clifftops stood out against the indigo sky.

Emma sat on the wide wicker sofa padded with cushions and curled her feet under her legs, her favoured position since she was a toddler.

'This is so far away, Emma.' Vivienne looked out across the water and took the seat next to her daughter.

'From where?'

'From everywhere!' She threw her arm around in an arc. 'From home, from Bedminster, from all our memories. It's another world!'

'I love it here,' Emma whispered.

'Oh, I get it, I really do. It is so beautiful. But seeing it makes me realise how far you've gone from me, from your old life.' Vivienne knew that the wine had erased many of the inhibitors that usually made her speech more guarded.

'My old life wasn't that great, Mum, if I'm being honest. Bits of it were – you and Aaron, of course, and I miss you both, I think about you all the time. It's been my wish to show you how I've been living, and here you are.' She beamed. 'But I was looking for something and I felt lost and then I met Michael and everything kind of fell into place.'

'Does he make you happy?' she asked tentatively.

'Of course he does!'

'Does he make you laugh?'

'Well, he's not a giggler like me, but he's solid and dependable and that makes me feel really safe.' She folded her arms across her trunk.

Both were silent for a second, as if considering this response.

Vivienne took a breath, again emboldened by the wine, which had lubricated her thoughts and her tongue. 'I guess I never thought you would settle down somewhere like this, it's so quiet, peaceful and beautiful, no doubt, but it feels more suited to someone like me who likes to potter and knit and sit with the dog, but you?' she shook her head, 'you have always been surrounded by friends, noise, laughter. You love the hustle and bustle and you love a natter! Good lord, Emma, I remember coming home from work one day and you were sat on the stairs, chatting away on the phone for an age and when I tapped my watch to tell you to get a move on, worrying about the phone bill, as usual, I asked you who you were chatting to and you covered the mouthpiece and told me it was a wrong number!'

'I remember that!' Emma laughed, 'it was a lady from Newcastle, she was sweet, told me about her allotment.'

'And that's my point: you are a people person, everyone loves you and even though I have only just arrived, my worry is that you seem a little quiet.' Vivienne raised her arms with her palms facing upwards into the vast expanse of darkness.

She looked to her left, as there came the unmistakable sound of Emma crying.

'I'm sorry, Mum.'

'Oh, love, why are you sorry and why are you crying? You're getting married! This is a happy time.'

'I'm crying because I do miss you and I do miss people and also because I'm a bit drunk,' she admitted.

Vivienne nodded. 'I know.' She reached over and kissed her child on the head, the novelty of being able to touch her after all this time apart was still wonderful.

'My life has just kind of happened,' Emma continued. 'I never planned it. But the further I get from Bristol, the more I understand how tiny the world is and I like knowing I can go home whenever I want to.' She sniffed and wiped her nose on her arm.

'But you don't, Emma. You don't come home. And you think home is crappy, and that makes me sad, not only because I miss you, but also because I think you might be looking for a home, looking for happy, and it's not a place. It never was. Happy is in here...' She placed her hand on her chest. 'I should know. I have lived in our crappy home in our little street for pretty much my whole life and apart from moments of self-doubt and the odd bout of loneliness, I have nearly always been happy.'

'Maybe I'm not like you,' her daughter said.

Vivienne took this as a slight, whether it had been intended as one or not. 'Maybe.'

'I wanted to spread my wings and breathe!' Emma opened her arms wide and threw her head back. 'I wanted to keep discovering, keep moving.'

'And I get that, love, I do. But my question is,

150

how do you know when to stop?'

'Well that's easy, when you find someone like Michael who shares your dreams and wants to take you with them.' She turned to face her mum. 'And if things get too much or we get bored, then we can move on, together. You heard him – China, America, it's all there for the taking!'

Vivienne nodded and pulled her girl towards her in a loose embrace as they listened to the sea below. It took a big gulp of courage for her to find the words that came next, 'I understand, and China and America sound wonderful, exciting, but I think there is a fine line between seeking adventure and running away. And for the record, when things get too much or are boring, they are often the most interesting bits, that's when you grow and learn and in those times, having roots that hold you steadfast to weather the storm is often better than to keep on running.'

'I love Michael, I do. I love him.'

Vivienne wished her daughter's words hadn't sounded so self-reassuring. She took a deep breath.

'You know I will always support you in whatever you choose. I think you are amazing and brave and beautiful. I never...' She paused, wondering how best to phrase things.

'You never what, Mum?'

She ran her hand over her daughter's scalp. 'I never want you to feel pressured into doing something that you don't want to. There are always options and there are no wrong choices, not in the long run. You can only go with what feels right or feels wrong and everything kind of figures itself out from there.' She kept her voice low.

'Are you talking about me getting married?' Emma cut to the chase.

'Not specifically,' she lied, 'but I wouldn't be doing my job if I didn't check that you *are* doing the right thing.'

'Oh, Mum, I am! I really am! Do you want to see my dress?' She leapt from the sofa, distracted by the idea, and took her mum's hands into her own, pulling her into a standing position.

'Yes, please!' Vivienne replied, with a little more enthusiasm than she felt.

Emma raced across the lawn. Suddenly, she dropped forward to plant her hands on the grass and rotated three hundred and sixty degrees with her feet in the air to perform a perfect cartwheel. Vivienne whooped and clapped, delighted by her athletic prowess and spontaneity, as Emma repeated the feat twice more.

'Is that a good idea on top of a big meal and wine?' Michael called from the table.

Vivienne watched her daughter shrink from his question, wrapping her arms around her slender trunk, as if embarrassed by the display. She nodded to Ellen to join them, trying not to notice the set of Michael's jaw, as he emptied his wine glass. It did little to erase her concerns.

The room Emma shared with her fiancé was like none that Vivienne or Ellen had ever been in. The bed was huge and sat on a raised deck at the back so that when you lay on it you got a clear view of the cliffs beyond the garden. French doors let the cool night breeze whoosh around the walls.

Opening a mirrored closet door, Emma lifted

the white gauze dress-cover from the rail and laid it on the bed before carefully unzipping it to reveal the stunning frock in which she was to be married. The bodice was fitted and fashioned from alternating panels of white lace and shirred white cotton. Spaghetti straps were delicately attached and the front was fastened with tiny pearlescent buttons. The skirt was full, again made from panels of alternating fabric, and its handkerchief hem was edged with lace.

Ellen sighed. 'It's very gypsy but also quite ballet-ish and maybe a bit hippy.'

Vivienne shook her head to rid her mind of Lizzie's comments.

'In a good way, though. Right?' Emma laughed.

'It's perfect for you, Em. You will look lovely.'

'You really will,' Vivienne said.

'I am keeping my hair loose and on my shoulders but wearing a flower crown – a florist up the coast is making it for me, using vintage dried pink rosebuds and some of the blue hydrangeas from the garden. I thought it was important to include part of Aropari in my outfit.'

'Has Michael seen your dress?' Ellen asked.

Emma shook her head. 'No, that would be bad luck. I have told him I'm going barefoot though, so he can probably guess that I'm not going to be all traditional.'

'Your mum's got flowers for her hair, too. We picked some up in Primark, didn't we, Viv?'

'I'm not so sure about them now, think I might be a bit old for flowers in my hair. They felt like a good idea standing in rainy Bristol while everyone did their Christmas shopping, but out here?

I'm not convinced.'

'Do you know, I have found it really hard to feel Christmassy this year, I think it's probably because my head is full of the wedding, but also it's not the same out here. The last couple of years away, I was in the city and working, so that was a big distraction and I had a happy Christmas by sharing the joy of everyone around me, but Michael's not a big fan of the whole festive thing. I think he sees it all as a bit of a waste of time so it's kind of put the kybosh on my own silliness for the season.'

Vivienne and Ellen looked at each other, not for the first time that evening hearing the sound of an alarm bell. This wasn't like Emma at all.

'It's made me think of Mendip Road, and the things that used to make it feel like Christmas. The smell of sausage rolls warming in the oven, the little foil trees you used to put on all the surfaces and the Carollers outside Asda in all weather. They were annoying because I had to walk in the road to get past them, but at the same time, the sound of their voices made my tummy jump with excitement, like it did when I was a kid, and Shaun always called for me to go ice-skating and when there wasn't any ice, we'd take his skateboard and whoosh down the path over at St. John's. The first time he suggested doing this we were only about eleven.'

'I remember.' Vivienne smiled.

'And I asked him why and he said that just because there was no ice, didn't mean we couldn't go out and fall over – a laugh was a laugh and a bruised bum was a bruised bum no matter how you got it, ice or skateboard. And he was right.'

She laughed.

'Don't you worry, girl. There are plenty of Bristol Christmases waiting for you in the future love,' Ellen reassured her. 'I reckon even old Michael would get in the mood after a couple of ladlefuls of my famous eggnog and a dance to my Christmas Mixtape under the mistletoe.'

'That's it!' Emma bounced and clapped, 'Elle you are a genius!'

'I know, I have been trying to tell your mother that for years.'

'I know what I am going to do,' she swallowed, 'I am going to give Michael a big slice of a Bedminster Christmas, right here in Tutukaka! I will cook the traditional big roast. I can cut up loads of white paper from the shredder to make fake snow. I'll cover a small space with tinsel and decorations, maybe a gazebo, hidden away in the garden and then, I'll reveal it to him on Christmas morning. I could make Santa's Grotto! And give him a stack of presents, silly things like chocolate and flashing Santa hats.' She smiled at her mum and her face lit up, as the ideas burbled from her. To Vivienne, she looked very much like the old Emma and it was good to see.

'Well, you've certainly got it covered. And if this doesn't turn our Michael into a Christmas lover, I don't know what will!' Ellen laughed.

'I do love him.' She ran her fingers over the pretty, white dress that lay flat on the bed and quite unexpectedly her tears fell again.

'Oh, love, look at you!' Ellen said. 'It's only natural to have jitters. I bet you haven't slept well for a while. It'll be the excitement and seeing

155

your mum again and all your plans, it must all feel a bit overwhelming.'

'It does.' She sniffed.

'Why don't you climb into this big bed and have a good night's sleep.'

Vivienne loved the way Ellen spoke to her girl. It was reassuring to know that should anything happen to her, Emma would always have this special relationship to rely on.

'I think I might.' Emma swiped at her tears. 'I'll just go and say goodnight to Gil and Michael.' She rubbed her eyes and smiled. 'It's going to be a lovely day, Mum. I'm having an arbour covered in flowers on the deck and we're putting the awning up in a day or two, which is where there'll be dancing. And I have a few other brilliant surprises...' She bit her lip. 'I can't wait!' She clapped her hands, and sniffed back her tears looking just like a child, trying to be brave.

'Oh, sounds intriguing.' Vivienne elbowed Ellen, who yawned.

'Tell you what, Viv, reckon my bed's calling me. I've come over all tired.' Ellen yawned again, as if to prove it.

Vivienne felt her own mouth stretching as she caught the tiredness that came off her friend in waves.

Having bid goodnight to their hosts and thanked them for a truly lovely welcome, she slipped into her pyjamas and climbed between the cool white sheets, discarding the wool blanket that had been folded over the foot of the bed – maybe Tessa's kind thought. She looked forward to meeting her.

Ellen bounced into her bed, running from the

bathroom in the darkness.

'Why are you running?' Vivienne asked.

'In case a monster grabs my ankles from under the bed.'

'You are not *still* scared of that, surely?'

'Why wouldn't I be? These fears don't disappear overnight.' Ellen pulled the sheet up over her shoulder and wriggled to get comfortable on the unfamiliarly soft mattress.

'Do you remember when you cut the legs off your bed and your mum went mad! I sat on the mattress watching you explain that you were scared of things hiding underneath it.'

'Poor old Mum.' Ellen sighed.

Vivienne's thoughts turned to the woman whose life had been far from easy.

It was after a silent minute, when their breathing had slowed, their eyes had adjusted to the dark and their ears had become accustomed to the strange night-time sounds of their alien surroundings that Ellen spoke, pulling Vivienne back from the brink of sleep. Used to sleeping in a room alone, she felt herself jolt awake.

'I know you're worried about her.'

'I am a bit,' she whispered. There was no point in being anything less than truthful with her friend, who knew her so well.

'But she's a big girl, and a smart one at that,' Ellen said, 'and she's done more in her little life than we ever have.'

'That's true, but it's not her I'm worried about so much as Michael. He seems so cool, not only with us but with her too. Have you noticed how she keeps seeking his approval, like a puppy who's not getting enough attention?'

'A bit, I suppose, but you mustn't go looking for things, Viv. If she's happy–'

'I know. I know,' she interrupted Ellen. 'And I might not have travelled like Emma, but I have lived, and I know what it's like to misplace your trust, to have your stability taken from you.'

'He's no Ray. I've told you that before.'

'I know you have.'

They lay still in the darkness.

This time it was Vivienne who broke the silence.

'I trusted him, Elle. I trusted him and he let me down and it changed something inside me, made me doubt everything I thought I knew. And even after all this time, it's left me with this cold kernel in my gut, so that I never feel properly warm. It's horrible. I couldn't understand why I was so different, how it had happened to me. My parents got married and stayed married, happy most of the time, as you know, and I just thought I'd be the same.' She took a deep breath and lowered her voice. 'When I was younger, and he had first gone, it felt like there was the possibility that my situation might change. I didn't feel properly on the shelf, but now, I don't know … I'm a proper reject.'

'Don't talk rubbish! You are no such thing. You live the life you choose to live. Things could be very different for you if you had a different head on.' Ellen's bed creaked as she turned to face her friend in the darkness across the room.

'I'm not so sure about that.' Vivienne huffed, slightly offended by the idea that she was somehow closed to the idea of change.

'You don't even see it.' Ellen raised her voice.

'Look at Pedro, he would give his left nut to get to know you better, and he's lovely and Bob likes him. You should go out with him. We'd get free teacakes for life.'

'Don't be ridiculous!' she snapped. 'He's friendly to everyone, not just me, and I am certainly not going to go out with someone just because my dog approves of him or because my loony friend wants a free teacake.' She tutted and closed her eyes.

'Half a free teacake,' Ellen corrected her. 'You always have the other half.'

Eight

Vivienne woke early and felt joy spread through her when she realised that she was in this warm New Zealand paradise and not her dark little bedroom on Mendip Road. She looked down to see that Ellen had slept on the floor. The sight of her friend curled up on the rug made her chuckle; she was far closer to the monsters under her bed than she had been when lying on it.

She spent an age deciding what to wear. Some of her clothes felt more appropriate for a resort, but this was someone's home and so she opted for a pair of sage-green pedal pushers and a white short-sleeved T-shirt with a green cotton cardigan slung over her shoulders, just in case. She slipped her feet into her sparkly silver jandals and laughed.

Emma burst into their bedroom. 'Morning!'

'Well, you sound a bit brighter today,' Ellen commented from the floor, where she lay on the discarded blanket and was coming to.

'Why are you lying on the floor, Elle?' She stared.

'Because I tried to get in with your mum in the middle of the night, but she was having none of it.' She sat up, trying to fully open her eyes.

'But why didn't you sleep in your own bed?' Emma noted the dishevelled sheets across the way.

'Because of the monsters,' Ellen answered matter of factly.

'Don't ask.' Vivienne kissed her daughter on the cheek. 'How lovely is this? Waking up in the same house as my girl.'

'It is lovely. I woke up so happy today. It feels good to have you both here to muck about with and chat to. I miss the gossip, the giggles, mates!'

Vivienne felt a flash of sadness at the prospect of having to leave her little girl behind when she left.

'I'm so excited, Mum.' Emma beamed.

'That's good, my darling.'

'About everything,' she added. 'I have made a few phone calls and reckon my Santa's Grotto idea is a winner, I'm going to make signs saying "North Pole this way" with a big arrow and really go for it. Michael will love it!' She clapped her hands together. 'You know that feeling when you know something and it feels like it might burst out of you, but you can't let it because it's a secret and it practically drives you nuts! That. See you outside for breakfast.' She smiled, and then left the room.

'What was all that about? She's a bit lively this morning.' Ellen spoke to the space Emma had occupied only seconds earlier.

'Haven't the foggiest. See you outside in a bit.' She left her friend to shower and dress and trod the cool hallway, still marvelling at the size and space of the magnificent McKinley home.

Walking past the study, she spied Gil sitting behind his desk with his back to the door. He looked at his watch. 'Yup, thanks, Jack. I've got Tessa coming home tonight, really looking forward to that...' She sped up, not wanting to eavesdrop, even unintentionally.

Michael was already at the table, tucking into scrambled egg on toast and a pint glass of fresh orange juice.

'Morning, Michael.' She spoke brightly, determined to try and get to know him in the few days before the wedding. 'I meant to ask you, are you having a stag do or have we missed it?' she joked, trying to picture Elle at such an event.

He swallowed his mouthful and gave a small shake of his head. 'I had a few beers with my mates from work, but to be honest, it's not really my thing.' He still seemed to find it hard to make eye contact.

'Oh, well, it's a good job you weren't in Bristol for our Aaron's then – they stripped him down to his boxers and tied him to a lamppost on College Green, poor love. That was his school mates – lovely bunch, but when they've had a few, you're best to steer well clear.'

'Sounds like it.' He gave a tight smile.

161

Not to be deterred, she tried again as she poured coffee from the cafetière into a spare mug. 'So are you looking forward to your first Christmas as a married man?' She tried to gauge just how indifferent he was to the season, knowing that Emma would give him a lovely surprise. She could hardly believe that in just a couple of weeks she would be back home, eating cold turkey in front of the telly and watching the EastEnders special while her little girl would be living the life out here, so very far away. She shook it from her mind.

'I'm working, I'm afraid. There won't be a Christmas for me. I haven't told Emma yet, but doubtful I'll be home between Christmas Eve and the twenty-eighth. We run a skeleton staff at this time of year and as the new boy, I felt obliged to volunteer, but it's just a day right?' He shrugged his broad shoulders and angled his fork for more food.

She struggled to remain composed, knowing how much trouble Emma was going to and more than a little concerned that at this early stage of their love affair, there was so little communication.

'And where is your hospital?' She pushed.

'Whangarei.'

'And that's commutable, is it?'

'About half an hour.' He took another mouthful and switched his attention to his phone.

'Only half an hour? So you *could* come home for Christmas?'

'It's not that straightforward, I'm afraid. I have to be on call, in the vicinity and sober, any emergency coming in doesn't really care that I am only half an hour away, minimum, they need me on

162

site, just in case.'

Vivienne felt her blood pressure rise. 'One thing I did want to ask you, Michael: are you looking forward to marrying my Emma?' She asked this rather more directly than she had intended.

Michael placed his cutlery on the plate and rested his elbows on the table. He swallowed and held her gaze. 'I love her.'

'Well that, as they say, is a jolly good place to start.' She grinned, briefly, and watched her daughter's fiancé stare into the middle distance as if the answer to her question might lie somewhere out on the blue, blue horizon.

'We work well together,' he began, 'and I don't like the idea of her not being around. We've had a lot of fun and I guess all couples probably struggle at some point when making decisions.' He coughed.

'What kind of decisions?' She was confused as to where this was heading.

'Oh, you know, a standard difference of opinion. No biggie.'

Vivienne had no clue as to what the difference of opinion might be. She pulled on all her courage to speak plainly. 'I want her to be happy, Michael of course and I want you to be happy too.' She smiled at her future son-in-law. 'I guess it's difficult for me, her mum, as I haven't had time to get to know you or to get to know you and Emma as a couple. It's all happened so quickly.' She gave a small laugh to try and smooth any awkwardness.

'It has.' He lay his phone on the table and looked at her. 'But they say you just know, don't they?'

'They do.'

'She is steady and calm. She likes what I like: to stay at home, drink wine, listen to some music, hit the ocean. We have a lot in common and that makes the future feel less daunting, you know?'

Vivienne nodded, she did know what he was talking about, but not who he was talking about. Steady and calm were the two adjectives she was least likely to use in any sentence when talking about Emma, and as for hitting the ocean? She pictured her little girl going quite hysterical on a trip to the aquarium when she spotted an octopus, and he had been in a tank.

'The wedding will–' he began.

'The wedding will what? Are you talking about me?' Emma disrupted the conversation, appearing on the terrace, smiling and with a plate full of crispy bacon and a stack of toast in her hands.

Vivienne silently cursed the interruption, suspecting that Michael had been about to open up to her.

'I'd better get going. Busy day.' Michael pushed his plate into the middle of the table and jumped up.

He kissed his fiancée on the lips and let his eyes linger on her upturned face, as his fingers skirted the side of her cheek.

'Safe journey – precious cargo and all that.' Emma gripped his wrist, as if unwilling to let him go.

He nodded at her and raised his hand at Vivienne before disappearing inside the house.

'Where's he off to?' she asked, sipping her freshly brewed coffee.

'He's collecting something for the wedding. Running around, you know. Chores.' Emma kept it vague, then handed her mum two slices of toast, pre-buttered, which she covered with homemade lemon curd.

Vivienne's stomach bunched with excitement. It was really something, to be eating breakfast on this glorious morning with the sun overhead and such a paradisiacal backdrop.

Gil strolled out, sunglasses nesting in his hair, and took a seat.

'Morning Gil,' she called.

'For you maybe, but for me this is lunch. I've been up for four hours, done the early morning round, put feed and water out and treated a home-sick lamb who's come from another farm, a different breed we are trying out.'

'You make me feel guilty!' she smiled.

'Don't, this is your holiday.' He raised his glass of orange juice at her in a salute. 'How was your first night on Kiwi soil?' he asked with a wide, ready smile.

'Lovely, thank you. I thought I'd feel a bit out of sorts with the time change and everything, but it's funny, after a good night's sleep, I'm brand new.'

'That's good news.' He clapped. 'I'm taking the boat out for a bit, doing all I can to get out of any wedding preparations. If I make myself available, she gives me a job to do.' He smiled lovingly at Emma, who poked out her tongue at him. 'Would you and Ellen like to come out with me? It's going to be a beautiful day – feels a shame to waste it.'

'Would I like to do what?' Ellen asked, arriving

resplendent in her navy maxi dress, a very large navy straw hat and oversized sunglasses. She looked lovely. It made a change to see her without the restrictions of layers and scarves to ward off the winter chill of home.

'I was just saying, I'm taking my boat out today, thought I could give you both a sea tour. There's no better way to get a view of the Poor Knights. And looking back into shore from the sea is something else.'

'What are the Poor Knights?'

'A group of islands about twenty-three kilometres out. The marine life is something else. It's famous for diving.'

'Is it a big boat?' Ellen asked.

'Not really. It's a speedboat, so there'll be no ice bucket and G & T on the deck, I'm afraid. But it's great fun for wave hopping and she'll get you where you need to go very quickly. Thought we might kill the engine and do a spot of fishing?'

'Oh yes, we can grill what you catch for supper!' Emma sounded like a proper Kiwi.

'You're 'avin' a laugh! You won't get me in a little boat, not for all the tea in China! What happens if you break down or you fall in?' Ellen looked genuinely worried.

'Well, if you break down, you call for help on the radio, and if you fall in, you get wet. It's quite straightforward.' Gil laughed.

'Are you always this laidback about things?' Ellen clearly couldn't decide whether this was a good or bad trait of his.

'Pretty much.' He picked up a stiffened strip of bacon and chewed it.

'I think it sounds lovely...' Vivienne paused. 'I've never been on a little boat before, and not too many big ones either, come to think of it. If I get seasick, can we come back?'

'Straight away.' He nodded.

'I'm not sure,' she hesitated. 'I don't want to spend time apart from you, Emma.' She was aware that their time together was precious.

'Actually Mum, I was going to suggest that you and Elle amuse yourselves for an hour or so anyway. I have a beauty appointment and one or two things to do that I am best left to my own devices for, then we can meet up back here?'

'Well, all right then.' She smiled at the prospect of the excursion, remembering her conversation with Ellen about being ready to grab a bit of adventure and be more daring. Well, this certainly fitted the bill on both counts.

'Tell you what, Elle, I'm going to the farm up the road to buy some fresh avocados – fancy coming with me and I can leave you there for a wander while I go and get my bits and bobs done and then we can both come back here and meet Mum. How does that sound?'

'I'd love that,' Ellen beamed. 'Sounds perfect.'

Gil drove the battered red flatbed truck along a narrow muddy track that wound its way down to the shoreline. The deftness with which he tackled the steep inclines gave her confidence that she was in safe hands. Conversation was minimal, as if they were both getting used to the other's presence. He parked under the spread of a spiny Douglas fir and pulled on a well-worn black baseball cap em-

167

blazoned with the ubiquitous Kiwi fern logo.

'This is my lucky fishing hat, so we won't go far wrong.' He flashed her a wide smile.

'Wouldn't be too sure – I might be bad luck,' she countered as she took tentative steps across the pebbly beach and out towards the jetty.

His eyes lingered on her face. 'I doubt that.' This compliment of sorts made her happy. 'Besides,' he continued, 'I brought you my second luckiest hat.' From his khaki and leather satchel he produced a second baseball hat; this one was navy and white and had a tree in a shield on the front. He placed it on her head and pulled down the peak. 'Now you're good. This is my Northland hat. You like rugby?'

'I guess I do now.' She adjusted the peak.

Vivienne trod the wide-open planks of the jetty, concentrating on not losing her footing in the gaps or slipping off the side into the dark, shallow water below. As Gil jumped down into the two-seater boat, she took in the steering wheel, what looked like a gearstick and the space at the rear – the whole thing couldn't have been more than twenty feet long. He threw his bags and fishing box into the back, then reached up towards the jetty to take her hand.

She felt ridiculously self-conscious and very nervous about stretching down to take his steady hand. He stood on the base, legs splayed to keep his balance, waiting patiently for her. 'It's okay. I've got you,' he murmured. She nodded, as she reached out towards him, still wary of falling. 'Take small steps and get as close to the edge as you can. That's it,' he said encouragingly.

But instead of letting him manoeuvre her down into the boat, she withdrew her arm back to her chest and dropped down into a crouch, from where she managed to lever herself in without his help.

Gil coughed and dropped his hand to his side. Both were a little embarrassed by her decision not to touch him, as if she might be making more of this than was necessary. Vivienne was grateful for the oversized sunglasses she'd grabbed in Tesco; she pulled them down to hide what was visible of her face beneath her cap.

'Welcome aboard!' he announced, and immediately the atmosphere cleared. He pointed to the caramel-coloured leather passenger seat. 'Right, buckle up!' He then coiled the rope that had held the boat fast to the jetty and clambered across to take his position in the driver's seat.

The boat swayed a little in the water and she instinctively gripped the side.

'You can relax, she's as stable as they come,' he said reassuringly. Still standing, he pushed a button on the dashboard and the engines jumped into life. She felt the shudder along the hull and under the soles of her feet. The smell of burning petrol hit her nose, and she noted with a little trepidation the plume of smoke that rose up from the back of the boat, but thankfully the smell and smoke quickly passed. Gil surveyed the ocean from his vantage point, the engine put-putted as it idled and then roared. She felt her body get pushed further back in the seat as the boat moved forward.

Gil smiled at his nervous sea companion. She swallowed a ball of excitement, knowing that this

169

day would be as wonderful in the retelling as it was to actually live it. She pictured Aaron and Lizzie sitting opposite her at the kitchen table while she dished up her predictable fish pie. *'Oh yes, that was quite some jaunt, a sunny day at sea on the Tutukaka coast in a speedboat. Yes! Me in a speedboat, can you believe it? It sure beats a rainy day in Bristol, no matter how many multi-coloured, glass droplet chandeliers you have to admire.'*

The broad black flag with the silver fern fluttered on the shiny flagpole and the sun scattered sparkling diamonds across the ripples of the cresting sea.

'So are we going to catch a fish?' Gil called as she adjusted her hat and nodded ahead.

She was both excited and petrified at the prospect of catching a real live fish! 'I don't mind catching one,' she shouted over the noise of the engine, 'as long as I don't have to unhook it or go near it or touch it.'

'You'll be a pretty rubbish fisherman with all those restrictions.' He laughed.

'I'd better stick to fish fingers then.'

He navigated the shallow bay with skill, raising his hand and nodding his greeting to all the fellow boat owners and day-trippers they encountered as they rounded the headland. Other boaties were either busy readying their vessels in the adjacent marina or were sitting in chairs and sipping iced drinks through straws. Gil pointed to a low-rise building hovering at the back of the marina with a beautiful mountain backdrop and a partially covered terrace.

'That's Schnappa Rock, the best restaurant on

the North Island, let alone in Tutukaka. It's owned by my friends Nick and Esther and the food is second to none.' A tall, dark-haired man came out of the front of the building, and stood on the terrace that overlooked the marina. The tables were already full of boaties and locals alike tucking into brunch in the sunshine. Gil raised his hand, 'Talk of the devil. That's Nick.'

Vivienne waved back, smiling at the friendliness of the welcome and hoping that Emma would be happy here. They passed a *Dive! Tutukaka* boat laden with passengers, tourists seemingly, all of them in wetsuits, some pulled down to their waists. They were peering into the water, presumably imagining what they might find down there in an hour's time. The dive master looked just the part with his long sun-bleached hair and mirrored shades. He raised his right hand to acknowledge his neighbour.

Vivienne relaxed a little and linked her hands in her lap. She watched as Gil took his seat, resting his bottom high on the back of it to give himself the best view over the narrow windscreen and stretching out his muscular legs. He pushed his sunglasses up his nose as he increased the engine speed and turned his face into the breeze.

It was only a matter of minutes before they were out in open water and he called out, 'Okay, are you ready to drive this beauty?'

'Oh god, no! No, I might crash it.' She giggled, crossing her arms over her chest, as if this might protect her from the prospect.

'I won't let you. Come on, it's a doddle.' He nodded towards the steering wheel.

'Really?' she screamed.

'Yes! Come on!' He leant across, still with one hand on the wheel, and climbed up on the seat, waiting until she had found her way into the white leather captain's chair and he was perched behind her. 'Take the wheel,' he encouraged.

'I'm scared!' she yelled.

'Don't be. We'll do it together.' He smiled.

She screamed again, and then, just like that, with her hands gripping the small steering wheel, she was driving the boat. 'Look at me!' she called.

'I'm looking.' He laughed, as he stood behind her, hands ready, just in case.

'I can't believe I'm doing this.'

'You're a natural.'

'Do you get to go out every day and do this?'

'Yup, if work allows and the odd evening too, if nothing needs doing on the farm or if I want to get away from it all. Tessa and I just head out. It's paradise.'

'Does she like the sea?'

'Oh, she loves it! Wouldn't suit me if she didn't – it's a big part of my life.'

He nodded and Viv felt an unexpected spike of envy shoot through her. What was she thinking? She berated herself for being so fanciful and allowing Ellen's silly chatter to take hold. They were newly acquainted friends and he was a charming host, nothing more. 'The everyday life of a sheep farmer in Tutukaka, eh?' She beamed.

'Something like that.' Gil chuckled. 'It's lovely to meet you both. And you know, you and Ellen can come out any time. I've got plenty of room. You are always welcome, and your family, of course.

You don't even have to plan, just pitch up any time.'

She smiled at the man's generosity of spirit. It was interesting to her that he had so little idea of just how different their lives were. Where this was a regular sort of day for him, her days were spent either on the till at Asda or pottering in the house, monitoring the laundry of her single life until she had enough for a full load, shopping for her tea, cooking her tea, knitting items of clothing that she wasn't sure anyone really wanted and taking Bob out in all weathers and of course, meeting Ellen to natter away the hours when time allowed. A very different life in every sense.

She tentatively turned the wheel to test the responsiveness of the boat. The back end kicked out as they arced to the right.

'That's it. Not too much or she'll run away with you.' He leant over her and steadied the wheel.

She felt the graze of his arm across her back and couldn't help the frisson that shot through her. She turned her head and he was staring at her. His mouth moved as if he was going to speak and he bent towards her. She jerked her neck to face forwards and sat up straight. It was an odd exchange. There was an undeniable crackle of electricity between them and her heart wouldn't stop pounding.

Get a grip, Viv. He's about to become Emma's father-in-law and he's with Tessa. This was to be her mantra for the next couple of hours. She hoped her body would catch up to the place where her mind had settled.

Suddenly, Gil reached forward and cut the

engine. The boat slowed and stopped, bobbing in the South Pacific Ocean. It was eerily quiet without the engine noise, and the gentle rocking induced a state of trance-like bliss. 'This is just brilliant. Thank you for bringing me out, Gil.'

'You're welcome. Shame Ellen doesn't have sea legs – reckon she'd have enjoyed it, if only for the view.'

'Possibly, but I tell you one thing, it'd be a hell of a lot less peaceful if Elle was on board. She only has two volumes: loud and really loud.' She smiled.

'I had noticed.' His eyes twinkled. 'You and her are close?'

'The closest. She's been my best friend since primary school.'

'Lucky ladies.'

'Yes, we are really.' The sun was warm and she reached over and let her fingers trail through the water. It was colder than she had anticipated. 'The water's chilly!'

'It is. We're not that far from Antarctica and we're not in the Gulf Stream, so we miss out on that nice warm water from the Equator.'

'Gosh.' She pictured the globe in the loft that her dad used to study and saw herself as a little X marked on it in the middle of the sea. 'It's strange for me, I always imagined that where there was a beach and the sun shone the sea would be warm.'

'Not always.' He smiled at her. 'And I wouldn't leave your hand in there if I were you, the piranhas will have your fingers off in seconds.'

'Ah!' She screamed and whipped her hand back inside the boat, showering them both in cool, salty droplets as she did so.

Gil bent over and laughed with his hands on his thighs. 'I can't believe you fell for that. As if we'd have piranhas!' He laughed again.

'Very funny.' She scowled mockingly. 'How am I supposed to know that?' She dipped her hand into the cool sea and this time hurled a cupped palm full of water in his direction.

Positioning himself in the seat next to her, he sat back with his head on the headrest and his legs stretched out in front of him. 'This is the life.'

She nodded. Out there on the water, the silences were far from uncomfortable. The sound of the waves lapping against the boat was hypnotic, as was the chatter of gulls overhead.

'It's so peaceful.' She closed her eyes and lifted her face towards the sun. 'It's not very often that I'm still like this; there always seems to be something to do, something to think about or fix. This is lovely.' She smiled. 'I can feel myself unwinding.'

'That's the idea. Michael has been on at me for years, for as long as I can remember, in fact, wanting me to expand the business, buy more land, diversify. He's never satisfied, but I try to explain to him that you only need enough. And this is enough for me.'

'I can see why,' she whispered, opening her eyes and looking at the Poor Knights on the horizon.

'We have a lovely home, a decent living and peace, and that's got to be good for your health and your mind.'

'I think you're right. I wouldn't mind a bit more peace; it feels like I always have one of the kids to worry about. If it's not one thing then it's an-

175

other. I thought I'd worry less about them as they got older, but I don't. It's just a different set of worries.'

'That's true.' He paused, 'I worry about Michael, chasing more, more, more...' He shook his head. 'Even the thought of it makes my heart sink.'

She thought of Lizzie, working Aaron hard so they could buy more stuff.

'I'm just not the type for the cut and thrust of acquisition. I have everything I want, right here.' He raised his hands and let them fall against his jeans.

'But Michael thinks you should be that person?' she asked, boldly.

'Yes. We are very different fish.' He smiled at the pun, as they bobbed on the ocean. 'I think Emma is good for him.'

She smiled, glad to hear this. 'I think he's certainly the stability she's been missing. He seems steady.' She was careful not to make steady sound negative.

'He is that.'

'That's something I've never had,' she confessed, 'not with a man. Emma's dad was a player, a rogue, really. He seemed so exciting to me when I was young, but we were mismatched, heading in different directions without even realising it.' *At least I never realised it...*

Gil snorted his laughter. 'Well, that's my story too, kind of. I thought I'd captured a spark with Michael's mum, but once I'd captured her, her spark faded and she withered until I realised that I wasn't enough for her, that this wasn't enough for

176

her.' He lifted his hand towards the air. 'And the moment, in fact the second I told her so and suggested she might like to be free of me, she lit up, like she was restored and had been waiting for me to set her free, and just like that, off she went. No way did I want someone to be with me through duty or, worse, pity. I realised that we had come at it from very different sides of the fence: she wanted the high life, fancy yachts and restaurants, and that's my idea of a nightmare. Anyway, all a very long time ago now.' He coughed and scratched the back of his head up under his cap, as if embarrassed to have been so open.

'I've never been on a fancy yacht or in a fancy restaurant. I come from a very ordinary family, you know – we drank tea and we talked about the weather. My dad worked at Wills Tobacco, a factory not far from where we lived, and none of us has ever had fame or fortune. As I say, just ordinary, but happy. And then out of the grey ordinariness of everything, Ray came along and swept me off my feet, quite literally. I was eighteen and I guess I was blinded, excited by the attention. His life felt a bit glamorous – well, compared to mine, it was. I mistook his deceit for mystery, his caginess for cool. He was a good talker and he knew how to hook me in. He was nice to my mum and dad, he knew that was important to me.' She paused. 'I don't know why I'm telling you all this. Boring, really.'

Gil turned in his seat and sat facing her, gripping the back of her headrest, as if this might aid his concentration. She could feel the heat from his fingers, only millimetres from her cheek. He

177

removed his sunglasses and held them in his hand. 'It's not boring, not at all. Carry on.'

She took a deep breath. 'The shine came off our relationship very quickly. He wasn't ready to settle down, at least not with me, and I couldn't see a way out of the life I was living, not with two small children. If I looked into the future, I just saw my life morphing into my mum's, but without the love and support she got from my dad, living in the same street, working in the same place and watching the telly all day and although I wanted more, I wasn't prepared to give up on us. Which I guess would have trapped us both, had he stayed, and I know that sounds selfish.' She looked into his eyes.

He smiled at her. 'I don't think it's selfish, I think it's admirable that you had that staying power. And don't be fooled – everyone wants a bit more out of life, especially when they're younger.'

She nodded. 'I guess so.'

'How did you meet him?'

'In the pub.' She groaned at the cliché. 'And I often wonder how my life might have turned out if I'd yawned just once more and said my good-byes sooner. I would have missed him, escaped, had a different life. Dodged a bullet.'

'Is that how it feels?'

Vivienne sat up straight. 'I shouldn't say that really. It's difficult. My kids...' She smiled involuntarily as she pictured their faces. 'My kids, no matter how old they get and despite the worry, are my best thing. They are everything, and I can't picture a life without them in it. I don't want to and so I feel torn. I have asked myself, would I have married him and gone through what I did

178

just to get them? And the answer is yes. Yes, I would. But I didn't know what I was getting into, not even a little bit. I had no idea that for him I was just temporary, disposable. And that's hard to accept that I was so deceived.'

She started to cry. Her tears came swiftly and without warning and she ferreted around in her pockets for a nonexistent tissue. Her embarrassment was acute.

'God, I'm so sorry.' She tried to hide her face with the back of her palm.

'Here...' He gave her his handkerchief.

Nodding her thanks, she blew her nose and wiped her eyes.

'Don't cry, Viv,' he whispered and placed his hand on her shoulder, squeezing gently.

'I'm crying because to say those things out loud makes me feel so sad. It's a horrible thought that I was nothing to him. And it's ridiculous for me to feel this way; we were on a collision course from day one. And when he left, I didn't yearn for *him* as such, but it was more the fact that I was robbed of the fight, the chance to understand what had gone wrong. He just disappeared and that hurt just as much.' This confession only caused her tears to fall faster. 'Sorry, Gil. Maybe I'm a bit jetlagged. I never really cry, and certainly not in front of strangers.'

'We're not strangers, we'll be family in three days' time.'

She nodded. This was true. 'I've been single for so long, I can't imagine my life being any different, despite Elle nagging me to get out there.'

They both gave short laughs at the thought of

the irrepressible Ellen.

'Does she say it loud or really loud?' he joked, trying to distract her.

'Both,' she managed. 'There are still times when I miss being part of a couple. I miss it more than I can say.' Again she felt the threat of tears. 'Oh, for goodness' sake, will you look at me?' she waved his handkerchief in front of her face. 'There's us supposed to be having a nice outing and I'm sitting in this beautiful place with tears and snot running down my face, spoiling it all.'

'You are not spoiling it, and for what it's worth, I do know how you feel.' He sounded genuine.

She sat up and tried to gather herself, feeling a little uncomfortable at having been so honest, knowing he would be greeting Tessa in no time at all. 'I'm sorry, Gil, let's talk about something else. I really don't know why I'm telling you all this. It's got nothing to do with you.'

She fiddled with the handkerchief in her lap and felt the burn of embarrassment on her cheeks, completely unsure as to how to handle this feeling of vulnerability. She glanced at the dappled surface and considered jumping in. Piranhas or not.

When she looked up, it was as if someone had flicked a light switch. A mass of dark cloud had come up behind them and hidden the sunshine.

'Reckon fishing will have to wait for another day.' Gil stood and indicated for her to move back into the passenger seat. 'It will probably pass, but I don't want you to be stuck out here in a storm. Not on your first jaunt.' He pushed the starter button and opened the throttle.

'Oh God, that makes two of us. I don't want to

be stuck out here in a storm either.' She wriggled down into the seat as he pulled the boat around and headed for shore.

'No need to panic, if it does reach us, I have been out in the rain a million times before. You are safe.' He spoke determinedly and it had the desired effect. She did feel safe.

It was as the boat edged towards the land that the storm caught up with them and the heavens opened. This was nothing like the cold, windy showers that skirted playfully across North Street and could be buffered with the careful angling of her brolly. This was something else entirely. It was like sitting in a warm shower with the tap turned to full. The squall hovered overhead, rolling from purple bruised clouds, sending the deluge in a curtain of rain that fell directly on top of them. Vivienne looked down at her clothes that clung to her body. She removed the soggy cap and ran her hand over her wet hair that was plastered to her scalp and blinked to free her eyelashes that were stuck together with rainfall. She blew out, watching the raindrops that dripped from her nose, shoot outwards.

'Hold on tight, nearly home!' Gil now had to shout, as the sound of the rain hitting the water was louder than she would have thought. She paddled her feet in the water that had started to gather at the bottom of the boat and wondered how much of a downpour it would take before the boat sank. Visibility was poor; it was as if a thick mist enveloped them and her heart raced. Gil stared ahead, his expression stern, as he concentrated on steering them, almost blindly, back towards the safety of the shore.

Suddenly with the end of the jetty in sight, he called across to her, 'Are you okay?'

She nodded and gave a double thumbs up, unwilling to admit to the enormous relief she felt at the sight of the gappy planks of wood that meant that soon there would be something solid beneath her feet. He reversed the vessel in a neat, well-rehearsed move and steered her alongside the mooring, before jumping up onto the sodden surface of the jetty to secure the boat at the front and back with the fat ropes that he quickly un-coiled and tied to the stubby cleats. He lobbed the two narrow fenders over the edge to protect the boat from the dock, as it bobbed on the choppy sea and walked along the jetty to the front of the boat, where he stood calmly and reached down for her hand. This time without nerves, she stood and with the rain running over her skin in tiny tributaries, she looked up and placed her hand inside his. Gil pulled, leaning back, anchoring her with his weight, as she climbed up and out of the boat. He kept her hand inside his, as they ran up the pebbled beach, towards the truck.

'Perfect timing.' He smiled, as they jumped into the truck. He removed his hat and rubbed his hair, scattering droplets of water over the dusty dashboard. 'Yes indeed, I would hate to have got caught in that.' He grinned, as he peered out of the windscreen and tried to look between the branches of the Douglas fir, as the storm raged on. Their breathing calmed, as their heart rates slowed.

Vivienne laughed as their bodies steamed in the

warmth of the vehicle, fogging up the windows and making the air thick with the salt-tinged vapour of rain.

'I'm soaked right through.' She pulled her t-shirt from her chest and it made a sucking noise, as it peeled away from her wet skin.

'It's okay. You are waterproof. Trust me.' He ran his palm over his face and shook his head.

They sat in silence listening to the sound of fat raindrops bouncing against the metalwork and watching, as leaves and twigs collected at the base of the windscreen.

'Do you think Michael wants to get married?' she asked bluntly.

He turned his head towards her and opened his mouth, clearly searching for the right words. 'He loves her.'

'And she loves him, I can see that,' she replied. 'But we both know, Gil, that sometimes it takes a little bit more than fairy dust and the heat of the moment to make a commitment like this.'

He nodded. 'It does, I know, and...' he paused.

'And what?'

He exhaled, exhibiting all the signs of the sort of stress she knew he worked hard to avoid. 'They are great kids, both of them.'

'What were you going to say?' she prompted again, squeezing the handkerchief that she had failed to return, which was now a sodden lump in the flat of her palm.

'I am a bit concerned. Not about Emma, not at all,' he was keen to emphasise this, just as much as she was relieved to hear it. 'I'm very fond of her, but I am worried about certain things...'

'What *things?*' She hated the vagueness of it all. 'I don't want her to get hurt. That's all I care about.' Her tone was urgent.

'I don't want either of them to get hurt,' he countered. 'Look...' He held up his hands. 'Michael is not a bad kid, he's a good man, but he's already married.'

'What?' she jerked her head to face him, as she yelled.

'To his job! Jesus!' Gil placed his hand on his chest and they both laughed at her premature hysteria. There was a moment of silence while they both digested this phrase.

'I guess what I am trying to say, rather badly, is that Michael will always put his work first and that's okay, if you are honest about it and the other person knows what they are taking on, but I am not so sure Emma does.'

'She knows his job is important, she told me as much.'

'Yes, she does, but I've seen enough of my son over the years to understand how important.' He blinked at her, 'As I say, I am in no doubt that he loves her, but I think Emma might be planning in her mind for a future that doesn't exist. And without her network of friends and family around her for support, I worry her spark might go out too and that would be the very worst thing I could imagine.'

'Yes,' she whispered, 'yes it would.'

The rain stopped and they both retreated into their own silent musings. Gil cracked the window a little to let in some air and started the engine. 'Guess we should think about getting back.'

She nodded, 'Yes, probably. Thank you for taking me out, I have honestly loved every second of it, even the rainy bit.'

Gil smiled, as he slowly reversed the truck up to the track in a well-practised manoeuvre. The engine steamed. 'Don't worry, Vivienne, I am probably just over-worrying. Maybe we need to have faith in the kids that it'll all be fine.' He gave a quick smile as he steered them towards home.

Strangely, his words had quite the opposite effect. Vivienne rubbed her forehead and placed the soggy, borrowed cap on the back seat; she had the beginnings of a headache. It was turning out to be quite a day.

She spied the familiar vast blue hydrangea plants just before they reached the entrance to Aropari, as breath-taking as they had been on first sight. They continued up the driveway and past the sign welcoming them home. As Gil pulled up the hand-brake, it was the unmistakeable sound of a dog barking that drew her from the moment. She thought for a second that her eyes might be playing tricks. It was Bob! But it wasn't, of course, it couldn't be.

'Tessa! Hello, you beauty! Hello there!' Gil leapt down from the cab and embraced his beautiful dog – his Tessa, his trusty sidekick, companion and seafaring buddy.

Tessa barked and nuzzled against his leg. 'Oh! Hello you! Welcome home!' He crouched low and rubbed the dog's pretty head.

She heard his words of earlier, recalled his happy face. *'If I want to get away from it all, Tessa and I just head out. It's paradise.'*

'Tessa is your dog?' she asked.

'Yup. Isn't she a beauty?' He petted the animal, oblivious to the lightness this revelation brought to Vivienne's spirit.

'Yes, she is. I have a dog that looks just like her, but he's called Bob and I miss him so much.'

'I'd miss her too. She's had a little op, been at the vet's for forty-eight hours. I must say, I didn't like her not being here.'

'You get used to the company, don't you?' She spoke absentmindedly, thinking of all the times she had taken comfort from the presence of her four-legged friend.

'You certainly do.' He looked up at her and quite unexpectedly she felt her stomach flip.

'Viv!' Ellen's shouts distracted her and she turned to the terrace to see her friend approaching with a basket of green fruit. 'Good Lord, look at the state of you two, you are soaked. What did you do, jump in?'

'The storm.' Vivienne pointed upwards at the sky that was already clearing to its beautiful shade of blue.

'Never mind that, will you look at these.' Ellen held up a huge avocado. 'I picked this straight from the tree, can you believe it? Look at them!' She was clearly impressed, and rightly so, they looked delicious.

'I didn't know you liked avocados,' she said.

'I don't, but that's not the point,' Ellen barked. 'I didn't know you liked going out in tiny boats, and getting rained on, but judging from your rosy cheeks, I'd say you rather enjoyed yourself. A day of firsts for both of us. Who knew?'

Vivienne gave her friend a hard stare. She was in no mood for her teasing in front of Gil.

'And I see you've met *Tessa?*' She emphasised the name with a knowing glint in her eye.

'Yes, she's smashing.' Vivienne turned her gaze on the animal, avoiding having to look at her friend.

'Isn't she just.' Ellen beamed. 'Emma and I have been hard at it. We're having a barbecue tonight, everything is under control.'

Vivienne smiled at her friend, who had slipped so easily into this wonderful Kiwi lifestyle.

'Michael not back yet?' Gil asked, a little sharply, as he straightened.

'Haven't seen him, but I know Emma spoke to him a little while ago.' Ellen grabbed Vivienne's hand to walk her back to the house.

'Viv,' Gil called after her.

She stopped and turned to face him. 'Yes?'

He placed his hands on his hips and looked skywards, as if searching for inspiration. 'Nothing.' He waved his hand in the air as if he might be able to erase the comment. 'Thanks for a lovely day.'

She smiled at him as he turned his attention to the back of the truck and began sorting out the redundant fishing tackle that they had neglected to use.

The two friends strolled back to their room.

'Tessa is a dog,' Ellen shouted, far too loudly for comfort. 'Fancy that.' She grabbed her friend's arm and squeezed it hard.

'Yes, fancy.' She wriggled free of Ellen's grip and

tried to sigh and look nonchalant, even though her insides were jumping with excitement.

'Reckon we might get you up to two notches on the bedpost by the end of the trip?' Ellen chortled.

'Don't be so ridiculous,' she shot back as she shed her rain-soaked trousers and sweaty T-shirt and headed for the shower. She couldn't, however, hide the smile that hovered around her mouth, even though Gil's unsettling comments about Michael and Emma had tempered her buoyant mood. She couldn't wait to speak to Emma later when they were alone.

'I think I might have a little nap after my shower.' She yawned.

'Good plan. I'll leave you to it, love. I have salad to chop, after all. Plus I want to give Trev a shout, let him know we're okay. I'll ask him to check on Bob too.'

'Thank you.' She yawned again and stepped into the bathroom.

After a blissful forty winks, Vivienne woke to find Ellen rummaging through one of the drawers, looking for God only knew what. She got up and began to get ready, giving her hair a quick tousle as she stood in front of the bathroom mirror. Her beauty regime was minimal: a little moisturiser or hand cream when she remembered and a smear of lipstick and blusher to liven herself up on a cold grey day. As this evening was very far from being either cold or grey, a simple spritz of perfume would do it.

'You need to make an effort, Viv.' Ellen was staring at her from across the bedroom. 'Your daughter is the star of the show and you are the mother of the bride. All eyes will be on you, you know; you can't just shove a top on and hope for the best. You've got to try harder. Why not accessorise, put your turquoise beads on or a few bangles. Pretty it up a bit.'

'Well, thanks for that, Gok! And what do you mean, all eyes will be on me? She doesn't get married for another three days – this is just a barbecue.' She pulled a face at her pushy friend, then picked up her toothbrush and scrubbed her teeth.

'I know, but I want you to look your best. You're not taking Bob for a run over at St John's, you are in Tutukaka, about to have dinner under the stars with a sexy, quiet, sheep-farmer cowboy. Who has a dog called Tessa. A dog!' she shouted. 'In case I have to remind you.'

'You don't have to remind me,' she mumbled, as she spat the white foam into the sink, rinsed with mouthwash and sprayed some more perfume under the collar of her loose shirt and over her bra. 'And give over, Elle. He is Michael's dad and we're here to celebrate Emma's big day, don't forget, not go speed-dating.'

'I know that, but there's no harm in making the best of yourself, especially with Gil around.'

Vivienne tutted at her friend's insistence, deciding not to admit to the frisson of joy she'd felt earlier, from simply being close to him. Plus, right now, her primary concern was to try and understand how things lay between Michael and Emma. She did, however, concede about her appearance. She dotted plum-coloured lipstick over her lips, and then pressed off the excess on some loo roll. She smiled at the turquoise beads that Ellen had looped over her neck and had to admit that they did indeed give her whole outfit a lift. 'Right, I'm all set for the red carpet!' She giggled.

Emma was positively glowing as she offered the tray of champagne cocktails round to each of them. 'I love you, Mum. I keep forgetting you're here and when I see you, it's like getting this big burst of happiness that fills me right up!' She burbled away enthusiastically, as her mum took the tall slippery glass between her palms.

'Well, I love you too.' She smiled.

Ellen sipped hers quickly. 'This is the life, eh, Viv?' she said and made her way to the terrace, where she plonked down on the wicker sofa to take in the early evening view.

Michael appeared, looking lovely, spruced up and freshly showered. Gil wasn't far behind him. Their arrival suggested they'd been in cahoots elsewhere in the house. Vivienne noted the swivel of Gil's eyes, the way he appraised her and smiled before taking a drink from Emma. Then he blushed slightly, as if he'd been caught.

'Careful, Dad, you oldies don't want to be mixing your drinks this early on of an evening – I'll be wheeling you to bed before eight at this rate.' Michael chuckled as Emma swanned past and kissed him on the cheek. He ran his hand along her bare arm. To witness this simple act made Vivienne happy. Maybe Gil was right, she needed to have more faith.

'Less of the "old", thanks, Michael. Trust me,

son, you'll blink and it'll be you getting ribbed by your cocky offspring.'

'Oh, I do hope so!' Vivienne joined in, loving the idea of having her wish fulfilled, imagining how brilliant it would be to become a granny. Emma laughed loudly and threw her head back.

The evening continued as it had started, with laughter, drink and fine food flowing. The communal salad bowls brimmed with ripe avocadoes, corn, chunks of cucumber and fat cubes of tomato, all tossed in a delicious balsamic dressing. Hot off the grill came gigantic prawns cooked in nothing more than a swipe of melted butter and a squeeze of garlic. Steaks were charred to perfection and dripped with a sweet, smoky barbecue glaze. To finish there was a slab of Mahoe cheese served with chilli-spiced oatcakes and a glass of warm red.

'Who needs a fancy restaurant, eh, Vivienne?' Gil raised his glass to her.

'Not us!' She laughed with the sheer happiness of being in this place, with these people, getting this spoilt.

As darkness fell, she followed Ellen to the loo. The cocktails had certainly had the desired effect and she felt the worries of earlier evaporating.

'Are we having the best time or what?' Ellen giggled as she peed and Vivienne held the door for her, just as they'd been doing since they were in single digits.

It was while they both washed their hands that she decided to confide in her very best friend. 'Something happened today on the boat.'

'Oh you little devil, tell me you kissed him! Hurray!' Ellen yelled, punching the air and hugging her friend.

'For goodness' sake, who do you think I am – you? Of course not.' She did however, giggle at the thought.

'So what did happen?' Ellen asked.

'Well ... nothing specific. But I suppose you could say, I felt something... When he was standing behind me, leaning over, we kind of shared a moment.'

Ellen roared her laughter. 'Shared a moment!' she repeated. 'What *do* you sound like? Shared a moment!' She laughed until she cried, wheezing against the sink and wiping her eyes, laughing afresh every time she looked at her friend.

'Well, I tell you what I'm *not* going to do, and that's share anything else with you if you are going to take the mick out of me.' Vivienne dried her hands on the towel in the cloakroom and did her best to ignore her chortling friend.

'I'm sorry, Viv, but sometimes you sound like a right arsehole and that was one of them times.' She shook her head again at her friend's turn of phrase. 'But luckily I love you anyway. And I am happy for you. Happy that you shared your moment.'

This time they both laughed, collapsing on each other for support.

'Don't say anything.' Vivienne felt the need to coach her mouthy mate.

'I won't.' Ellen tutted, indignantly, 'cross my heart.' She drew the requisite cross on her chest.

As they left the bathroom, feeling a little more composed, Emma rushed over to them and grabbed her mum by the arm.

'Mum...' she began, standing only inches from her, as if she required her full attention.

'What is it, love? Are you okay?' Vivienne could sense Emma's anxiety; saw the way her eyes darted and her breath came in short bursts. She was also aware that the buzz of conversation had died; it had all gone very quiet outside. 'Is something wrong? What's happened?' Her heart started to race.

'Nothing is wrong and nothing has happened.' Emma gave a brief smile. 'But I need you to trust me and I need you to close your eyes,' she whispered.

'Oh no, it's not pin the tail on the donkey, is it? I'm rubbish at that.' She snorted.

'No, it's not that, but keep them closed and let me guide you, please...'

Nine

'Keep your eyes closed, Mum!'

'They are closed, for goodness' sake.' She giggled, walking with her hands stretched out in front of her and with Emma holding her arm. 'You know how I hate surprises. And I'm worried I might fall – don't lead me near the cliff edge or let Ellen trip me up.'

'We're nowhere near the cliff edge. We're back on the terrace. Trust me.' Emma spoke calmly.

'I don't appear to have any choice!' she yelled,

193

as she held on tight, giggling at the absurdity of the situation.

There was the sound of footsteps and she heard an unmistakeable gasp as Ellen took a sharp breath. That made her smile; whatever Emma had made or done had certainly made a big impression on her friend. She pictured the Santa's Grotto Emma had been discussing, was this it? The big reveal? Her excitement built. Or maybe it was something less Christmassy and more to do with the wedding, and probably the thing that Michael had been involved in fetching today. Her mind raced with possibilities. *A table centrepiece? Flowers? The cake!*

'Okay, I've got you,' Emma cooed. 'In a few seconds I'm going to let you open your eyes, but not until I say.'

'For goodness' sake, stop mucking around! I'm getting very impatient.' She flapped her hands with excitement, nerves and apprehension.

Emma counted her down. 'Three, two, one... Okay, open your eyes.'

Vivienne slowly opened her eyes and continued to hold her daughter's hand. She blinked a couple of times and looked at the ground, shaking her head slightly, as if this might help her adjust to the change from dark to light. The candles seemed to burn extra bright, making everything around her blur a little. She beamed in anticipation – until she looked up.

Her smile disappeared in an instant and her heart seemed to swell and then shrink inside her ribcage. She thought she might fall and gripped Emma's hand even harder to keep steady. She stumbled backwards and Ellen rushed forward and placed her arm across her back. Her breath came in short starts and the sound of her blood racing around her veins was loud in her ears.

There, on the lawn, not ten feet in front of her, wearing jeans and a blazer, brown boots and a white shirt, was a man, a large man with a paunch resting on his tightly cinched belt and the florid complexion of good living beneath his tan.

He smiled at her with the same bright, film-star gnashers, albeit a little dulled by age and time. His thick crop of dark hair was lighter and higher on his forehead than she remembered and his twinkly eyes sat in the inevitable fine folds of crow's feet. The changes were evident, but it was still, unmistakeably, her husband.

'Hello, Viv.' He took a step towards her.

She opened her mouth to speak, but no words came. She stared at him, as if he had just risen from the dead and popped up right there, on the other side of the world. Her body shivered and her blood ran cool. She felt light-headed and it took all of her energy and concentration to remain upright, gazing at the apparition before her.

Emma grinned and gave a little clap, then moved until she was standing in front of her. 'I found him, Mum! Can you believe it, I found my dad!' She sniffed away her tears. 'We chatted on Skype for the first time a few weeks ago. I've been absolutely desperate to tell you, but I've pictured this moment over and over. He lives in Australia, has done for years, and guess what? I've got half-brothers and sisters, isn't that just amazing? Can you believe it? My dad is going to give me away!'

Vivienne stared at her daughter, who was gabbling, filling her brain with information that was coming way too fast for her to process. The words remained a jumble of unintelligible sounds in her mind. She watched, as Emma walked over to the man who had abandoned them and threaded her arm through his. The familiarity of her action took Vivienne's breath away. Her chest felt tight. And still she couldn't find any words.

Ellen, however, was not at all tongue-tied. Confident now that her friend wouldn't fall over, she removed her arm from Vivienne's back and walked forward. Her tone was sharp and she pointed her finger.

'You've got some nerve, Ray Lane. You think you can just turn up after all these years without so much as a by your leave and pick up where you left off? Cos if that's the case, I'll have an egg-fried rice and some chicken chow mein or had you forgotten? You went out to get takeaway and she never saw you again! You walked out, left her with two little ones!'

'You always were a gobby bird, Elle – reckon your mum must need a medal by now.'

'She died, Ray.'

He looked down at his boots and put his hands in his pockets.

'And that's not the only funeral you missed. Your in-laws died too and what about all the kids' birthdays, Christmases? In fact everything since Emma was four and Aaron only a bit older.'

'It's okay, Auntie Elle, I've forgiven him.' Emma squeezed his arm, pulling him closer to her, defending the man whose actions were, to everyone

196

else, indefensible.

Vivienne cocked her head and looked at the beaming Emma, who had good intentions written all over her hopeful face. She clearly wanted everything to be amicable. If only it were that simple.

Ellen swallowed. 'That's all well and good, Em, but maybe it's not your job to forgive him, sweet girl. It wasn't you that had to pick up all the pieces of what he left behind and try to build something secure out of it; it wasn't you that cried yourself to sleep night after night, wondering what you were going to do. For all he knew, your mum was on the streets, and you and Aaron too.'

'Enough!' Michael shouted, raising his hand. 'This is exactly what I have been dreading.' He stared at his fiancée.

'It'll be okay, Michael, everyone will come around.' Emma gave a small nod, sounding much younger than her thirty-one years.

He shook his head, as if unconvinced, before turning to address the strangers in his family home. 'This is supposed to be a happy time. We are getting married. In case you had forgotten, this is our day, our time.' He looked back at his love. 'Emma thought that because so much water has flowed under the bridge, you would all be able to move on, make a fresh start.'

'We can. I know it,' Emma breathed, her smile now a little faltering.

'I know you have the best intentions, Emma, but it's not always that easy, love.' Gil spoke up from behind Vivienne, near the door, his voice gruff. 'This is real life, not a fairy tale where you can airbrush the hurt and waltz off into the night, slapping each other on the back and remembering the good times. It was hard enough for me when Michael's mum left, but at least we discussed it, made a plan. If she had just upped and left, well, I can't imagine how you start to forgive that.' He glared at Ray, then gave Vivienne a small smile.

Vivienne turned on her heel and walked slowly from the terrace, her arms in front of her, as if there was a still a possibility that she might fall. She couldn't stand there staring at the man for a moment longer.

'I'll come with you, Viv.' Ellen fell into step beside her.

Vivienne stopped and shook her head, laying her hand gently on Ellen's arm. She didn't know what to say or who to address or what the hell was happening, but the one thing she did know, was that she wanted to be alone.

As she made her way on unsteady legs across the vast lawn, the sound of Ellen haranguing Ray and then Emma's defensive tones drifted towards her on the evening breeze.

This can't be happening, this can't be happening, God help me...

She wished for silence to think. She sat on a chair in the middle of the wide deck with her eyes closed and took deep breaths. It helped. A little. Despite the tremor to her limbs, she felt a bit less fuzzy. A warm wind was blowing up from the shore. She pulled her soft pashmina around her shoulders and kicked off her sandals, liking the feel of the bare wood against the soles of her feet. Concentrating on her breathing, she tried to steady her racing pulse.

'I ... I don't believe it,' she muttered, shaking her head. 'I don't believe it.' She pictured Emma's face shining with joy as she stood by his side and found it hard to feel angry at her daughter.

Ray had reappeared as if magicked, just as he had disappeared – in an instant. The last time she had heard his voice was when he called goodbye from the front door. 'Shan't be long!' Those were the last words she'd heard, his singsong tone giving no indication that he was off. She could no longer remember how she had responded or even if she had.

It was a Saturday night; that she remembered. Emma was playing on the floor and Aaron was cuddled on her lap; *Juliet Bravo* was on the TV and she was looking forward to the food that would be arriving piping hot in a matter of minutes. It was a real treat, takeaway food, and not having to cook was a small, but welcome reprieve from the monotony of her busy life. This was how it was for them, feast or famine. He was either rolling in cash or scrabbling in his pockets for stray coins.

As the minutes turned to hours, the fake smile she put on for the children faded and her facade of calm cracked. She left the kids with Mrs Lewis, Shaun's mum, and ran through the streets, arriving spent, to beat her fists on Ellen and Trevor's front door, tears falling and her voice loud, a rare display on her part. 'Where is he, Trev?' she screamed. 'I know you know! You bastard! You're as bad as him. What am I supposed to do now? What am I supposed to do?'

Ellen had opened the door and she had sunk to her knees on the front step. With her friend's arms around her, she sobbed. 'It's all right, my babber, I've got you,' Ellen had soothed.

And even now, all these years later, it was Ellen's words that punctured the still of the night: 'Little kids ... her mum ... bloody phone ... not good enough!' She managed a tight smile at the sound of her friend, the kind tigress. Her very best friend in the whole wide world; a sister.

She had no idea how long she sat there alone. Minutes, maybe an hour, but she was suddenly aware of someone approaching. The walk was familiar with its faint swagger, it was the one that had accompanied her down the aisle of St Aldhelm's on a sunny day, a plastic day when everything had been fake – the flowers, the promises and the picture of a future that he'd allowed her to paint.

Her stomach lurched. It took all of her effort not to throw up. It was surreal. Ray was coming towards her. *Ray...* Back from who knows where, like a thing in the night. She wrapped her arms around her trunk and pulled her pashmina tight, still shaking.

He climbed up onto the deck and exhaled before dragging a chair next to her and sitting down. Now he was so close, she recognised the shape of him even without turning her head. She could smell his scent, which she had quite forgotten, a mixture of cigarettes, soap and his own natural smell. It did something to her brain and she hated the twist of longing that this misplaced sentimental surge fired inside her. She felt like being sick. To sit so close, to feel his presence, took her back to the days after he'd left. The pain in her chest had been very real. This man, *her husband*, had gone and she didn't know why. Gone, without any explanations, without giving her the opportunity to understand – that was almost as soul-destroying as his absence.

'This is some set-up, huh?' His voice had an Australian accent and she wouldn't have recognised it in a crowd or over the telephone. That in itself was strange.

She looked out to sea, to where she'd bobbed on the water earlier that day, happy, oblivious and laughing in the rain.

'Emma says Bedminster is quite gentrified now – can't believe it. We used to say we lived in lower Ashton, trying to make it a bit more upmarket.' He laughed softly, his manner quite different to the loud, bellowing confidence he'd exuded in his youth. There was the slightest wheeze to his exhale, a rattle in his smoker's chest.

'They knocked down the gasworks.' It surprised her how easily the small talk slipped from her lips; and why this particular fact, she didn't know. It was the first thing she thought of.

'Oh, Viv, you sound the same – that lovely comforting accent of home. I'd forgotten it.'

She ignored the compliment. *It's not your home! Home is where you live, where you stay!*

'Emma tells me Aaron is married?'

She nodded.

'And you are still in Mendip Road?'

She nodded again, staring ahead.

'I haven't been back to the UK for over twenty years, Bristol even longer,' he said, as if they were chewing the fat in the pub, stranger to stranger.

201

'Emma's quite a girl. You did a great job there, Viv.'

She turned slowly to face him, wishing he would stop talking about *her* family. She noted the small changes to his profile, the way his ears and nose seemed larger, the hooding of his eyes, the slight droop to his tanned face, the jowls. Time had robbed him of his tautness; he was now slack, his skin a size too big for his frame. She realised that the Ray she'd pictured in her head, the one she repeatedly saw waltzing off towards a better life, didn't exist and probably hadn't for a long while.

'What do you want?' she managed, her voice still small.

'I don't want anything. I just thought you might like to talk.' He raised his palms and tilted his head and even this conciliatory gesture made her blood boil in anger.

'I don't mean right now, I mean what are you doing back in Emma's life, what's going on?'

'Nothing's going on, Viv.'

The way he spoke her name was unnerving, rude and unwelcome. It was as if this was just another day of their married life and just another discussion, her nagging, him defensive.

'Then what is it you're doing here?' She hated the slight quiver to her voice.

'I came to give Emma away.'

'But you gave her away years ago – twenty-seven years, to be precise. You gave us all away, just walked out.' Her eyes blazed.

'I'm sorry, Viv.'

'What?' She screwed her face up.

'I said I'm sorry.'

Her laughter was louder than usual and gutsier.

She shook her head and tried to stop the strange sounds that were erupting from her throat. It took minutes before she could compose herself. She sat up straight and took a deep breath.

'Oh good Lord. Those two little words – you always did think they could make everything better.' She sighed.

'I don't know what else to say to you, don't know what will make things right.'

'Well that makes two of us.'

There was a beat of silence while they considered how to proceed, both glad of the darkening night, which offered a little anonymity and a little extra courage. It was Ray that eventually spoke.

'I didn't know how to handle it. Didn't know how to handle anything back then.' His legs jumped and he rested his palms on his thighs.

'You took the coward's way out, Ray. You let everyone down, did a runner and left me to pick up the pieces. For days I thought you might be hurt, knocked down, injured. I went to the bloody police – I thought you might be lying in a ditch or at the bottom of the Avon Gorge! Can you imagine what it was like for me, having to phone them and tell them I had made a mistake, you weren't missing, you'd just left? God, the humiliation.' She covered her eyes with her hand, feeling again the hot wave of shame. 'Or what it was like trying to tell my mum and dad that you'd gone, had had a change of heart, met someone else, after they'd ploughed all their savings into our wedding, helped you in so many ways, made you part of our family...'

She hated the catch to her voice and lifted her chin to look up at the stars, as if this angle might stop the tears that threatened. She didn't want to give him the satisfaction, hoping he knew that any tears were for her parents' sacrifice and not for him, never for him.

'I was young,' he began.

'I was young!' she shot back. 'But I had to grow up a bit quick.'

'The woman I met...'

'Suzanne.' She helped him out, wanted to show that she wasn't entirely in the dark; it made her feel a little less vulnerable. 'Suzanne from East-ville Market.'

'Yes, Suzanne.' He paused. 'She was important to me. More than just another girl.'

Vivienne stared at him. Clearly he had no idea how insulting or revealing his words were. Was that what *she'd* been, just another girl? And how many more were there?

'She was the one. I loved her.'

Vivienne blinked at him. 'Are you serious? You want me to sit here and listen to how much the woman you left me for *meant* to you? I was your wife!'

She heard him sigh deeply in the darkness. 'No! I'm trying to tell you that I didn't do it lightly, that she was important, she changed me, it wasn't some whim. I just didn't know what to do. I couldn't think straight.' He sighed again. 'I can tell I'm making a mess of this.'

'You think?' she snapped.

'I just want to be straight with you.'

'Well that'll be a first.'

She heard the creak of his chair as he stood up, saw his silhouette walk past her towards the cliff edge. His walk had changed: the swagger was not so pronounced and his left leg had a slight roll to it, as if he had a problem with his hip.

'I've grown up a lot since then, Viv, and I am trying to explain. I'm not asking for forgiveness and I don't expect it, but I would like you to listen.'

'I'm listening,' she spat.

'You were everything I thought I wanted.'

I thought I was everything you wanted...

'And then, I admit, I started playing around when the kids came. I was sick of having no cash and feeling so useless at home, and it was exciting for me.' He paused. 'I'm not proud of it, believe me. I didn't think about the consequences, not really. I thought I was Jack the lad, but the truth of it was I was a scared kid with no idea how I was going to support you all, no idea about anything. It was like walking a swaying tightrope across the Avon Gorge and I was just waiting to fall. I'd look at the little un's and know that I was going to let them down, that I couldn't give them what they needed and it killed me. And then I met Suzanne and it was like, POW! The thunderbolt moment.'

Her tears slid down her face as she sat in the dark on the other side of the world from where it had all happened. Hearing this blunt confirmation of her supplanting, even after all these years, it hurt. Her distress was a surprise to her and an embarrassment. She already knew about his dalliances, Trev having confirmed what she'd long suspected, but it was still uncomfortable, hearing

205

this simplistic confession from her husband, especially the implication that she had been one of many. And it was offered in a rich confetti of words, seemingly without any understanding that his leaving had ripped her to shreds.

'It's hard for me to say this to you,' he continued.

She heard him swallow and recalled him making that same sound in the darkness, as he lay down on the mattress alongside her, with the kids asleep in the room next door.

'It's late. Where have you been, Ray?'

'Nowhere. Go back to sleep.'

It was as hard for him now as it had been then, to admit that he wanted to be somewhere else.

She remained quiet, not wanting to make it any easier for him.

Ray sniffed. 'You know, Viv, it felt like you hadn't been interested in me for a long time.'

'Whose fault was that?' Her retort was almost automatic. 'You were never there, never helped me, I was exhausted.'

He ignored her. 'Suzanne was very interested in me. She wanted to know about me, talk to me. She liked my mates, my jokes.'

Well, good for her. 'I don't know why you're telling me this. If it's just to ease your guilt, fine, but I couldn't care less. I hoped I'd never seen you again and you popping up like this, it feels horrible. I thought you were behind me, behind us. And it's thrown me. I'm supposed to be here celebrating my daughter's wedding. I was having such a lovely time, and now this!' She closed her eyes briefly. 'You have no right to be here, Ray. No right at all.'

He shook his head, clearly not interested in any wider discussion. 'Suzanne is dead.' He paused. 'She died,' he repeated, as if this might help the facts sink in.

Vivienne's primary feeling was sympathy for the demise of this woman she had never met, but there was also a measure of fascination. She wondered what it was about Suzanne that had made her so wonderful; what did she have that had been so lacking in her own personality? What was the thing that caused the thunderbolt?

He continued. 'And just when I was coming to terms with my loss, figuring out how to go on without her, struggling to make sense of it all, I received an email from Emma. It felt like a lifeline, a second chance. I just couldn't believe it.'

She could tell by the curve of his words in the night air that he was smiling.

'It felt like a chance to start over.'

She braced her feet against the deck, trying to quell the tremor of fear in her legs. It was only just occurring to her that he might want to have a bigger role in her kids' lives. She pictured him in Mendip Road, back in his old stomping ground, bumping into her in North Street, eating his breakfast in Pedro's.

Please God, no...

'Will you come back to Bristol at any time?' She hardly dared ask.

'No.' His response was instant and she breathed out, relieved. 'My life's in Adelaide, South Australia, has been for a long time. We run an outdoor-pursuits business. We have a shop, tackle, bait, outboard engines, boats, that kind of thing.

Been going for years. Although with the rise of online availability for what used to be specialised, the last few years haven't been that kind to us, we are struggling a bit.'

How easily you became a 'we'. Traded us in. She pictured him opening the door of a morning, greeting his customers, and all those people he interacted with had no idea of his other life, his other family, at that very moment, turning out the lights for bed.

Her snort of laughter was involuntary. 'It's funny, really, I remember you not wanting to jump over the Malago in case you got your daps wet.'

He laughed wryly. 'Things change. People change,' he breathed.

'Some do,' she conceded. 'But not many. Emma said you have other children?' Her tone was calmer, but still clipped.

'Yes, two boys, twins who are twenty-four, and my daughter, who's just turned eighteen.'

She felt a flicker of sadness for Suzanne, the woman she had never known, who had been forced to leave her children too soon. This, however, was tinged with an unattractive spike of envy, which she would later berate herself for, at how lucky those kids were to have grown up with a dad in their lives. Hearing him use the words 'my daughter' and knowing it wasn't Emma he was referring to was galling, even after all this time.

'Did Suzanne know about me and the kids?'

'Yes. Yes she did.'

'Did she never want to get married?' She instinctively fingered the wedding ring on her finger. A symbol that made her blush, as if she had stolen something from this other woman, the chance to go through the marriage rite, forgetting for a second that it was Ray who had caused the mess.

'We discussed it at the beginning and at the end, but I told her it didn't matter, it was just a piece of paper.'

'Well, yes,' she cut in, 'that's all it was to you. You made that very clear.'

'I don't want to argue with you, Viv.'

'So you said.' Her voice was sharp. 'Did you ever think about Aaron and Emma?'

'Of course I did! Especially when the others were born. It took me right back – it was hard.'

She felt little sympathy. He'd only ever been a phone call away.

'I watched the twins and longed to know how Aaron was getting on.'

Vivienne sat back in the chair, thinking of all the times in the early years that she had seen her son shrink from his dad's comedic jibes, all the inappropriate comments that had knocked his confidence and made him feel small.

'I feel sad and sorry.' Her tone was curt.

'What are you sorry for?'

She watched his outline turn towards her and shook her head. 'Lots of things. Sorry for your loss, believe it or not, and for all the wasted bloody years, for you and for me.'

'It wasn't all bad when we were together, was it?' he asked quietly.

'I don't know, Ray. Sometimes, if I take the kids out of the equation, I can't seem to see much good. But they are like my compensation, aren't they? They are more than good – they're perfect.

They've grown into lovely people and I'm very proud of them. But any good there was between us...' She drew breath. 'I'm afraid you erased that when you went, wiped the slate clean.'

'I guess that's fair enough.' He sniffed and swallowed, collecting himself as he folded his arms. 'Thing is, Viv, it was all right for you, you knew how to be a family, you'd had good practise, growing up with your mum and dad, all that stability.'

'Oh no, Ray, don't you dare! Don't give me that "I was left to me own devices" rubbish. Because living with people, being married to people, being part of a family...' She pictured Aaron's hurt expression, remembered her dad taking her hand as she cried at the kitchen table– *It'll all be okay, love, you'll see.*' 'It's all about being kind, and leaving in the way you did was the least kind thing you could have done. All it would have taken was a letter, a note, anything other than leaving me high and dry wondering why I wasn't quite good enough. A little bit of kindness would have made all the difference in the world.'

Ray took another step towards the edge of the cliff as the garden lights came on.

Ellen's booming voice travelled towards her from the lawn. 'Keep him there, Viv! I'll push him off, we'll say it was self-defence or an accident.'

She couldn't help the burst of laughter that erupted from her. Even in this, the direst of circumstances, when she was finding things far from funny, Ellen knew just how to lighten the mood.

Ray turned towards her and she was surprised to see the remnants of tears on his ruddy face. 'I tell you what; some things don't change. Ellen bloody Nye, a gob bigger than the Cheddar Gorge and an attitude wider than the Clifton Suspension Bridge.'

'And thank God for that. She's been the one constant in my life since I was five.'

'Don't reckon you'll ever shake her off,' he nodded.

'No, I tried that in Hong Kong, but she found her way back to me.'

His voice, for a second, had sounded pure Bristolian and she felt the smallest flicker of affection for him. It was like bumping into an old acquaintance in an unlikely place, someone she hadn't seen for a while, and remembering something about them that she had particularly liked.

She rose and took Ellen's arm, walking on shaky legs back to the house, without giving him the satisfaction of a goodbye. Emma, Michael and Gil were nowhere to be seen; presumably they'd retired to a sofa somewhere with a brandy to mull over events. This suited her quite well. She didn't particularly want to see anyone.

Vivienne rubbed night cream into her face as she stood in front of the mirror in the en-suite bathroom. It had been one hell of a day.

'You all right, girl? You're very quiet,' Ellen asked as she ran a brush through her hair and set out her clothes for the next day, as she always did.

Vivienne nodded. 'Yep, just exhausted, ready for my bed.'

'Me too. I can't believe it, Viv, I really can't. I phoned and told Trev earlier, and he was gobsmacked. Hardly said a word, think he was shocked.'

'I bet. I spoke to Aaron, too, briefly, and he was very quiet. It's a lot to take in. I said I'd call him again tomorrow. He'll no doubt have lots of questions when he's had time to digest it. I could hear Lizzie shouting in the background.'

'Did he want to speak to Ray?'

'No, he didn't ask to. He said very little actually.' She pinched the bridge of her nose and wiped away the last of the cream on the back of her hand. Her make-up-free face had a dewy sheen.

'I don't mind telling you, though, Elle, it's unnerved me, it really has. Just a few minutes in his company and I'm reminded of everything I found so intoxicating about him – that little twist of charm that had me wrapped around his finger. I can see it in him.'

'You don't still fancy him, do you?' Ellen said, leaning forward, eager to hear every last detail, reminding Vivienne of their teenage selves all those years back.

'God, no! Of course not.' An image of Gil shot into her thoughts. 'But I can see now that the Ray I knew doesn't exist any more. This man has a grown-up family and a business in Adelaide, a place I couldn't even point to on a map. For all these years I have wondered about him, even hankered to see him, just out of curiosity, and yet, sat out there on the deck, I realised that I feel nothing. I've been clinging to a memory.'

'I think...' Ellen started, then stopped herself.

'You think what?' It wasn't like her to be so reticent.

212

'I think that maybe you clung to that memory because it stopped you having to go forward, that maybe it felt like the safest option.'

'An excuse, you mean?' She turned from the mirror and looked at her friend.

'No, not an excuse ... a cushion, to soften any further blows.'

'When did you get so poetic?' Vivienne scoffed.

'When I started travelling the world!' Ellen roared. 'I'm an international jetsetter, don't you know.' She did as she always did, tried to lessen the pain with her humour, provide a sticking plaster of laughter, which sometimes made things feel a little bit better.

'Oh, Elle,' she murmured, falling into her friend's arms, 'what am I going to do?'

'You don't have to do anything,' Ellen cooed, holding her close. 'Nothing at all.'

There was a sharp knock on the door. Vivienne pulled away from her friend and wiped at her tears, then yanked her oversized pyjama top down over her bottoms. She pulled a face at Ellen and placed a finger on her lips in an attempt to get her to be quiet. 'Yes?' she called out.

'Can I come in?' It was Gil's unmistakeable, hypnotic bass.

Vivienne ran her palm over her make-up-free face and looked down at her night attire. A quick glance in the mirror confirmed that there were shadows of exhaustion etched below her eyes. She grabbed the wide, pale pink pashmina, her new favourite thing that she had picked up on their whistle-stop tour of Stanley Market, and wrapped it around her shoulders like a shawl. 'Sure.'

Ellen jumped on her bed and hid her face in the pillow.

She opened the door to Gil, who was leaning casually against the frame. He stood up straight and placed his hands on his hips, his denim shirt-sleeves were as ever rolled to the elbow.

He pointed along the corridor and said, in his typical slow, considered manner, 'I was just going to get a drink and take it outside. Thought you might like one too, unless you're calling it a night?' He was either oblivious or uncaring of the fact that she was in her pyjamas.

'No, not at all, I was just going to read for a bit,' she lied. 'A drink would be lovely.'

Gil eyed Ellen over her shoulder. She was still lying motionless with her face in the pillow.

'Ignore her.' Vivienne jerked her thumb in the direction of her friend.

He gave a small nod.

The night was still. The darkness was punctuated by the buzz and flutter of bugs attracted to the subtle lighting that surrounded them. Gil sat down in the wide rocking chair that stood under the porch on the terrace and she took up position in the matching chair next to him. He'd grabbed two tartan wool blankets from the closet in the den and now handed one to her, which she placed over her thin cotton PJs.

'He's staying in a B & B along the coast,' he offered, as if she'd asked. 'The kids are getting him settled.' This explained Emma and Michael's absence. 'I didn't know whether to tell you he was inbound. I was in a very difficult position: Emma was so excited about the big surprise, but personally I thought she was being naive. It's not her fault, I'm not blaming her – she has a good, good heart and was doing what she thought was a positive thing. Michael is as suspicious as hell of the guy, suddenly popping up like a mole on the lawn after all these years, and she was dead set on doing it her way. I couldn't tell you. I wasn't even sure he'd show up, thought it might all be talk. I guess I hoped that might be the case.' He sipped his glass of wine.

She sat back against the cushioned rocker and closed her eyes. 'You must rue the day you invited us lot into your lovely home. I know you like peace, and we've brought nothing but drama. I bet you'll be glad when we've all gone home.'

'Not at all. But I must admit, it's usually a lot quieter than this.' He gave a low whistle and Tessa loped from the hallway and came out to sit by his side. 'There's a good girl.' He rubbed her silky ears with his wine-free hand.

'Ah, makes me miss my Bob. He's my companion of an evening. We sit in front of the telly and I chat to him.'

He nodded. 'We do the same, but instead of the telly, I look at that.' He pointed at the vast canopy of stars above them. 'I never get sick of looking at it and it's ever changing.'

She stared up at the celestial display and suddenly felt very small. 'You have been so kind to us all.' She sipped the chilled glass of white wine. 'Thank you for everything and I'm sorry again for the upheaval.'

He batted away the compliment before asking

his question. 'Do you think maybe this is a chance to patch things up with Ray?'

'You mean as friends?'

'Or more, possibly?' He kept his eyes on Tessa's coat under the porch lights.

'Oh good God, no! Absolutely not. Not at all.' She shook her head vigorously, keen to emphasise the point. 'I was saying to Ellen earlier, I don't know him and he doesn't know me. It was eight years of my life when I was too young to know any better.'

'But you've been single ever since?'

'Yep.' She nodded.

Gil gave a nervous cough and swirled the wine in his glass. 'That's a long time and I guess I wondered if, despite what you said when we were out on the boat, it might be because you still hold a candle for him.'

'It's not. No way. Ellen thinks I've been using him as a cushion, to soften any further blows, hiding myself away.' She shook her head and then drained her wine glass.

Gil reached for the bottle on the floor and refilled it.

'Thank you.' She took another sip and noted how the dry, sharp, floral aftertaste whizzed up the back of her nose and bounced back down onto her tongue. It was delicious and quite unlike anything she had tasted at home, though that could of course have been down to the setting or the company or the fact that she'd already had three cocktails and one hell of a shock.

'I'm trying to keep calm for Emma's sake. I want her to have the best wedding and I don't want to cause a second of tension for her and Michael at this lovely time, but deep down, I feel bloody furious!' She took a bigger glug this time. 'He has no right, Gil, no right at all. It was me that got up with her at all hours, fed her, clothed her, walked her back and forth from school in all weathers, saved up for her braces, took her on day trips. Saved up for every little thing she needed from shoes to shampoo, me!' She patted her chest. 'And yet he just pitches up and prepares to waltz her down the aisle as if nothing was amiss. It's just not fair!' She was aware of her raised voice and took a deep breath.

Gil took his time, unhurried as ever. 'Life's not fair. I wanted to be married forever, I wanted Michael to take over the farm–'

'But he's a doctor.'

'Aye, and that's amazing, but my sheep won't care what he's doing if he isn't here to see them right. What he does is noble and selfless, I get it, but I had a dream that my boy would continue everything my dad worked for, and everything I've achieved. But...' He took a sip of his wine. 'He was never interested in the farm as anything other than a hobby, a way to earn pin money while he was at home on holiday. It's just how it is.'

'So you'd rather he farmed than worked in medicine?'

Gil took a while forming his response. He stretched his legs out and crossed them at the ankles. 'I want him to be happy, to live a good life and I see how stressed he gets and that's not healthy. This life, living here...' He gestured at the vast black night. 'This is paradise. There's no stress, no boss, it's just me and the seasons, my land and my animals, and I think it's about the happiest anyone can be. I wanted that for him.'

'You are right, Gil. This is like a little slice of heaven.' She tucked her feet under her thighs.

'Do you want some socks? I have some clean ones in the laundry that'd do you.'

'Oh, that'd be lovely, thanks.' She unfurled her legs, wiggling her chilly toes in the cool night breeze.

Gil left the creaking chair with Tessa trotting after him, to return minutes later with a pair of soft, downy socks that were going to be way too big for her.

He crouched down on his haunches and gently took her right foot into his hand before resting it on his thigh. The feel of his fingers against her skin, this smallest of contact set her whole body aglow. It was exhilarating, exciting and scary all at the same time, a feeling she had quite forgotten. The joy rippled along her limbs until she shivered and then smiled.

His actions were so unexpected they left her speechless. He opened the sock and placed it over her toes, carefully pulling it over her foot and her ankle and patting it into place. Each touch of his hand to her skin, especially her feet, which very probably no one had touched since she was a child, sent delightful tremors right through her. They seemed to emanate from the point of contact and fill her right up. He then took her left foot and repeated the process, slowly, before sitting back in his chair.

Vivienne's breath came fast and a blush of longing spread over her. She leant forward, wondering what to do next – thank him, kiss him? She was as anxious and uncertain as she was elated, unsure how to proceed while her brain whirred beneath a fug of confusion and the mist of wine. She was glad it was dark and that she was at least partly in shadow. It felt good to be hidden, lest he should see her expression and take a guess at the swirl of emotions inside her. This was new territory and she had no idea what to do or say next. She wished Ellen had given her instructions – her friend the tart, who had slept with fourteen times more men than her.

They were both quiet for some minutes.

Eventually she spoke her thoughts. 'I wish everything was simple.'

'It can be.'

'Doesn't feel like that right now.' She rubbed her forehead. 'It's like I've been under his spell for all these years, not realising how much time was spinning by, and look at me now! Getting older and in the same position I was in when he went.'

He turned towards her. Leaning forward, he rested his elbows on the arms of the chair.

'That's what bullies do, they tell you they are going to do this and they are going to do that and the only way to stop them is to tell them you're not going to put up with it any more. It really is that simple. They only have the power if you give it to them. He bullied you and you have given him power for all these years. You need to choose differently now, think differently.'

'You make it sound so easy to start over.'

'It can be, Viv.' He said it again.

'I think for Ray and me this can be as hard or as easy as we choose to make it.' She looked into the hazel eyes of the kind sheep-farmer cowboy who made her smile. 'I just want everything to be okay for Emma and Aaron and for Emma and Michael.'

'We'll do everything we can.' He nodded.

Her heart flexed at the way he used the word 'we' so comfortably. She rested her back against the chair again, noting the attractive stubble on his chin and his long eyelashes.

'I can't think straight, Gil. I feel like I'm falling to earth at a million miles an hour and there's so much filling my head right now...'

He nodded. 'You have a lot going on, that's for sure. But you are not having to face any of this alone and that should ease your burden a bit.'

'That's kind, but you don't have to take on my family's dramas. We've disturbed you enough and it's nothing to do with you.'

'But I want it to be something to do with me.' He swallowed. 'Look at me, Vivienne.'

She slowly looked up at him. He leant over towards her chair and let his fingertips rest on her jaw.

'I want it to be something to do with me because I like you.'

'What do you mean, you like me?' Her voice was small, shaky.

He hesitated. 'I mean, I like you. I've liked you from the first time I met you.'

'That was only thirty-seven hours ago.'

'Yes.' He shook his head in disbelief. 'I felt like we connected and even though that sounds like something Emma should be saying with her funny ideas, it's true.'

She blinked.

'Did you...' He paused. 'Did you feel the same?'

She let a smile play around her mouth in response and gave a small nod.

He shook his head. 'And I'm sure this goes against every bloody rule in the book, seeing as you're about to become my son's mother-in-law, but I can't help it. I like you and I want to get to know you better.'

Vivienne reached up and held his wrist. 'I can't tell you how happy I feel right now – and shocked and nervous and flattered and scared, really scared.' She took a deep breath. 'I feel completely out of my depth. I'm out of practise at all of it. And I'm still a married woman, because Ray just disappeared, left me stranded.'

Gil sat back and stared at her pretty face. 'Of course.' He looked confused. 'It's probably not the done thing for us to be chatting in this way. In fact, there's no probably about it. But it's where we are and as I said, it can be simple, if we let it.'

Her brain whirred. *What's the point? I'll be gone in a week, far, far away, back to my little house in Mendip Road. There's no point at all. It would just make things weird, possibly forever, and that would be a shame, for us all.*

'I don't want things to get weird,' she whispered.

'I think things are already a little weird,' he replied calmly.

He reached forward and placed his hand on her leg and left it there. She placed hers over the back of his, feeling the warmth rise up under her palm.

221

It felt lovely; illicit and lovely.

'Sitting here next to you makes me feel very happy,' she whispered.

'It makes me feel happy too.'

She felt his hand increase its pressure on her thigh. She smiled and squeezed it. He turned his palm and gripped her fingers and that was how they sat, in silence, getting used to each other's presence.

Vivienne let the butterflies flutter around in her stomach. 'I think the last time I held hands with someone like this, I was about ten.'

'Who was that with?' he asked, his voice gentle as the night.

'It was with Daniel Marks. He was nice, sent me a Valentine's card and signed it.'

'Smart man, leaving you in no doubt as to who you should be holding hands with.' He nodded his approval.

'I felt very lucky. I was never popular at school, not really, and certainly not with the boys. Not that I was fussed – I always had Elle, she was enough.'

He laughed. 'I can imagine she would be. And I can't believe you weren't popular. Unlike me, who had to fight the ladies off with a stick!'

'Did you?'

'No!' He laughed. 'I had a lazy eye. I was shy and skinny, and not that into cricket, which was an offence punishable by exclusion. I was what you might call a late developer.'

'Have you had girlfriends?' She felt bold asking. *Not counting Tessa...* She smiled.

'Nothing serious since Michael's mum. The

odd fling, but things just never clicked for me.' He shifted in his seat. 'I've never really had the confidence.'

Vivienne nodded. 'I know how that feels. I remember at school they chose Kelly Kimber to be Mary three years running and I was desperate for the role. I knew all the words and practised my sad face for when the innkeeper sent us on our way. I used to walk around my bedroom with a pillow up my nightie practising being pregnant. I was a natural.'

'Why didn't you get a go?'

'I didn't actually tell anyone I wanted to be Mary. I was too shy to speak up, nervous.'

'For what it's worth, I think you would have made a great Mary, but then I think you're great, full stop.' He squeezed her hand.

She stared straight ahead, nervous, embarrassed and swallowing the firecracker of joy that was sparking inside her.

'I'm just very ordinary, Gil. I ain't no Kelly Kimber.'

He sat back and stared at her profile. 'I won't forget seeing you for the first time when you arrived.' He shook his head. 'I was taken by your calmness, your kindness. You are lovely to be around.'

'It's all an act, you know.' She looked at him.

'What is?'

'The smiling, happy me that tries to make everything seem better.' She sipped her wine.

'I don't believe that.'

'It's true. I have lived for all these years with everything pulled taut, scared, waiting. Ellen's

223

right, I have held this cushion up to smother any advances, soften any blows.' She was suddenly overtaken by a wave of fatigue. 'I think I need to get to bed, Gil. I'm rambling and I want to make a better impression on you than this.'

'I like listening to you ramble, it can get quiet here at night.'

She picked up on the suggestion of his loneliness.

'Thank you for the loveliest day,' she whispered. 'Oh God, I can't believe that Ray is here in Tutukaka, I can't believe I've seen him.' She released his hand and rubbed her eyes, as if she might wake soon.

'Don't think about him tonight. Get a good sleep,' he soothed.

She stared at him. 'Gil...' she began softly. She wasn't sure what had occurred, but she felt the beginnings of happy and she wanted him to know that. But her thoughts were cut short by the arrival of Michael's 4 x 4, which swept along the curved driveway, its lights shattering the peace and causing Tessa to bark. It came to rest on the tarmac apron at the front of Aropari Farm.

'Hey, Mum,' Emma called out as she jumped down from the cab and made her way over to the porch with her characteristic skip. 'I wasn't sure you'd still be up. Are you mad at me? I thought it would be lovely for you, but I guess I didn't think it through. I just want everyone to get along.'

She sat on the ground and placed her head on her mum's lap. Vivienne stroked her beautiful fine wavy hair away from her face.

'No, darling, how could I be mad at you? I

think you only ever do things with the best intentions, but I must admit, I'm a little shocked.'

'I think you should give him a chance. He's changed a lot, Mum. He really regrets not seeing Aaron and me – he said as much. And Bailey, Trent and Ashley, that's his kids; they know all about us and really want to meet us. I think it will be great. It's exciting!' Her gabbled enthusiasm made her seem a lot younger than thirty-one.

Vivienne looked up and held Gil's stare, thinking of this new, perfect life her happy girl envisaged and silently hoping that she wasn't going to get hurt again. 'It will be great.' She briefly closed her eyes and smiled at him.

'I feel like the luckiest woman alive. I'm getting married to this incredible man, and my mum and my dad are here to see it. I can't believe it.'

'I love you, Emma.' She bent forward and kissed her child's head.

'Love you too.'

'I'm going to bed.' Michael sounded tired.

'I'm coming too,' Emma called, as she jumped up and linked her arm inside his. 'See baby, I told you Mum wouldn't be mad, it's all going to be okay!'

Vivienne noted the slight stiffness to his posture, as he marched his fiancée across the lawn and they disappeared inside the house.

Ellen was snoring, deep in sleep, when Vivienne crept into the bedroom. She peeled back the duvet and laid her head on the pillow. What a day. She pictured Ray, sleeping only minutes away in a B & B up the coast. The reality of seeing him had still not sunk in.

Gil's words played in her head on a loop. *I've liked you from the first time I met you ... felt like we connected.* It made her heart soar.

She wiggled her toes inside the soft wool socks that he had put on her feet. No man had ever done anything like that for her. Her pulse fluttered and she wondered what kind of woman would be everything *he* wanted.

Ten

The next day felt very different. Gil had, as ever woken early, done his rounds and was busy taking in a feed delivery up on the main pasture. Everyone was a little quieter, busying themselves with wedding chores that ranged from polishing glasses and washing cutlery to sweeping the terraces. Vivienne had stared at herself in the mirror and noticed a difference in her appearance, not only the first hint of a bronze glow from having spent time in the sunshine, but also a blush to her cheeks and a brightening of her eyes, as if she had woken from a long, long sleep, refreshed. Her limbs felt loose, her senses acute.

Emma had left a long list and they all pitched in, motivated by their love for her and their desire to make her day the best it possibly could be. Michael had been tasked with putting up the strings of lights in the porch and placing solar lanterns in and among the plants and trees around the grounds.

Ellen was busy tying minute pink ribbons around the white tulle-wrapped sugared almonds that were to be given as wedding favours. She sat patiently at the table with everything she needed laid out like a production line. Her tongue poked from the side of her mouth as she tried to perfect the tiny bows. She only stopped occasionally to flex her palms and holler 'Damn these sausage fingers!' which made them all laugh.

Vivienne sat barefoot at the breakfast bar, writing out name places on miniature cream folds of stiffened card. She used an unfamiliar ink pen and tried to write in a curly script, flapping each one dry when it was finished and worrying that her calligraphy might not be up to scratch.

Vivienne and Gil skirted around each other. Any physical contact came with a new awkwardness; the previous night's openness, bolstered by champagne cocktails and glasses of white wine, now stung their tongues and made them both overly self-conscious. They were, after all, fundamentally still strangers. When she did catch his eye, his smile was warm, if fleeting, and the leap in her stomach was just the same.

Emma had opted to spend the day with Ray in town; they collected the gazebo lights and had lunch down by the water's edge in Whangarei. Vivienne managed to avoid interacting with him all day. She and Ellen had agreed a strategy: she would keep out of his way, get through the wedding day and never have to see him again, once Emma was hitched. He lived in Adelaide and she in Bristol and they were hardly likely to run into each other, and for that small compensation, she was grateful.

'How many of those have you managed, Ellen?' Gil called across from the kitchen as he carried a tray of silver wine coolers to the countertop.

Ellen counted out loud. 'Fourteen.' She shouted her response. 'Hey, Viv, did you hear that, fourteen! One for each—'

'Guest!' Vivienne yelled, cutting in with urgency.

'Only another twenty-seven to go,' Gil said encouragingly.

'You have got to be kidding me!' Ellen snorted and banged the table. 'Another twenty-seven, at my age? I don't think so.' She roared her laughter.

Gil stared at her and then looked at Vivienne, who shrugged her shoulders, as if she had no clue.

After the previous night's drama, supper was a far simpler affair. Emma and Michael went down to Schnappa Rock for some time alone, no doubt tempted by the special of New Zealand Green Shelled Mussels in a Thai Green Curry sauce. They were also keen to finalise the menu and numbers with Nick and Esther who were providing the catering for the big day.

Vivienne assumed Ray had gone back to his digs, caring little where he was, as long as he wasn't near her. She, Gil and Ellen picked at the lunch leftovers: plates of salad with slivers of cheese, slices of cured ham, pickles and fresh sourdough bread, and fruit salad for pud. The informal grabbing of plates and sitting in the sunshine, proved to be one of the nicest meals they had.

She and Gil stole surreptitious glances over the top of their wine glasses, while Ellen, as ever, provided the background music with her constant stream of chatter. She had to admit, the slightly clandestine nature of their interactions only served to heighten the way she felt about him.

Both she and Ellen were hit with a bone-deep tiredness mid evening. They wished Gil a pleasant night and very soon after completing their night-time beauty rituals and teeth cleaning, climbed between the crisp, white sheets of their twin beds.

'I'm too tired to think straight.' Vivienne yawned.

'Sames,' Ellen muttered.

'Night-night, Elle,' she whispered, feeling the pleasant heaviness to her limbs, as a deep sleep threatened.

'Night-night, Viv,' Ellen whispered back. Then, 'Just one thing, Viv.'

She slowly turned her head towards her friend. 'What?' she croaked.

Ellen flung back the covers to reveal herself in the neon-pink string bikini and scanty vest that she must have secretly picked up during their Primark shop. 'Gil and Vivienne, sitting in a tree! K-I-S-S-I-N-G!' she shouted, leaping up and jumping on the bed, the thin triangles barely covered her modesty, as she hollered so loudly, Vivienne was sure the whole of Tutukaka would hear.

She sat up, laughing loudly despite her tiredness. 'Don't move!' she instructed. 'Let me get my camera!'

'Not on your life!' Ellen dived under the sheet, string bikini and all, and lay very still, and when their laughter finally subsided, a good twenty minutes later, they both fell into a deep, restful sleep.

A sharp rapping on the door woke her. Vivienne sat up and took a couple of seconds to remember where she was. She rubbed her eyes, as if this might speed up the process. The room was bright and a little too warm; she leapt up and opened the French doors, welcoming in the morning breeze, before scurrying back to the safety of her bed. The sound of Ellen completing her morning toilette came from the bathroom.

'Hello?' she called out.

Michael walked in. His chest heaved and his jaw was locked. He narrowed his eyes at her and without preamble or even a morning greeting or a smile, said, 'I can't find Emma. I've looked everywhere.'

'What do you mean, you can't find her?' she repeated, thinking that there were only so many places to look.

'I mean, I went to bed and when I woke up, her side of the bed was untouched and I don't know where she is. All her stuff is here, including her phone.' He scanned the room, as if hoping that she might be hiding close by.

'You haven't seen her?' he quizzed, more irritated than concerned.

'No.' She shook her head. 'Maybe she made her bed and has gone for a walk?' Vivienne knew it sounded illogical, but it was the best she could come up with given her current level of lucidity. 'What time is it?'

'It's nearly seven.' He didn't need to check his watch and had clearly been counting the minutes since waking. He ran his fingers through his hair.

'She didn't come to bed and she hasn't slept on the sofa. No one has seen her. I asked Dad before he went out to do his rounds.' He drew a fractured breath, obviously worried. 'This isn't like her.'

Vivienne looked up at him, surprised yet again by how little he understood of her daughter's true nature. With her bursts of energy, her love of spontaneity and her penchant for doing the unexpected, this was *exactly* like Emma. She knew she was just as likely to be found chanting in a wood or sitting on the beach watching the sunrise.

'Did you check she hasn't gone to where Ray is staying?' This was her first reaction, unpalatable though the idea was, even saying his name left a bitter aftertaste, as a bubble of jealousy ringed her thoughts.

'I already called him. She's not there. He said he'd head over.'

Oh good...

He snorted with frustration. 'I would have thought she might have left a note.'

'She'll turn up, love.' She smiled, ignoring the flip of worry in her gut, not so much at her daughter's absence, but at just how little this man seemed to know her. 'I'll get dressed and we can make a plan, okay? Call her friends...'

He nodded at her, smiling briefly. 'Okay.' He paused. 'She hasn't really got any friends here, only me. And anyone we know in Auckland would have called me, I'm sure. Plus she wouldn't have got that far, I don't think.' He was clearly flustered.

'Oh.' She found it heart-breaking to hear confirmed that Emma, arriving freshly minted from

231

her travels and her six months in Auckland, might not know anyone in Tutukaka. She wondered how many of the people she had invited to the wedding, were her friends, and how many would leave her a crumpled envelope of congratulations, with or without a sticky thumbprint in the corner.

As Michael shut the door behind him, Ellen came out of the bathroom. She was fully dressed, thank goodness.

'What was that all about?' she asked.

'Michael can't find Emma. Her bed wasn't slept in and she didn't leave a note or anything and her phone is still here, apparently. She's not in the house and he's getting fretful. He's looked everywhere.'

Ellen opened the bathroom door wide. 'Not quite everywhere.'

Vivienne craned her neck and saw an unmistakeable mop of blonde hair poking over the top of the bath.

'Emma?' She raced into the bathroom and there was her girl, curled up in the big tub with a pillow under her head and the blankets from their beds under and over her.

'It's not as comfortable as it looks,' Emma whispered.

'Why are you hiding in here?' She looked Emma in the eye. 'Michael is really worried – that's not funny.' She adopted her stern voice, the one that used to see her kids come running when they'd misbehaved. She had a sudden image of the two of them standing in front of her in their school uniforms, both blaming the other when a fight in the sitting room had resulted in a smashed ornament and a nasty purple egg on Aaron's head.

'I snuck in last night and you were dead to the world, so I chatted to Elle for a bit and she made me a bed in the bath.'

'Why are you avoiding Michael? I don't understand.' She was trying to make sense of it all when Emma sat up in the bath, placed her head on her raised knees and started to cry.

'Oh, Emma! Don't cry love. Come on, this is the day before your wedding, you can't be crying.' She instantly felt guilty for her earlier tone.

'I think you better get out of the bath and talk to your mum, Emma.' It seemed that Ellen was already better informed than she was.

'I don't want to see anyone,' Emma managed through her tears.

'You don't have to. I'll go and tell Michael that you've turned up and you are chatting to your mum in private. He'll understand. Take all the time you need.'

'Thanks, Elle.' Emma nodded and flung off the blanket, then clambered from the bathtub and came into the bedroom to sit on the end of her mum's bed.

Ellen winked knowingly at her best friend and left the two of them alone.

Vivienne placed a pillow behind her head, budged up along the wall and patted the space beside her. Emma climbed up and sat next to her, with her back against the other pillow, nestling next to her mum.

'I can't remember we snuggled up like this, probably when you were a teenager,' Vivienne reflected.

'No, I think it was when Fergus left,' Emma reminded her.

'Oh yes, Fergus.' She smiled at the memory of the bespectacled lad with his chip fat powered van. 'Right, Em, what's going on here?'

Her daughter took a deep breath, as if preparing to perform. 'I love Michael,' she said.

'Yes, and he loves you.' She was glad to get the preliminaries out of the way.

'He is everything I have ever dreamt of, Mum. He is smart and sensible and he makes plans and knows where he is heading.'

'They are all wonderful gifts, that's true.' She was still struggling to see the problem, so far.

'But it was something you said – that you can only go with what feels right or feels wrong and everything kind of figures itself out from there.' Emma paused and wiped her nose.

'I did say that, and it's true. And what I most want is for you to be happy, that's the main thing. And if what makes you happy is being here in Tutukaka with Michael working hard towards your future, then that's it.'

'And this is the most beautiful place I have ever been.' Emma confirmed, 'but...' She bit her lip.

'But what, love?'

'I am not like Michael.' Her tears fell afresh.

'Well, that's okay! You don't have to be like him. Some of the best relationships are between people who are polar opposites. They each bring such different things to the table that they fill in each other's gaps and it makes things interesting, keeps it fresh.'

'But what if I don't bring anything? Literally

nothing!' She patted the sheet over her legs.

'That's not possible. You are the kindest, loveliest girl and he loves you, everyone does. Making someone happy is the biggest gift you can offer.' Vivienne knew she was treading a fine line between supporting her child and helping her figure out the solution, without overly imposing her own thoughts and concerns.

Emma pulled up her knees under the sheet and rested her folded arms on them. 'I don't know anyone here, Mum. It was different in Auckland; I met people through Hai, but now Michael's at Whangarei Hospital, I can't exactly go and hang out with him at work to meet his friends ... it's so quiet.' She turned to look at her mum. 'I miss having a best friend around, like you and Elle. People who've known me forever, who I don't have to be on my best behaviour with. Seeing you and Elle here together, it's brought it all back. And I know it sounds stupid, but one of the things I miss most about Bristol is people coming and knocking for me, school mates and people I grew up with. You know, just being able to chat in the street. It made me feel at home.'

Vivienne gave a knowing sigh. 'I love that too, and you *will* have that here when you've been here a little longer. So are you saying the problem is that you're lonely?'

'A bit. Yes.'

'Well, if that's the case there is no reason to worry Michael by hiding from him, but it's certainly something you need to talk to him about.'

'I guess.' Emma plucked at the sheet.

Vivienne sighed. 'But if the problem *is* Michael,

then that's a whole other conversation,' she paused, 'I think you're suffering from a muddle of things, Em – pre-wedding nerves, and you and Michael are only just starting out in so many ways, getting to know each other, you are having to settle into a new place, and it must be strange to have your dad here. It's a lot for you to deal with. A lot for *anyone* to deal with,' she corrected.

Emma nodded. 'It is all of that, but also...'

'What, love?'

Emma's tears came again. 'It's not only my loneliness that's the problem, Mum. I...' she swallowed, 'I don't know if I want to marry Michael!'

Vivienne rubbed her daughter's back. 'Is this what we call a case of the jitters?' She struggled to find the right response, aware of the weight that might rest on her opinion.

'I don't think so. I don't know!' Emma bawled.

'Don't cry. It's okay.' She spoke softly, belying her rising sense of panic and worry. 'No one is going to make you do anything, Emma. This has to be your decision and it has to be the right one.' She remembered Ellen's words about her own mum's reaction to her getting engaged to Ray all those years ago. *'You were smitten. For her to wade in with any opinion, either way, would have caused problems between you and your mum.'*

'It's hard to know what advice to give you, my love. But I do know this: a marriage isn't something to enter into lightly. You have to be as sure as you possibly can be. And if you have any doubts,' she let this trail.

'I know that, Mum.' She took a deep breath and seemed to calm a little. 'The thing is, and I know this makes me sound like a loon, I think I have presented a face to Michael that might not be truly mine.'

'What do you mean?' She caressed the flicked-up ends of her daughter's fine blonde hair.

Her words came slowly. 'I don't think I'm always myself in front of him. I've been realising that more and more since you've been here. You know how much I like kidding around, planning things, having fun, just like you and Auntie Ellen, and... Michael's not like that. I think you've noticed that, haven't you?'

She glanced sideways at her mum, but Vivienne kept her thoughts to herself.

'And last night, when he and I went out to dinner together, at Schnappa Rock, suddenly it all seemed a bit...' She swallowed. 'A bit over-whelming.' She paused. 'The food was amazing and that was lovely, but he was talking about his work schedule and how we needed to fit hiking around his rota and he was tasting the wine and all I could think about was how much I wanted to run up the jetty on the Marina, rip my clothes off and jump in and I knew he would have been horrified. I had to hide my thoughts from him, and that made me quite sad.'

Viv gave her a gentle hug of encouragement.

'And after we got back here last night, I started thinking about how I often dilute other thoughts and ideas because I know that's what he wants to hear. I want so badly to be the person he loves that I think I might have been hiding the real me, and I'm worried that if the real me comes out, he might not like it. I don't think he wants a wife that's going to strip off and run up the jetty.'

Vivienne felt a terrible sadness at hearing her child's words. 'The thing that bothers me most about what you've just said, is that you would even consider trying to change yourself into what someone else wants you to be. You should never, ever try and shrink any part of you to fit what you think a man, or anyone else, might want. Never! Not your body, your thoughts, your ideas, your plans or your dreams. Nothing. And if you are doing that...' She gulped the incendiary words that hovered in her throat.

'I can't marry him, Mum. Can I?' Emma turned and looked at her and there was a beat of stillness while they both understood the enormity of her statement.

'I don't know, but I do know the person you marry has to love all of you, including your crazy...'

The door opened and in walked Ellen.

'How are we doing?'

'We are having a good chat.' She nodded over Emma's shoulder.

'I don't think I can marry him, Elle, at least not right now. I need a bit of time to think about what I want and I think we need a bit of time as a couple to get to know each other; properly get to know each other, the real us, without having to hide anything. Mum said some things that got me thinking and it doesn't feel right, no matter how much I pretend that it does. I think I was panicking a bit because I'm thirty-one–'

'Oh, ancient.' Ellen cut in.

'I just wanted my life to be sorted by now, I wanted to know the plan.' Emma sighed.

'Well, we'd all love that, Emma, but I'm afraid life doesn't come with a book or a timetable, you can't just flip to page one hundred and fifty-five and find out what happens next.'

'I wish we could sometimes,' Vivienne said.

'Ooh no, don't be daft!' Ellen pulled a face. 'That'd be awful. It's the not knowing what's coming up next that makes things exciting.'

'I think Mum's right, I've been hiding what makes me me...' She stumbled on her next words. 'And ... and I'm not sure Michael would want the real me.'

'Oh Lordy! Is this my fault?' Vivienne hated the thought.

Ellen gave her a sideways look. 'I would say so, yes.'

'Ignore her, Mum.' Emma smiled briefly. 'It's no one's fault, it's just how it is. But I must admit, I don't know what to say to him. I'm scared.' She closed her eyes, as if imagining the conversation.

There was a knock at the door and Michael walked in. 'What on earth's going on? I was worried sick when I woke up and you weren't there! Where have you been?'

'Just here. Hiding in the bath.' She shrugged, implicating the two women, who looked at each other. 'I'm sorry, Michael,' she whispered.

He sighed and knelt down so he could see her face behind the curtain of hair.

'Could we... Could we go for a walk, do you think?' she whispered.

'A walk?' He shrugged his shoulders. 'Sure. If you want to.'

'I do.' She climbed from the bed and placed her

hand inside his, looking back at her mum and Ellen as she and Michael left the room.

Ellen sank down on her bed. 'I'm a nervous wreck.'

Vivienne nodded. 'I just want her to be happy, Elle. I can't stand the thought of her making a mistake.'

'He does seem nice enough, and let's not forget, he is a real doctor.'

'Yes, he does and he is.' She looked at her friend. 'But I don't care what he does for a living if he isn't right for Emma, everything else becomes irrelevant and being *nice enough* sounds like faint praise. Not that it matters what we think, it only matters what Emma thinks. And you were right, by the way. Nothing my mum could have said would have stopped me marrying Ray. But I think the fact that she isn't desperately longing for tomorrow speaks volumes.'

'Imagine coming all this way for a wedding that doesn't happen.' Ellen twisted her mouth.

'Firstly, we don't know it's not going to happen – we mustn't jump to any conclusions right now. And secondly, no matter what happens, I wouldn't have missed this trip for the world. It's been incredible.' A vision of her bobbing on the ocean in the pouring rain with the storm raging overhead, as she sat in Gil's little boat, popped into her head, just before the sound of Ray's loud voice filtered through from the hallway.

'Although I must admit, there is one guest I would rather not have had to mix with.' She curled her lip.

'I'll come out with you.' Ellen swung her legs

off the bed.

'No, you're okay, Elle. I'm a big girl. I managed to hide from him yesterday, but I can't do that to-day and tomorrow.' Flinging on her cropped jeans and a loose-fitting long-sleeved T-shirt, Vivienne went to face the music.

'I'm proud of you girl.' Ellen smiled at her mate, as she left the room.

It was strange to see Ray sitting at the breakfast bar in the kitchen and Gil with his back to him, busy at the stove. They both turned to look at her. Her cheeks flared under their scrutiny and she felt uneasy at being in the company of both of them at the same time.

'Morning.' Gil smiled, returning his gaze in-stantly to the Italian stovetop coffee maker.

'How are you doing, Viv?' Ray's Australian ac-cent still took her by surprise. It was so far from the voice that she remembered.

'Fine.' Her nod was brief; she was irritated by his presence.

'Have you spoken to Emma this morning? I got a call from Michael and he sounded ready to flip.'

She hated the way Ray spoke with such ease and familiarity not only about Emma but also Gil's son, and the fact that he did so in Gil's company.

'She's fine, thank you.' Her curt response was tempered by a glance at Gil; she would talk to him in private, later. 'There's no need for you to hang around, Ray. It's all under control, so if you have plans...'

'Hear that, Gil? I think she's trying to get rid of

241

me.' He spoke over his shoulder.

His manner, the way he saw fit to objectify and talk over her in the name of humour, buddying up to the nearest male to try and assert himself, reminded her so powerfully of her life with him that she felt her fingers flex and her muscles cord in anger.

'I tell you something, Ray...' She inhaled, ready to tell him exactly how she felt, when the terrace door slammed and Emma rushed through the hall, heading for her bedroom with her hand over her mouth. Michael followed swiftly behind. All three turned to face him.

'You can all stop staring at me and you can crack on with packing up your fancy outfits – the wedding's off. I'll start phoning around. Dad, can you call Schnappa Rock, apologise to Nick, tell him not to bring up all the food, I can't bear to think of the waste.' He looked anxious, a whole jumble of emotions clearly hovering near the surface.

'Where's Emma?' Ray asked.

'Probably packing. Who knows? Not me. I don't know much, apparently.' He looked up at his dad. 'Not even the "real her", whatever that means.' He raised his arms in the air, his palms splayed.

'She probably just needs a bit of time.' Vivienne didn't know what to say, or how to make it better.

'Now there's a coincidence, that's exactly what she said,' he snapped.

'There's no need to be sarcastic, Michael,' Gil interjected. 'Viv's only trying to help.'

'Is that right? Seems that since she and her friend arrived, the things they've said have been far from helpful.'

'That's enough!' Gil yelled.

'It's okay, Gil.' Vivienne tried to sound soothing. 'I understand Michael's hurt and this all feels like a big mess. We all need five minutes to calm down.'

Michael gave a snort and, grabbing his sunglasses, he swept from the room.

'I'll go and talk to Emma.' Ray slipped down off his breakfast stool.

'Oh no you don't!' It was her turn to snap, 'I've told you, if there is somewhere you need to be then please don't feel you need to hang around on my account.' She fired off the words, as she made her way to Emma's room.

She knocked and waited, until a small voice called out, 'Come in.'

Pushing the door slowly, she spied Emma curled into a little ball in the corner of the vast bed, her fists bunched up under her chin and her eyes red and swollen. The beautiful dress hung over the wardrobe door inside its gauze sheath.

'Oh, Emma.' She walked over and knelt on the floor, cradling her child to her chest.

'He ... he is so mad at me! And ... and I was only telling him the truth, that I'm scared and that I think we need more ... more time and that he doesn't really know me.' She hiccupped.

'He's not really mad, just hurt and embarrassed, and in the heat of the moment it can often sound the same. It'll all be okay, love, and, either way, you were very brave to have the conversation, very brave to question what you were about to do.'

'I don't feel very brave, I feel very stupid.'

'Well, you are not.' She kissed her scalp.

243

'I don't want to lose him, as a friend. I do love him, I really do.' Her tears fell again. 'But I don't think we are right for each other, Mum.'

'You have only known each other for such a short space of time, and it's far better you decide this now than further down the line, trust me, that was the mistake I made with Ray. Marriage has to be based on honesty and friendship and trust. Better to wait and get it right than rush and make a big mistake.'

Michael marched into the room. 'Oh, I didn't know you were in here, Viv.'

'Just checking she's okay, but I'll leave you two to it.'

She untangled herself from Emma's grip and walked to the door.

'You know, Michael, I'm not interfering. This is between you two and you're both grown-ups. But I do think that being able to be open about how you're feeling, doubts and all, is one of the most important things there is. Even if what the other person has to say is something you don't particularly want to hear.'

He gave a small nod. 'I guess.' He stared out of the window and his voice now had a distinct quiver to it. 'But I kind of think that if she's not ready now, if she has doubts, or feels she can't be herself with me, then she'll probably have the same doubts and we will be in the same situation in another month or another year.'

'I'm really sorry, Michael.' Emma sounded desperate.

'Me too.' He gave a half smile.

Vivienne left them to it.

Gil and Ray were still in the kitchen and they had been joined by Ellen, who was busy emptying the dishwasher and hunting in the cupboards, trying to locate where the crockery and pots lived. Gil was cooking eggs in a skillet.

'How is she doing?' Ellen paused from her task.

'She's sad, as you'd expect, but chatting to Michael now. He's naturally upset and it's horrible to see, two lovely people who have jumped a bit too soon and are now trying to mop up the mess.'

Gil turned to her and gave her a sincere, if brief, smile that made her gut flip. It was in her mind a direct message that all was well between them, despite the distressing development.

'I feel sorry for them both,' he ventured.

Vivienne nodded at him.

'Well I feel sorry for me!' Ellen pointed at her chest. 'I came all this way, got my hair done, we both did, not to mention Viv's Siberian hamster experience. I bought a new frock and a fancy fascinator and now there won't be so much as a vol-au-vent passed around and, more importantly, there'll be no pictures of me in my finery. I wanted them for Facebook.' She pulled a sad face.

'Tell you what, if you get dressed up, I'll take pictures of you if you like, Elle,' Ray offered.

'No, thanks. You'd probably run off with my camera.' She closed her eyes and carried on refilling the dishwasher with coffee cups and plates.

'That's a bit harsh,' Ray said. 'I'm a business-man nowadays. Strictly legit.'

'Ray, you wouldn't know legit if it jumped up and bit your arse,' Ellen countered. 'The things my

Trev has told me about your antics...' She tutted. 'I'm lucky you never got him into real trouble.'

'Ah, Trev. I miss him.' He shook his head and smiled, as if picturing the good old days.

'And he misses you too, like a hole in a bucket,' she scoffed.

'Anyone for eggs?' Gil held up the skillet in an attempt to divert them from their acid-laced banter.

Vivienne felt a swell of awkwardness at this strange reunion that was happening in his kitchen, under his nose. Ellen and Ray were carrying on as if they were in her house in Mendip Road. She was acutely aware that they were Gil's guests and the idea of him feeling excluded worried her.

'Me, please.' She walked forward and grabbed a plate. Breakfast was the last thing she wanted, but it was a way to show unity.

It felt surreal to her, the four of them sitting around the breakfast bar talking about the weather, the food, anything other than the fact that she had been thrown into a jovial catch-up with the man who had abandoned her, and that Emma had pulled the plug on her nuptials. She felt quite light-headed.

'So, what do we do now?' It was Ellen that broached the topic, typically unafraid to tackle the elephant in the room.

'Well, from my perspective, you continue to enjoy your stay,' Gil said. 'We take care of the kids the best we can and, when it arrives, we work out how much cake needs to be eaten per person until we've got through the whole lot.'

'Now that sounds like a plan,' Ellen said.

'I suppose I should think about getting back to Oz.' Ray looked at the other three, who said nothing to try and stop him.

'I can give you a lift to the airport, no worries,' Gil offered, avoiding eye contact.

'Cheers for that mate!' Ray raised his coffee mug in a salute.

There was a second of silence. It seemed to Vivienne that, like her, everyone was considering how very different this trip had turned out to be.

'I have one question...' Gil paused. Everyone looked at him, sipping their coffee. 'What's Viv's Siberian hamster?'

Vivienne sprayed her mouthful over the breakfast bar, and Ellen laid her head on her arms and laughed out loud.

It was only when Emma appeared from the hall that they all sat up straight and rather sheepishly went quiet.

'Can I get you a drink, Emma? Or something to eat?'

Vivienne noted the kindness with which Gil spoke to her, his nearly daughter-in-law.

Once again, Emma broke down in tears. 'I'm sorry, Gil. For everything.'

'You don't have to apologise, love. You and Michael will work things out, however you're meant to. Life's too short not to do the right thing.'

Emma walked over to him and put her hands around his waist in a grateful hug.

'What's the plan, love?' Ray asked.

Emma shrugged. 'I don't really have one, not long-term, but Michael and I have agreed we need

247

to spend time apart to get our heads straight.'

'I was just saying, I should probably think about getting home, back to Oz.'

'Can I come with you?' she asked brightly, as if her dad had thrown her a lifeline.

Emma's request came out of the blue. Vivienne bristled. She had assumed that Emma would come home to Bristol, at least for a bit. She'd pictured the two of them sitting on the sofa on Christmas Day, sharing the tin of Quality Street while they listened to the Queen's speech.

Ray opened his mouth and looked up at the ceiling. He shifted awkwardly on the bar stool and pulled at the collar of his polo shirt. His hesitation was cringe inducing.

'I know the kids would love to meet you and it would mean the world, spending some time together, getting to know each other a bit better. I could even get you working in the shop.' He gave a nervous laugh.

Emma nodded her enthusiasm. 'That sounds really good!'

'But I think it would be best to wait until after Christmas. Ashley – that's my daughter,' he added, 'she's a bit of a live wire and what with her mum passing so recently, she needs careful handling. I think you turning up might be a bit of a shocker.'

'I agree with Ray,' Ellen cut in. 'When people aren't where you expect them to be, either popping up unexpectedly or doing a runner unexpectedly, it can be a bit of a shocker.'

Vivienne acknowledged her friend's support with a slow blink.

Emma swallowed and picked at her fingernail,

looking for any distraction to mask her hurt. Yet another blow on this horrible day. 'That's okay, I understand.' Her voice was very small. 'I'll call you over Christmas and we can sort something out for the New Year, maybe?'

'Yes, maybe.' Ray looked away and downed his coffee. 'Let's do that.'

Vivienne stared at the bloated let-down that was her husband. His promise of wanting to be there for Emma, made only a day or so ago, reminded them all that this was what he did, what he had always done: said one thing and did another.

'Do you know, I think I was right, Ray. People do change, but not many. And certainly not you.'

Emma looked at her mum. Her expression was one Vivienne had seen a lot when she was a child: searching, wanting her mum to make everything better.

'You come home with me, Em.' She closed her eyes and smiled.

'Well, this is nice, are we all having a nice catch up over breakfast?' Michael's anger frothed, causing them all to look up.

'Michael, I...' Emma began.

He held up his palm. 'I tell you what, Em, save it. I've heard just about all I can take today. It feels like I'm the only one whose life is falling apart while you all chat over brunch. I'm going back to work.' He addressed his dad. 'I'm going to stay in digs for a while. One of my mates has a spare room, it's right by the hospital.'

'I think you should stay here, son. You need to be near people, Michael,' Gil said.

'I will be, Dad – my patients and my friends.

That'll do me for a while.' He nodded.

'I'll speak to you later. Drive steady.' Gil spoke earnestly.

'Bye, Michael.' Vivienne struggled for anything more poignant to say.

Emma got tearful again as the two exchanged a lingering look. Then Michael threw a sports bag over his shoulder and left.

Ray downed his coffee and slapped his thigh. 'Right, I better go back and pack up my stuff at the B & B.' He smiled in everyone's general direction. 'About that lift?' He flicked his head towards Gil, who was sipping his coffee with one hand on his hip.

'Sure, I'll drop you back at the B & B and they can call you a cab to Auckland from there.' Gil threw the remainder of his drink into the sink with some urgency, as if suddenly hit by a nasty after-taste.

No one mentioned the less than subtle rescinding of his offer to give Ray a ride all the way to the airport.

'I'll come with you, Dad. We can chat while you pack.'

It tore at Vivienne's heart to see Emma so keen to make every minute count, knowing they were on a timer.

Ray took the hint and stood up. 'Bye then, Viv.'

'Bye then,' she echoed, looking at him only briefly. She felt very little emotion at bidding him farewell, and there was no fanfare, just an ordinary parting. She was surprised by how low-key it all was, when what she had craved for so many years was the chance to say goodbye.

Eleven

Gil jumped into the cab of his truck, off to check on the farm, as he did twice daily. It was now late morning and the last lull in the day before the heat really took hold.

'Can I come with you?' Vivienne asked, approaching the driver's door as he threw an empty bucket and a large bundle of twine into the back of the cab.

'Sure,' he said nonchalantly, closing his door and waiting for her to climb in.

She wound down the window and drank in the view as the truck dipped and rose over the uneven terrain of Aropari. There seemed to be sheep almost everywhere, grazing on clumps of grass or sheltering behind gorse bushes and standing very still as if playing hide and seek. They bleated as they spied the red vehicle, which was as familiar to them as the man driving it. Gil maintained that each sheep's bleat was unique. Leaning his tanned arm out of the open window, he made a clicking noise with his tongue and they seemed to respond.

As the truck climbed higher, her body sank back into the leather-upholstered seat. She gripped the sides, wanting to hold onto something.

'You're quite safe, the ground flattens out in a bit.' He laughed, looking straight ahead. And it did, suddenly, as the truck crested and emerged onto a plateau.

She was quite unprepared for what lay before her. It was utterly magnificent. It was as if she was sitting on the top of the earth. She let go of the seat and sat forward until her face was as close to the windscreen as she could get.

'Oh, Gil! Oh my word.'

He slowed to a stop and cut the engine, pulling on the handbrake. Vivienne jumped out and walked forwards, propping herself against the bonnet with her hand shading the sun from her eyes. 'I have never seen anything like it in my whole life.'

She let her eyes sweep left to right and back again, trying to take in the spectacular vista. The arcing dips and swells of the land held dense woods, clustered together amidst the green, green grass, with soaring mountains in the distance and the rugged coastline unfurling to the left. The blue sky was flecked with light clouds and the sea sparkled beneath the sun's rays. It was like standing in a painting of heaven.

'I cannot imagine what it must be like, being able to come up here every day and look at this.' She turned to face Gil, who was staring at her, not the view.

'You can see why I prefer sheep and land to people.' He smiled.

'I must admit, I still feel guilty that we've come here en masse and shattered your peace. I feel sad for Michael and Emma and I don't want you to think badly of us. I hate to think of all the plans having to be undone.' Her voice rattled with nerves.

'It's not so difficult: a few phone calls and a group email and that's pretty much it. And what we can't cancel, we shall have to enjoy. Apparently Ellen's already got her eye on the top tier of the cake.' He gave her a short smile. 'It's Emma and Michael I'm worried about too, not anyone else's opinions or having to cancel the caterers. That's the easy bit.'

'You are right, absolutely. And you are a good dad, you know. Michael's lucky to have you.'

Gil smiled, 'I don't think anyone has ever said that to me before, I really appreciate it.' He coughed, clearly choked by her compliment. 'I've only ever done my best, picked up the slack after his mum left and muddled through, but most of the time it's been guesswork.'

'It's the same for all of us,' she acknowledged. 'I said to Emma, you can only ever do what feels right at the time.'

'I think it would have been easier doing it with someone by my side.'

'Oh, tell me about it,' she laughed. 'It'll be strange getting on that plane with Emma in a couple of days' time. I reckon she might find the cold weather a bit of a change, after this.' She was of course delighted that her daughter had decided to come back to Bristol for a while, giving her and Michael the space they needed and a chance to think everything through. 'I'm a bit torn, Gil.'

'In what way?' He looked at her, awaiting her next words, his expression reminiscent of a child with his hands cupped for sweets.

'Oh, you know, I wouldn't have wished this outcome on them, but it will be lovely to have her back, even if it is only for a little while.'

He exhaled, as if disappointed. 'You can't clip

their wings, eh?' he muttered.

'No, not even if you want to.'

'And what about you, Viv?'

She liked the way he had slipped into calling her by this familiar abbreviation, the same as Ellen did, establishing them as friends.

'What about me?' She kicked the ground, a little coyly.

'Are you looking forward to packing up and heading home?'

She put her fingers into her jeans pockets and stared at the view, taking a big lungful of the pure, beautiful air. 'Yes and no.'

'Keep it vague, why don't you?' He laughed. They were both a little nervous.

'I mean, I'm looking forward to getting Emma home, and to seeing my Bob, of course.' She smiled at him, knowing he'd understand that. 'But the thought of leaving here, going back to the gloom of a cold, drizzly winter, back to work ... I don't know, it's not that appealing.' She held his gaze briefly.

'Well you could always stay here for Christmas?' He spoke softly and with clarity.

'What?' She didn't know why she asked him to repeat himself, having heard him perfectly. Maybe it was to give her a moment or two to consider her response.

'I said, why don't you stay here, with me, for Christmas.'

'I...' Vivienne felt a nervous giggle in her throat, which she swallowed. Was he mad?

'So, what do you think?' His voice was a little more strained now, as if nerves were affecting him too.

'I feel warm here, Gil.' She looked out towards the sea, committing the view to memory.

'Well, it is a beautiful day.' He nodded at the tranquil water glittering in the sunlight.

She shook her head. 'It's not the weather, it's in here.' She placed the flat of her palm on her chest. 'I feel alive, like I'm waking after a long, cold sleep, and it feels lovely.'

'Is that a yes then?' He smiled.

'Oh, Gil.' She shook her head. 'No. It's a no. And I appreciate your offer more than you know. But I need to get back to Bristol, to my little life on the other side of the world. It's where I live, where I'm from, where my house is and my lovely son. This place is paradise. Everything here feels different.' She shrugged. 'And you are...' She searched for the right words. 'You are someone very special. But Emma needs me and Aaron too, it's Christmas, a big deal, we have set ways...'

'I see.' He paused. 'So if I was asking you to stay for a while in say, May, that would have made a difference? Or just before Easter, or Valentine's?' He gave a wry smile.

She smiled back at the handsome, quiet, sheep-farmer cowboy. 'I can't, Gil. I can't just stay here. It's been a wonderful holiday but that's it. I need to get home.'

'Well you don't have to, you could make a few calls, send an email, that's the easy bit remember?'

'Easy for some, maybe, but not for me. My life doesn't work like that. I have an ordinary life – I work in Asda and I walk my dog, that's it!'

'Well, I don't do much more here. I work the

farm, walk my dog, take my boat out, ordinary stuff.'

'Maybe the world feels a little less ordinary when you've got glorious sunshine for half the year and good New Zealand air to breathe.' Her words, spoken to Ellen as they'd sat in Pedro's with the rain trickling down the window, had never felt more poignant.

The ringing of Gil's phone made them both jump. He looked at the screen. 'Home,' he read, before taking the call.

Despite standing at some distance from him, she could hear Ellen's booming voice on the other end: 'Gil? I'm in a right pickle here. Emma's gone off on a bloody bike ride, of all things, and there's a man here with a gert big tent thing who wants to put it up on your lawn. I've told him there's no point, but he's pulling out ropes and whatnot nonetheless. A shedful of flowers has been dumped on the front porch, looks like Kew bloody Gardens out here, and the cake is listing in the heat. I think I might need a bit of help!'

'We're on our way, Ellen.' He ended the call and opened the driver's door of the truck. 'Seems like some of those phone calls and that group email I mentioned didn't quite reach everyone. We'd better get back.'

Vivienne climbed into the cab. 'I'm sorry, Gil,' she whispered.

'Oh, don't be, we'll sort it out. It's not a big deal. We can send the gazebo back and distribute the flowers to everyone in town, how's that sound?' He avoided her gaze as he swung the truck around at speed and headed down the steep hillside, bumping in and out of the ruts without another word.

Both were acutely aware that the state of affairs at the house was not what she'd been apologising for.

Ellen stood by the porch in her white trousers and pink-and-blue paisley tunic, looking quite lovely among the pots of flowers that had been delivered. 'What am I supposed to do with this lot?' she asked, bending down to admire the gorgeous terracotta pots of hydrangeas and cream and pink roses.

'Let's move them up to the deck,' Vivienne suggested, 'then they'll be out of the way. Plus they'll look pretty.'

She was happy to be kept busy, quite unable to process the fact that Gil had asked her to stay for Christmas – as if that was at all possible for someone like her – and at the same time lamenting the fact that she only had a few more days in his company. She and Ellen spent the next hour ferrying the pots, one by one, up to the deck and placing them in clusters in the corners, where they did indeed look splendid.

'I need a rest!' Ellen flopped down on the wicker sofa and lay back, closing her eyes.

Vivienne took the seat next to her. 'The view from the top of the farm is something else, Elle, like heaven.'

'Ooh I'd like to see that, funny though, Gil doesn't seem half as keen to spend time alone with me.' Her friend chuckled. Vivienne ignored her.

'I sometimes wonder where I'll end up,' she thought aloud, as she watched the boats glide by in the early afternoon sun. The *Dive! Tutukaka* boat passed at speed across her sightlines, heading back to the marina by Schnappa Rock. She wondered what it might feel like to dive up at the Poor Knights. There was so much on the planet that was alien to her.

Ellen picked up the thread. 'If you could end up anywhere, where would it be?'

She shrugged. 'Dunno. It's hard to picture anywhere other than Mendip Road. But I sometimes think I might quite like the Lake District.'

Ellen laughed and then quickly checked herself, glancing at the flowers that had been meant for a celebration that was no longer happening. 'I don't know why that's funny!' she whispered. 'I guess I thought you might say Redland or Weston-Super-Mare – you know, really push your boundaries. I wasn't expecting the Lake District. Whereabouts?'

'I don't know. I've never been.'

'Me neither.' Ellen sniffed.

'I saw a programme about it a few years ago, and I think about it sometimes. The rolling hills, the mountains and the beautiful lakes. It looked like a film set, gorgeous, like proper patchwork. And so much space! I thought I'd like to live there in a cottage, with a goat and Bob.'

'Well I never, you dark horse, what a woman of mystery. I never knew you'd like a goat. I thought I knew everything about you.'

'Well there you go.' She smiled. 'I thought I knew everything about you, but apparently I didn't. Fourteen...' She shook her head and tutted.

'Oh don't start on that again.'

They giggled like teens.

'I imagine the air in the Lakes to be like nectar,

a bit like this. I bet you can really breathe.' She closed her eyes and inhaled deeply.

Ellen gave her a sideways glance. 'You know you wouldn't like living there. Too far from me.'

'Blimey, Elle, I've never eaten watermelon on a tropical beach, or sipped champagne with a view of Paris or slept for twelve hours and woken up feeling like a queen, but I bet none of those things are horrible. Just because I haven't done something or seen something, doesn't mean I won't like it. I'm sure I would.'

'What's got into you, Mrs?' Ellen sat forward and stared at her mate.

'Nothing. It's just been a funny old day.'

'It has that.'

The sound of muffled tears floated on the breeze behind them. Both sat up and turned to see Emma, newly returned from her bike ride and staring at the stunning floral display that surrounded them on the deck.

'Dad got off okay, I checked. He's on his way back to Australia right now.' She swiped at her tears.

Vivienne and Ellen exchanged a look of relief. There'd been a lurking doubt in Vivienne's mind that Ray might have hung around.

Emma had now started crying in earnest.

'Oh, love!' Vivienne stood up and beckoned her over. 'Come and sit with us.'

Emma plonked down between the two of them. 'This is supposed to be the night before my wedding and look at me!' She sniffed.

'You can't have it both ways, Emma. You can't have a change of heart, tell everyone to get off the bus and then cry about it,' Ellen said firmly.

Both Vivienne and Emma stared at her.

'What? I'm only saying!' Ellen yelled.

There was a beat of silence while Vivienne waited to see how Emma would react. To her credit, she sat up straight and looked directly at the woman who had been an aunt figure all her life. 'You're right, Elle. I need to get it together.' She exhaled, tipping her head back and straightening her shoulders, as if limbering up. 'I think, Mum, that I might go up to Auckland tonight, say my goodbyes to Michael on the way and then go and see my friends. I can meet you both at the airport for our flight. Would that be okay?'

'Of course, love. You do what you need to. We'll be okay here, won't we, Elle?'

Ellen crossed her arms over her large chest. 'I don't know, Viv, first Michael, then Ray, now Em – we only need Gil to do a runner and we've got the place to ourselves.'

The three laughed at the absurdity of the situation.

'I don't know if I want to be here on my own with those two, I'll feel like a prize gooseberry.' Ellen spoke without thinking, as was often the case.

Emma turned to her mum. 'What's she talking about? Surely you don't fancy Gil?' Her expression was hard to read, but if she had to call it, looking at the set of her eyebrows and the twist to her mouth, Vivienne would have gone for extreme disapproval.

'Of course I don't!' she protested, giving a small cough to clear her throat. 'That's just Elle's idea of being funny, which she isn't. Ever.' She glared at her friend, who began to sulk.

After helping Emma pack, they stood in front of the house.

'See you at the airport.' Emma gave them a small smile, as she climbed into Gil's truck. Driving her to Whangarei would give Gil the chance to check on how Michael was faring, he had offered right away.

'Thanks for taking her, Gil. We'll see you later. Can I get you something to eat when you get in?' Vivienne asked, aware of the echo of domesticity in her offer and the way her cheeks flamed accordingly.

'No, you're all right. I'll grab something on the way home,' he said mournfully, avoiding her stare.

'We'll see you later then,' she whispered.

He gave a single nod.

Emma waved out of the window until the truck turned around the wide bend of the drive and disappeared into the dusk.

Vivienne and Ellen stared into the space they left behind, standing in silence as the squawks of the seabirds below rose in what sounded like a chorus of farewell to Emma, who had lived among them for a short time.

Ellen turned to face her friend. 'Fancy a bit of cake?'

'Why not.'

The two linked arms and made their way into the kitchen.

As their conversation became punctuated with

more and more yawns and repetitions, Vivienne knew it was time for bed.

'What a bloody day.' Ellen sighed as she climbed into her bed. 'And I've eaten too much cake,' she moaned, rubbing her stomach inside her pyjamas. 'I shan't be putting my pink string bikini on any time soon.'

'Amen for that.' She whispered, 'I hope Emma's okay. And Michael.' Vivienne thought about the young man who was the reason they had come to Aropari in the first place, and then she thought about his dad. 'It's good that Gil is going to take a break on the way home. It's harder to concentrate when your head's a muddle and you're tired, and some of those twisty roads are a bit tricky. I hope he doesn't think we're rude not waiting up for him, but I'm beat.'

'He won't mind, I'm sure. And don't you worry. I'll bet he knows those roads like the back of his hand.'

'Yep, probably.'

'Wonder where Ray is. Will he be home by now?' Ellen spoke through her yawn.

'Don't know. Don't care,' Vivienne said as she picked up her toothbrush.

'Don't know. Don't care!' Ellen imitated her with a squeaky, irritated voice that, despite her tiredness, made her laugh.

Vivienne slipped between the sheets and was glad to see the end to the day. She ran her palm over the pillow where Emma had earlier cried and sent her thoughts of love and positivity out over the ether, just as she had every single night for the last four years, only tonight her prayers had a little less further to travel. To Aaron too she said goodnight, sent love and hoped that his decorating chore wasn't too taxing, the poor love. Her final thought was of Gil. She lay with sleep lapping at her, picturing the landscape at the top of Aropari and hearing his words in her head, words that echoed with possibilities: *'Why don't you stay here, with me for Christmas...'*

It was a little after midnight that she twisted in the white cotton sheet, letting her slender limbs dangle from the mattress, eager to catch even the slightest breeze that might flutter through the open French doors and across the terracotta floor. She changed position yet again, casting the sheet to the middle of the bed and hating the dull, taunting whut, whut sound of the oversized wooden ceiling fan that seemed only to swirl the heat around and offered nothing by way of relief. She wished she'd asked how to put the air conditioning on before everyone had left.

Ellen was snoring, as ever in the deepest sleep. Vivienne pictured her face squashed against the window of the funicular in Hong Kong, her mouth open as she snoozed, oblivious. It made her smile.

A mosquito whined from a dark shadow, hovering tantalisingly close and yet invisible. She waited for it to land, swatting at her skin in anticipation of its arrival. Mosquitoes loved her. All it took was a quick circuit of St John's on a summer's evening and she'd be covered in bites, returning home to dab at them with calamine lotion. Ellen took great pleasure in referring to her as 'an-all-you-can-eat bug buffet'.

She sat up in the bed and blew upwards into her fine fringe, trying to cool down. It was too hot for her to sleep. The pleasant summer warmth that had earlier soothed her bones and massaged her skin had become a strength-sapping heat that made doing even the smallest of tasks quite tiring and rendered sleep nearly impossible.

Flinging back the sheet, she tiptoed past her sleeping friend and opened the door. She trod the hallway, liking the feel of the cool slate floor under her bare feet. She ran herself a large glass of cold water and stared at the cake mountain on the countertop.

'Oh, Emma...' She sighed.

Taking her drink, she padded across the hallway and out onto the front porch. Her gaze narrowed and she could make out a shadow standing on the deck.

It was Gil.

He had put on the outside lighting and small wells of light danced between the flower displays. It looked magical. She approached slowly, without giving too much thought to the fact that she was wearing her cotton pyjamas.

As if sensing her, he turned around, clutching his wine glass to his chest.

'Hey.'

'Hey.'

She walked across the grass and trod the high step up onto the deck and there they stood, side by side, looking out at the bruised, purple ocean and the dark, forbidding sky.

'Am I disturbing you?' she whispered.

'Not at all.' He shook his head.

'It's so hot. I couldn't sleep.'

'Gets like that sometimes. I can never sleep after a long drive; I find it hard to switch off. I think there'll be a storm tonight. It certainly feels like it.' He kept his eyes on the horizon.

'Did you see Michael?'

'Yes.' He nodded.

'How was he?'

'As you'd expect.' He took a slug of his wine. 'He was pleased to see Emma and they were both tearful and hugging.' He shrugged, as if this was a topic he found difficult. 'And I've thought about it a lot on the way back, but I don't honestly know if they were tears of joy at being reunited or tears of sadness at the prospect of separation or just the tears of goodbye. Sometimes it's hard to tell.' He glanced at her. 'Would you like some wine?'

'Sure, thank you. Funny, isn't it, at home I wouldn't dream of getting up in the dead of night and having a glass of wine. Cocoa maybe or a cup of tea in extreme emergencies, but never wine.'

Gil topped up the glass he'd been drinking from and handed it to her. 'Yeah, well, you're not at home, are you? You're here, where everything feels different, so you might as well make the most of it.' His tone was clipped.

She took a sip as they stood quietly, side by side. There was a flash of lighting followed by the crack of thunder out on the horizon, but not a drop of rain, yet.

'Do you think Emma is afraid to let herself be happy?' he asked, his voice softer.

'That's a strange thing to say.' She took another drink of the cool, crisp, white wine.

'I don't think it's strange.' He shook his head. 'I think it's a very real possibility that she might constantly be on the move and on the lookout for the next thing, unable to settle, because somewhere along the line she's learnt that nothing lasts forever and maybe it's easier not to try because that path only leads to disappointment.'

Vivienne held the glass to her mouth and took a large gulp before handing it back. 'Are you saying that's what I've taught her?' The very idea made her insides jump.

He took the glass from her without meeting her gaze. 'Not intentionally, but...'

'Go on,' she urged, wanting to hear his thoughts, as much as she dreaded it too.

'I think Ellen might be right: you've been hiding, using what happened to you so long ago as a cushion to soften any further blows. And maybe Emma thinks it's the safest way to live, maybe that's what she has learnt, not to hang around long enough to get too attached to anyone or anything.'

'It was Ray that ran out, not me! If it's leaving that's been her example and set the pattern–'

'No! No, Viv, you misunderstand me,' he cut in. 'I'm not having a go at you or blaming you.'

'Well that's what it sounded like, a bit.' She sniffed, really not wanting to give in to the tears that threatened.

Gil placed his wine glass on the floor and turned, taking two steps towards her. Reaching out, he took her hand. There was an undeniable spark of electricity between them, just as there had been before. She ignored the second flash in the sky and the crack of thunder that seemed a little closer now than the first. She felt her mouth go dry with nerves and her heart raced. He placed his fingers on the third finger of her left hand and touched them against the thin gold wedding band. He wiggled the ring a little, easing it over her knuckle, and then gently slid it from her finger.

'You don't need to wear this...' He paused. 'You aren't married to him. And you don't need it to protect yourself or to give you status. You need to set yourself free, Viv. You need to live that life.'

He turned her hand over and placed the thin sliver of gold in her palm. She looked down and ran her thumb over the little circle that sat in the middle of her hand.

Her tears came then, a steady stream, all beating the same path, and she cursed the display and the fact that they were spoiling this lovely moment, as she stood on the deck among the flowers with their heady, sweet bouquet, the sea below and the stars above and the wine working its magic, with the sexy, quiet, sheep-farmer cowboy standing in front of her.

'Don't cry, Viv. Please don't cry. You are amazing. You are beautiful and I really would like you to stay here. With me, for Christmas.'

He leant in to kiss her. It surprised and thrilled her. She arched forward, standing on tiptoe to return the kiss and as she did so, her fingers opened and the gold band slipped from her hand and fell between the wooden planks of the deck. She didn't even notice, as she reached up and knitted her fingers in his hair.

And then it came, the thunderbolt she had waited for her whole life. Her heart leapt and her stomach flipped and she was filled with a new sensation. It was like coming home. Pulling away, she looked into his face.

'I'm happy,' she managed, and without too much thought she leant forward to return the kiss. With her hands on the side of his head, she kissed him squarely on the mouth. It was a revelation: sweet, pleasant, gentle. She had quite forgotten the sheer joy of being lip to lip with another human being.

He let his hands travel over her, waist and hips, reciprocating with another kiss.

The two retired to the wicker sofa, giggling like a couple of kids let out for the evening. She lay with her head on his shoulder.

'Here.' He lifted her head and placed a cushion under it, before putting his arm around her.

'How come you're so nice to me?' she asked.

'Because I hate to think of you having anything less than the nicest possible day. That's what you deserve.'

'I've never felt this hopeful, Gil. I feel like it's all there for the taking.' She looked out at the dark night, watched the stars twinkling over a landscape that held no history for her and was a long, long way from home.

'That's because it is.' He smiled and twisted his neck to kiss her arm that lay on his shoulder.

Vivienne sat up and turned to face him, their hands still entwined. 'I can't stay here with you for Christmas, Gil. You know that, don't you? I just can't.'

He stared at her, hanging on her every word.

She continued. 'But I will never, ever forget how

you have made me feel. You are beautiful, in every sense, but I can't just stay on here now, lovely as it would be to spend Christmas in this heavenly place, with you. What about Emma – she can't stay here, can she? Not after all that's happened. She wants to get home and I understand that, she's been gone a long time. And I can't just leave her to settle back in Bedminster on her own, she's going to need a bit of looking after. And I promised Bob I'd be back in a fortnight.' She wriggled her toes and sighed. 'There's other people to think about, Gil. I can't just be putting my happiness first.'

Gil closed his eyes and breathed through his nose. Bringing their entwined fingers up to his mouth, he gently kissed the back of her hand.

'But that's exactly what you should be doing, Viv. For once in your life, put yourself first! It's only Christmas, for goodness' sake, only one day and just a roast. Another three weeks here, that's all I am asking – time for the two of us to get to know each other a bit more.'

He ran his fingers over the side of her face and flashed her a twinkling, smile. 'And, you know, maybe what Emma really needs is the chance to stand on her own two feet for a few weeks, back home in Bristol. A chance to reconnect on her own terms, not with you making it all happen for her. She'll feel better for making her own decisions and will be able to see her brother, and get re-acquainted with Bob. I can't see the problem, Viv. Like I said, it's time to live that life.' He squeezed her hand. 'But I won't pressurise you again.'

Viv's heart was pounding in her chest. She

could picture it all, there was sense in his words, but it just wasn't her. She was not the sort of person to spontaneously fall in love with a sexy sheep-farmer cowboy and decide to stay on a few extra weeks, never mind if other people were a bit inconvenienced.

A cool wind blew across the terrace; it felt pleasant, stirring the heat of the night. 'That's a nice breeze.' She closed her eyes.

'Yep, reckon the storm is heading away from us.' He looked out to the horizon.

She leant forward and kissed him. 'I want us to just enjoy right now because I know that when I am walking Bob on a cold, drizzly night, memories like this will keep me warm,' she whispered, lying once again with her head nestling on his shoulder.

'Yup.' He kissed her scalp. 'Let's just enjoy the right now.' He sighed.

'I won't ever forget tonight,' she said. 'And when I die, I will think of this moment and it will bring me peace.' With her eyes closed, she smiled, knowing this to be true.

Twelve

Ellen lay face down on top of her suitcase, like a flailing turtle, desperately trying to do up the zip. 'I don't know what's happened, I'm only going home with what I came with and I can't close my case.'

'What are you like?' Vivienne asked, a little halfheartedly, as her friend wriggled and threatened to topple off the bed. She was tired after the dramas of the preceding days and was dreading the long journey, which seemed much less appealing without the prospect of holiday happiness at the end of it.

'You look like you've got a case of post-holiday blues. It's always hard to go when things have been so lovely, but this hasn't all been lovely, Viv, and it's time we got back and started sorting out the knots in the fairy lights.' She looked at her watch. 'Plus the sprouts will want putting on about now.'

She gave a short laugh at Ellen's attempts to cheer her up.

'We'll have a giggle on the way home, you'll see – only two hours at Kong Hong airport but still enough time for you to try and ditch me again.'

'Maybe.' She gave a weak smile.

'Lord above, I tell you what, if you're going to be this miserable, I might just get myself a pair of headphones and a Walkman and ignore you all the way home.' Ellen tutted.

'Good luck finding a Walkman – this isn't the eighties.'

Ellen poked her tongue out at her friend, before continuing to gabble. 'How long do you think it will be before we stop, once we've set off for the airport? I need to plan my loo breaks.'

'I don't know, Elle. Maybe you should just sit on a towel.'

'Okay, Miss Snarky! It wasn't me that had to put on Nicola Brown's gym knickers.'

'It was Ribena!' she yelled.

'There's no need to shout,' Ellen replied, at little

more than a whisper. She stood up and looked at her friend. 'Look, Viv, I know you're going to miss being here and your little flirtation with Gil. It's been good for you and it's been great to see you so happy, it really has. I hope it's made you realise that there's more to life than working and walking Bob. It's like I said, you need to get out there.'

Vivienne ignored her; too stunned by the way she felt to even know how to explain that this was so much more than a little flirtation. Gil might have described the obstacles in their way as surmountable, but to her they felt like the exact opposite.

She left the bedroom without looking back, pulling her suitcase behind her, as she walked past the vast kitchen and cathedral-like hallway of Gil's magnificent home, barely glancing up, as if it was already a memory, as if she couldn't bear to look at what she would be leaving behind. Making her way to the back terrace, she cast one last look at the deck, still beautiful under the weight of the wedding flowers, and took even more snaps of the sea beyond, knowing that no photograph could truly capture the magic of Aropari.

'All set?' Gil called from the truck. He placed their cases in the flatbed of the truck and stepped back. Ellen buckled up into the middle seat, next to him. He had reverted to being a little cool and this she understood to be his way of keeping a lid on things. She got the distinct sense that, like her, he couldn't wait to get the journey over with.

It was a less than happy drive along the state highway; not even the grand vistas and Ellen's rambling chatter could distract her from the fact that in a little over two hours she would be saying goodbye.

The signs indicating Auckland International Airport came up sooner than she'd imagined, and they turned off the highway. The modern, sloping-roofed building looked much smaller than it had when they'd arrived, but then she'd been distracted by the intoxicating sight and sound of Emma. She looked up at the large white triangular canopies that bore the words *City of Sails*. It made her think of her time in Gil's boat, when she'd dipped her hand into the cool, salty water while wearing his Northland hat and they had got caught in the rain. She knew that that day, in fact all her days at Tutukaka, would sustain her through the long shifts on the till at Asda, a welcome diversion from the cold draughts that invariably blew in under the door and chilled her toes. She also knew that there wouldn't be anyone waiting at home to pop soft wool socks onto her feet and give them a warm.

Gil lifted his hand, acknowledging the traffic cop who was pointing at the drop-off sign. 'Two minutes!' he called out, quickly jumping out, pulling down the tailgate and removing their two heavy suitcases containing wedding outfits they had never got to wear and plastic flowers for their hair bought in haste. He placed the cases side by side on the kerb and hopped back into the driver's seat. 'Cheers then!' he shouted from the open window. Then he indicated and pulled away from the drop-off zone, into the stream of traffic. And just like that, he was gone.

'But...' Vivienne felt her chest heave as her

breath came in irregular bursts.

'He couldn't stop, love. He had to get off, that policeman was watching him. We'd already said our thank yous and goodbyes on the journey, you know that.'

'But...' She stared after the truck, watching it disappear out of view. 'I wanted to say goodbye properly. I ... I wanted to talk to him!' She was aware of how desperate she sounded. She gripped the handle of her handbag and fought the desire to cry.

Ellen rubbed the top of her arm. 'You can write to him or email him.'

'I don't want to write to him! That's not enough!' She raised her voice, snapping at her friend, as she shrugged her arm free and her tears finally gathered.

'What's the matter with you?' Ellen bent low and spoke softly.

'I'm not ready to go,' she managed, wiping her eyes with her fingers and swallowing as she fought to regain her composure. 'I'm not ready to go home yet.'

'Oh I know, love. Everyone feels like that after a lovely holiday, everyone wants just one more day and then another and another. It's what Trev always says, why can't we just stay here, just you and me in the sunshine? Lord, we've even looked in estate-agent windows, working out how much our house would fetch, and then picturing our evenings walking on the beach with a sangria in our hands. And it sounds lovely, idyllic, but it's not real life, is it? Real life is what's waiting for us at home.'

Vivienne looked up at her friend. 'But don't you see, Elle, that's just it – you have Trev, you've always had Trev, but I don't have anyone waiting for me. And now I might have found him and I don't want to go home. Why can't *this* be my real life? Why can't I stay here for a little bit longer, why can't I have Christmas here with Gil?'

'Christmas? Don't be daft, we need to get home. And you are not alone, you've got me. And you've got Aaron and Lizzie – okay, bad example – but you've got Bob and now you've got Emma coming home!'

Vivienne stared at the slip road that wound out of the airport complex, hoping for a final glimpse of the truck, but he'd gone. 'I want to stay a bit longer. I need to talk to him, I need to figure out whether it *was* a thunderbolt or whether it was just the wine and the stars.' She placed her fingers over her eyes, as if trying to block out the distraction of the busy airport terminal, and sighed. 'I know I'm not making much sense.'

'No, you're not. I don't know what you mean.' Ellen shook her head.

'I mean, Elle,' she wiped her mouth with the back of her hand and swallowed her tears, 'that Gil has asked me to stay here with him for Christmas and I want to. I really do.'

'But...' Ellen's eyes narrowed and her lips moved, as if she was desperately searching for the words that would express how she was feeling. 'You can't.'

Vivienne placed her hand on her friend's arm. 'It's okay, Elle, I'm only going to be a Skype screen away, and it's not forever, just a couple of

275

weeks. I just think I can't afford not to explore the way I'm feeling. What if this *is* my one shot, what if I'm being given this one chance? I need to see him again, but I'll be home in the New Year with tales of my adventure.'

Ellen stared at her; it was a while before she spoke. 'But supposing you're not?'

'Don't be daft, of course I will be. But I think I need this time with Gil, and I need to think about me. I like him. I really do.' She smiled.

'And that's what's worrying me. I think he likes you too.' Ellen swallowed.

Vivienne couldn't contain her joy at hearing her friend confirm this. 'Really?' She felt the swell of excitement that her fourteen-year-old self had craved, confirmation that one of the nice boys liked her too. 'Well, that's a good thing, isn't it?' She cocked her head.

'I don't know, Viv. I want you to be happy, of course I do, but I want you to be happy around the corner from me, where I can see you every day and meet you in the park and walk along the Malago or go and get a coffee, share a teacake, just like we always have...' She let this trail.

'And that's what will happen! That's my life, that's our life. Things aren't going to change. Besides, I've got my Bob waiting for me. But for the next couple of weeks I can have fun! It was you that told me I needed to live a bit.'

'I know, and I only want you to be happy, I do, but I can't imagine not having you near me, Viv. You've been there my whole life, you're my best friend and I love you.'

'Oh for goodness' sake, now look what you've

276

gone and done!' Vivienne blotted the tears that fell down her cheeks and her friend sniffed. 'It's just over Christmas, Elle. That's all. And you and Emma can travel back together and it will be good for Emma to stand on her own two feet at home. She can have space to figure out what comes next.'

'She can come to me for Christmas, of course.' Ellen sniffed. 'I'll get an extra cracker.'

'That's great and you can fetch Bob from Pedro's and give him a cuddle from me and air the house, even get the bread and milk in for when I come home, which I will do, soon.' She leant forward and kissed her friend on the cheek.

'Mum! Elle!' Emma called out, as she jumped off the bus that had pulled up in front of the terminal. With her rucksack on her back, her hair braided at the front and her tanned, ringed toes wiggling inside her jandals, she looked like any other traveller.

'Hello, lovey.' Vivienne threw her arms around her daughter. 'Are you okay? How are things?'

Emma pulled a face. 'Things are pretty much as they were. Michael and I are still on hold, but we are talking, which is something and we have agreed that no matter what happens, we will always be friends. I do love him, but maybe not in the way that I should and maybe he doesn't love me in the way that he should.'

'He doesn't love your crazy.' She smiled.

'Exactly.' Emma blinked at her mum.

There was a silent hiatus as the three stood on the kerb.

'Shall I tell her or will you?' Ellen sniffed.

'Tell me what? Is Dad okay?'

It was interesting to Vivienne that this was Emma's first thought. She saw the V of concern above her nose. 'Fine, as far as I know.' Emma's shoulders sagged in relief. 'It's nothing bad, just a slight change of plan. I've decided to stay here for a bit longer.'

'What? Why?'

'I want to talk to Gil.'

Emma tilted her head and furrowed her brow in confusion. 'What do you mean; you want to talk to him? Do you want me to call him for you? I've got his number right here.' She started to rummage in her bag, looking for her phone.

Vivienne composed herself and kept her eyes on her daughter. 'No. I mean I want to talk to him myself, face to face. I think I might like him, Emma. In fact, no, that's not true, I do like him and he likes me.'

'Is this some kind of joke?' Emma laughed nervously.

'No.' She paused. 'I came out here to see you get married and, believe me, this was the very last thing on my mind. But the moment I saw him–'

'I don't believe this.' Emma stood with her hands on her hips, looking at Ellen, as if hoping she might provide the punchline.

'Don't look at me! I knew they were having a bit of a flirt, but I thought it was something and nothing. I'm as shocked as you are.' Ellen folded her arms.

'So...' Emma rolled her hand in the air. 'Have you and Gil been...' She stopped again to find the right word. 'Have you been *seeing* each other the whole time you've been in Tutukaka?'

'No, we haven't *seen each other* at all, but we have told each other how we feel and he did ask me to stay, for Christmas, but I said no because I couldn't see how that would work, not with you coming home and work and things, but then, when I saw him drive off...' She shook her head, not wanting to cry again.

'So why this change of heart, then? Why do you want to stay now?' Emma asked.

Vivienne sighed. 'Because when he drove off,' she continued, 'I felt sadder than I have in a very long time. I felt robbed, hollow, and it got me thinking. I think I *have* been hiding away, afraid to put my head above the parapet or take a risk. And I think you might have been a bit like that too, Em,' she ventured.

'What a crazy thing to say to me! I am the most adventurous person I know – just give me a ticket and time to pack and I'm off.' Emma shot her hand out like an arrow firing into the distance. 'I go anywhere and everywhere and I meet people and I try things – everything!' She snorted her disagreement.

'But that's just it, Emma. If you run in a circle long enough, it's hard to see where you are on that journey. Sometimes, the hardest thing is to stop, sit still and see what comes to you. You have to trust that things will be okay and you have to stop running.'

Emma didn't mean to cry, but her tears fell nonetheless. She walked forward and held her mum in a warm embrace. 'I'm glad I'm going home, Mum,' she whispered.

'Look after Bob for me and tell Aaron that I'm fine, more than fine, tell him I am great and I'll be back before you know it, okay?' She pulled away and smiled at her beautiful girl.

'Okay.' She nodded.

Vivienne turned to her best friend and smiled. 'I think you might be right, Elle. It's the not knowing what's coming up next that makes things exciting!'

'I wish I'd never bloody mentioned it now.' Ellen grinned at her friend.

'I'll see you in a couple of weeks.' She pulled the handle on her suitcase and prepared to wheel it to the bus stop.

'You'd better.' Ellen narrowed her eyes. 'Look after yourself.'

'I will. Cross my heart.' She drew the cross on her chest.

Ellen blinked quickly. 'I know you said a while ago you quite fancied hooking up with someone who owned a wool shop, but I didn't think you'd go one step further and try and find someone who made sheep.'

Vivienne doubled over, laughing. 'You are a one-off, Elle. He doesn't make sheep!'

She walked calmly and confidently to the layby where the buses came and went, watching as Ellen and Emma made their way, hand in hand, into the terminal. She felt a wave of nervous excitement in her stomach.

The bus wheezed into the spot and the driver opened the doors.

'Hello!' she breezed. 'How long is the drive to Tutukaka?'

'About three and a half hours.'

'Right, better get a ticket then.'

'Is that one way or return?' the driver asked.

'Oh, return. Definitely a return. I'm only here for Christmas.' She smiled and opened her purse.

By the time the bus pulled into Tutukaka Marina and Vivienne had retrieved her suitcase from the hold, it was mid afternoon, only a few hours before dusk would be drawing its blind on the day. She glanced at her watch. Emma and Ellen would be in the air right now. She tried to ignore the flip of nerves in her gut as she considered the fact that she was all alone on this continent and had no idea how Gil would react to her return.

Walking past the Ocean Hotel, with the busy marina to the right, she made her way to Schnappa Rock, where she knew Nick and the team would mind her suitcase and let her phone Aropari from their landline. She hurried past the outside tables where families and divers sipped cool drinks in the sunshine and looked out over the water.

Dialling the number with a trembling finger, she held the receiver under her chin and waited. There was no reply.

'He's not there.' She spoke out loud.

'You looking for Gil?' Nick asked as he finished seating more hungry yachties desperate for the good organic fare.

'Yes.' She nodded.

'I think I saw him down at his boat as I came around the headland. Want me to drop you off?'

'Oh, Nick, thank you.' She smiled. 'That would

be great.'

As Nick's car bumped down the familiar track, she felt her heart race at the sight of Gil's truck sitting in its regular spot, under the shade of the Douglas fir.

'I can't thank you enough.' She smiled as she shut the car door behind her, and then watched as he reversed back up to the road.

Treading cautiously along the pebbled beach, she kept her eyes on Gil, who, oblivious, purposefully loaded his fishing gear into the back of his boat from the jetty. Tessa, his seafaring companion, sat alongside him.

'Gil!' she called.

He froze, immediately stopped what he was doing, then turned slowly towards the voice that had called him from the shore. He stared at her as she approached. She wished he would say something, do something!

She was almost upon him when he stepped down into the boat and began rummaging in his khaki and leather satchel. 'You'll be needing this.'

He tossed her his Northlands baseball cap, which she caught and placed on her head.

'There are dolphins in the bay. We need to hurry if we want to see them.'

He reached up and she took his hand, letting him help her down into the boat. And as he did so, she felt the spark travel up her arm and shudder through her body. The thunderbolt.

She took the seat next to him and sat back.

Gil started the engine, navigating his way out of the bay and past the marina to the left of them. Nick waved from in front of Schnappa Rock, as he parked up. Gil opened up the engine and they roared out into the deep water, heading in the direction of the Poor Knights.

'Look!' he called suddenly, pointing to the left of the boat.

Vivienne followed his arm until she saw them. She sat up tall in the chair and stared at the pod of dolphins cutting through the waves. 'There must be at least ten!' she shouted, captivated by their shiny, sleek skin, which seemed to glisten in the sun's rays. They dived one by one, coming out of the water, as if in slow motion and leaping high against the wide, bright blue sky, as the crystal droplets flew from their bodies.

'Oh, Gil!' She didn't realise she was crying until she tried to speak. 'It's the most beautiful thing I have ever seen.'

'All part of the everyday life of a sheep farmer in Tutukaka.' He smiled at her, turning the boat in an arc to loop back on the dolphins so they could watch them all over again.

'Welcome home, Viv.' He winked at her.

'Oh, Gil, I'm not staying for too long. I can't. I have to get back, this is just for Christmas,' she whispered.

'I know.' He smiled and leant in for a kiss. 'I know.'

Thirteen

Trev pulled Emma's rucksack from the back of his car and placed it by the front step of the little house in Mendip Road. He banged his hands together to try and ward off the December chill.

'You sure you're going to be okay?' Ellen hugged her tight.

'Yep, I'll be fine. I'm so tired, I'll probably just take Bob for a quick stroll and then crash out.' She dipped down and rubbed the silky fur of the dog she hadn't seen for four years. He'd gone from puppy to big boy in her absence. It had been almost comical, earlier, to see Pedro so upset at having to give up his houseguest. They had both clearly had a lovely time.

'Okay, well, look, you've got my number and if you need something or if anything is bothering you, just shout and I'll be round in my slippers in no time.'

'I will. I promise.' Emma nodded. 'God, it's so cold.' She zipped up the micro fleece that her mum had given her and rubbed her arms.

'Aaron's been in, checked things over and put the heating on, so the house will be toasty.' Ellen flicked her eyes across to the building.

'Thanks, Elle. See you tomorrow!' She waved and made her way inside.

Trev clicked his seatbelt and turned to his wife.

They were alone now for the first time since he'd collected them at Heathrow.

'I missed you.' He nodded as he started the engine.

'I missed you too, but not all the time, only a little bit of the time, when I remembered you. The rest of the time I was having too much fun.' She paused. 'Robbie okay? Still with this wife?' She sucked in her cheeks.

'You haven't been gone a fortnight!' He laughed.

'I know, love, but he's a fast worker.' She sighed.

'Oh, don't. I just want him to have what we've got. It's a lovely way to live.' He smiled at her.

'Good Lord, Trev, I'll have to go away more often.' She pulled her coat around her shoulders.

'And that's a bit of a turn-up, Viv not coming back with you.'

She nodded and looked out of the steamed-up window at the grey buildings of home. 'She'll be back soon enough.'

Trev pulled up outside their house and switched off the engine.

'Ah, home sweet home.' She turned to him. 'Are we getting out, or what? I'm desperate for a cuppa.'

He hesitated, pulled the key slowly from the ignition, jiggled the keys in his palm and coughed to clear his throat. 'I think that with Viv away, Elle, me and you should spend a bit more time together – you know, like go for a walk or go to the pictures or something.' He glanced at her, looking like the slight boy of thirty-odd years ago who had needed a drink just to get up the nerve to ask her to dance.

'What like a date?'

'If you like.' He blushed.

'I'd like that very much.'

'I sometimes think that for our whole lives we've been tied to the Lane family, and I know you and Viv are close, and I wouldn't want to change that for the world...' Ellen stared at him, unsure of where he was going with this. 'But when we were young, I was in Ray's shadow, he called the shots and I did his bidding. It wasn't a good friendship, not in hindsight. Then when he left, you felt responsible for Viv and you spent all your time with her, helping with the kids and whatnot–'

'She needed me to.'

'I know, I get it, and I'm not moaning. I'm not.' He raised his palm. 'I just think that it's about time we put Ellen and Trevor first. You and me.'

Ellen nodded and her response came in a quiet voice. 'All right then, Trev. You and me.'

He reached over and pulled her to him, kissing her gently on the mouth.

The text alert on her phone beeped. As Trev climbed from the car, Ellen reached for her phone.

The message was simple.

Make that two notches.

She replied instantly.

Tart. X

Emma flicked on the hall light and placed her rucksack by the radiator. The place was indeed toasty. She smiled at the prospect of being able to thank her big brother in person tomorrow. It would be lovely to see him. After the last few days she could suddenly care less about falling out with Lizzie. Life was just too short.

It wasn't the temperature, but the quiet that sent a shiver down her back. When the air was still and there was a hush all around, Tutukaka had felt like the closest thing to heaven, but here, in a house cluttered with things waiting to be used, crying out to be admired by people, it had the opposite effect. It made her feel lonely. She pictured her mum living here alone for the last four years and swallowed a wave of guilt that she hadn't called or written more often.

Emma tried to shrug it off – she'd only been in the house for five minutes and had yet to unpack.

She walked from room to room, putting on the lights and drawing the curtains. The first thing that struck her was the smell. It was a scent she had almost forgotten, the smell of her childhood: a mixture of books, food and the lingering perfume of the three generations of women who'd all lived under that roof. It was the scent of her family history and it was in the very fabric of the building; it sent a longing for childhood through her veins. She ran her fingers over the mantelpiece in the sitting room, cringing at and yet fascinated by the clusters of photos that had sat in the exact same spots for as long as she could remember.

Picking up one of herself in her mum's arms, she scrutinised it. Her mum looked so young and happy. She pictured herself coming home from school on so many nights and flopping down on the saggy sofa with the TV remote in her hand. She smiled at the ghost of her younger self who'd figured life would be so straightforward. She had imagined marrying a boy from up the road, moving into a house near her mum and having babies, lots of babies, and the idea had delighted her!

Staring at the photo of her mum, she whispered into the ether, 'I want to stop, Mum, I do. You are right, I'm tired of running in circles.'

Carefully placing the picture back in its spot, Emma went into the kitchen to pop the kettle on. The place was, as ever, neat and tidy, but worn. Everything had an age to it that in a certain light might be mistaken for grubbiness: the scoured circles on the top of the stove, the cracked sealant around the big window and the marbling on the old lino from a thousand sploshes and spills. It was, however, far from crappy. It was home.

With Bob following at her heels, she took the big mug of tea into her palm and sat down on the bottom stair, having quite forgotten the joy of sipping a hot cup of tea in a cold climate. Pulling the telephone on its curly cord into her lap, she unfurled the piece of paper from her pocket and dialled the long, unfamiliar number.

She cleared her throat and sat up straight, waiting. Finally it connected, emitting the instantly identifiable ringtone of a foreign country. It rang and rang.

'I'll give it five more rings, Bob.' She counted in her head. *One... Two... Three...* And just as she was deciding on the best message to leave on the answerphone, someone picked up.

'Hello?' The male voice sounded young and impatient.

'Oh, hi!' She smiled, happy to have got through. 'Can I speak to Ray, please?' she chirped.

There was a slight delay on the line.

'No, sorry, you can't. It's just gone midnight.'

'Oh God.' She closed her eyes, cringing. 'I forgot the time difference. I'm used to phoning from Auckland and I forgot. Did I wake everyone up?' She realised that she was probably speaking to her brother.

'No, you're good. I'm a friend of his son's. Ray's out with his daughter – they went for dinner and a late movie. Can I take a message?'

Emma tried to hold the phone steady. She tried to picture what it might be like to have a dad who would take you out for supper and then a film. A dad who was around...

'Hello? Can I take a message?' the voice asked again.

'No. I'm sorry to have bothered you.' She slowly put the phone back in its cradle and set it on the floor.

She sat there just long enough to finish her mug of tea and for her bum to go numb, when a knock on the door roused her. She twisted the unfamiliar lock to find Shaun Lewis standing on the doorstep with his hands jammed into the pockets of his jacket.

'All right, Em?' He spoke as if he had seen her yesterday and not four years ago, when she was last home.

'All right, Shaun?'

'Bloody cold, innit?' He shivered.

She nodded. Yes, it was.

'Thought you were off in New Zealand, getting married?' his tone was matter of fact.

'I was, but it didn't really work out.'

'Bummer.' He sniffed.

'Yep, bummer.'

'Your mum not here?' He peered past her, towards the kitchen. 'My mum wants to know if she's got any mixed peel. I don't even know what that is to be honest.' He shook his head and jogged on the spot to keep warm.

'No, she's not, and I wouldn't know where to look.' She shook her head, as her tears gathered and spilled down her cheeks.

'What you crying for?' He grimaced.

She shrugged her shoulders and wiped her nose. 'Lots of things,' she whispered.

'Well, it's nearly Christmas, so you can cut that out for a start.' He sniffed. 'Fancy a lunchtime pint up the Rising Sun?'

Emma sighed and grabbed her mum's old jacket from the back of the door. A pint in the pub sounded like a plan.

'Why not.' She bent down and spoke to Bob. 'I'm nipping out, Bob, but I shan't be long. See you in a bit. Be a good boy.'

She closed the door behind her and linked arms with Shaun, as they walked up Mendip Road heading towards Cotswold Road.

'You had a nice time away, then?' Shaun asked casually.

'I've been gone four years, Shaun, that's a big deal, it's not just time away, that makes it sound like a holiday. I've been travelling.'

'Four years, blimey, that's a long time. I'd get bored. Didn't you want to arrive?'

'What do you mean?' She looked up at him.

'Well, four years of travelling, that's like going round in circles, isn't it? Reckon it's about time someone got their arse into gear and got a job.'

Emma laughed out loud. 'Did my mum tell you to say that?'

'No!' He laughed too, although he wasn't sure what they were laughing at. It felt good nonetheless. They walked speedily along the pavement.

'Sorry to hear about you and Nat.' She squeezed his arm. 'I liked her.'

'Ah well, Nat's a good girl and all that, but she wasn't for me.'

'You don't sound too upset about it all, Shaun. If you don't mind me saying.'

He stopped walking and looked at the girl who had been his friend since primary school. 'That's because, as I have always told you, thing have a habit of turning out right in the end.'

Emma smiled at him and hoped that this was true.

'Malago's frozen. Means we don't need to go and dig out the skateboard. I dare you to walk on it!' He nodded towards the twist of river just out of sight.

Emma paused and looked at Shaun.

'I will if you will.' She glanced to the left, planning her route.

'You're on.'

With that, she ran across the road and into St John's Burial Ground, across the grass and down the bank, chased by Shaun, and screaming as she went.

Ellen shivered. It was a cold day. The frost had hardened on the pavements and everyone was bundled into layers, walking with their heads pulled into their shoulders, neckless, hoping that this might increase their temperature by a couple of degrees. She rang the doorbell of the house in Mendip Road and was surprised when Shaun Lewis opened the front door. 'All right, Mrs Nye?'

'Not bad, Shaun, you?' she asked, as she walked into the familiar hallway.

'Elle!' Emma called from the kitchen. 'Look, I've put all the little foil trees out. I found them in the loft and we're sorting the fairy lights. We're making Santa's Grotto in the front room, Shaun's helping me with the sign.'

He held up a marker pen, as if proof of his role was required. Ellen smiled at the way Emma had roped Shaun into her plan. She smiled; it was obvious that the boy didn't mind her crazy. The radio was turned up, the lamps were on and Bob was sprawled on the rug in front of the fire. Ellen tried to remember the last time the house had felt so alive and figured it was when they were in their teens, getting ready to go out of a Saturday night, with Viv's mum in the kitchen cooking supper and her dad in his chair, with the telly blaring in the front room.

'I only popped in to see how you were doing?' She felt a wave of emotion at being inside this house without her best friend in it. She didn't like it one bit.

'I'm doing great. Aaron and Lizzie and her parents are coming over for Boxing Day, please tell me you and Trev and Robbie and everyone can make it too? I am making homemade sausage rolls and I am stealing your eggnog recipe. Might even do a trifle.'

'We'll be here love, don't you worry.' Ellen smiled. 'Heard from your mum?'

'I had a text the day before yesterday, but truthfully, Elle, I've been so busy since we got back, time's flying. We went to listen to the carol singers yesterday outside Asda, it was lovely, got me in the mood.' She gave a little shimmy.

'Well, good for you. Anyway I'm not staying, only wanted to check on you.' She felt as if she was gatecrashing.

'No, don't go, please stay and have a cup of tea!' Emma pleaded.

'I can't love, got to get back to Trev, maybe tomorrow.'

'Yes, come and knock for me and we can take Bob for a wander.'

'Will do.'

Ellen let herself out of the house and walked the familiar route to Pedro's without any great sense of urgency. It didn't feel the same.

She pushed open the door and took up her seat with her back to the window, but a couple of minutes later she moved to Vivienne's seat opposite, with a view out on to the street. It gave her some comfort to be sitting in her friend's chair and to know Vivienne would be back in her rightful place again soon. Her return home couldn't come soon enough. Ellen missed her dreadfully. There were a dozen times in the day when she thought of something she wanted to share, something that only her best friend would truly appreciate.

'Hey, Ellen!' Pedro swanned over to the table with his tea towel tucked into his Christmas apron. 'What do you think?' He plucked the fabric, showing her the garish picture of a fat Santa holding a cup of coffee.

'Very you,' she said.

'How's Bob? I do miss him. It was lovely having that little fella around.'

'He's great, keeping an eye on Emma. He'll be glad to have Viv home.' She nodded.

'Bet he's not the only one. You look like you lost a quid and found a penny.'

She smiled. That was exactly how she felt.

'I know what will cheer you up – a nice latte and a toasted teacake. What do you say?' he smiled.

Ellen wasn't used to feeling so melancholy. 'Actually, Pedro, I've changed my mind. I think I'll just go home. See you soon, though. Thanks, love.'

She stood up and bustled her way between the tables and back out into the cold. The thought of sitting alone at their table and watching the world go by was more than she could bear.

'All right, Elle?' Mr Figgis waved from the other side of the street. She waved back. 'Where's your mate?' he asked, looking up and down the road to see if she was close by.

'She's ... she's on her way, be back soon!' She tried to sound bright, as she hurried home, hoping she wouldn't bump into anyone else en route.

As she placed her key in the front door, she heard Vivienne's voice coming from the kitchen and her heart leapt. Beaming, she shrugged her arms from her coat and unwound the scarf from her neck. She was back, the dark horse! Chatting to Trev! Her heart swelled with happiness, how she had missed her.

She hung her coat on the hook by the door and was hurrying down the hall when Trev shouted out to her. 'Elle! Quick! It's Viv on Skype. She's only just called, come on!'

Ellen's heart sank. The disappointment was huge. She had thought the wait was over. She walked in and stood behind her husband, resting her hand on his shoulder and listening. She bent low and gave her friend a small wave. She could see the darkness through the window and did the calculations: it would be half ten at night. Vivienne was wearing a soft tunic, one they'd picked up in Primark only weeks ago. It felt like a lot longer. The windows and doors were all open. Ellen knew it would still be hot and as she briefly closed her eyes, she caught the scent of hydrangeas, as her memory played a trick on her. It was, as ever, intoxicating.

Vivienne was sitting at the breakfast table in the vast kitchen at Aropari. She bent her head, as if peering into the camera and gave a small wave back to Ellen, who had come into the room and was now standing behind her husband. Trevor showed no sign of shifting from his seat. Not just yet.

'Well, good for you, girl. Good for you. That's a turn-up for the books! It's a bit of a shock, but I do understand.' He chuckled.

Vivienne tried to gauge Ellen's expression. She hadn't had a chance to talk to her yet, and Trev was rather robbing her of the moment.

'I should have said this a long time ago, Viv,' he said, 'but I'm sorry.'

'Don't be daft. What are you sorry for?' Vivienne lowered her voice. Despite the slight flickering on the screen, she could see his pained expression, his hesitation. He looked to the side, avoiding her gaze. 'I knew Ray was up to no good.'

'With Suzanne, you mean?'

He nodded. 'And others.'

'I guessed as much. Not at the time, of course – I didn't want to think about it then – but I've had a lot of opportunity to think about it since. I was quite naive.'

'Not naive, Viv. Lovely. You were lovely and he was a shit and he didn't deserve you.' He swallowed. 'I fell out with him long before he went, argued with him, told him he was an idiot, but he didn't listen to me, didn't listen to anyone.'

'Thank you for that Trev.' She shrugged. 'And for what it's worth, I don't blame you, not in any way. I did a bit, maybe, for a while, and I'm sorry for that.' She rubbed her face. 'What a carry-on.'

'Yep.' It was that.

'I suppose Elle's told you all about him pitching up here as if there was nothing amiss.'

'She did.' He nodded.

'Hey ho.' She sighed. 'You know, it was all a very long time ago. I think it's time we all moved on, no hard feelings. Look after my mate for me, won't you?'

'Always.' He smiled and slid from the chair so that Ellen could sit down.

Vivienne watched him creep from the room and close the kitchen door behind him.

And there she was, her best friend, filling the

screen. Sitting in the kitchen that she knew so well, as familiar to her as her own. In the background she spied cups that she'd drunk coffee from and then popped into the dishwasher on countless occasions. On the fridge sat a magnet saying *Bring me chocolate and no one will get hurt* that she'd picked up as a gift for Ellen when they were in Morecambe. It was a weird feeling to have Ellen beamed into the kitchen of Aropari, all the way from her hometown, three streets from where she'd grown up and over eleven thousand miles from where she was now.

Vivienne had told herself to be strong and to stay calm, but at the sight of her friend her resolve melted. Her sob came instantly and powerfully, knocking the air from her lungs and leaving her breathless. Her tears fogged her vision and made her nose run. There was the unmistakeable sound of identical sobbing, carried across the oceans to where she sat.

The two women stared at each other, separated for the first time since they were children.

Vivienne shifted closer to the screen and, lifting her hand, she placed her palm flat against the screen. Ellen did the same and there they sat, with fingertips separated by ten millimetres of technology. Rivers of tears snaked down their faces and their breath came in stuttered starts, as they sat there without saying anything, both trying to process their immeasurable sense of loss.

Ellen knew what was happening. Vivienne didn't have to speak and she didn't have to ask. If she was honest, she had known it was going to happen from that moment on the kerb outside the airport when her best friend had confidently strolled towards the bus stop, as if walking towards a brighter future. She opened her mouth, but the gulping sobs robbed her of breath and the ability to speak.

They sat like this for some minutes, until eventually, almost spent, they both ferreted around for kitchen roll and blew their noses and wiped their eyes.

'Merry Christmas, Viv,' Ellen managed.

'Merry Christmas, Elle.' Her words were faint.

Both felt the next sob building in their chests, blocking their throats and misting their eyes.

'Goodbye, Viv.'

'Goodbye, my Elle.'

Fourteen

One year later

Handing him a glass of wine, Vivienne watched as Gil rummaged on the shelves of the fridge for snacks to take out to the deck. She pushed open the sliding glass door that led out to the terrace, smiling at the view that greeted her, wondering if she would ever get sick of it, and feeling smug, knowing that she wouldn't. To watch the seasonal shifts in the landscape of Tutukaka had been her greatest joy, and now it was summer and the green lawn was edged once again with magnificent hydrangeas. The little goat bleated at the sight of her and trotted on the grass, leaping with joy.

She knew exactly how he felt.

Seabirds swooped and called, as the sun prepared to sink below the horizon, bathing everything in a pinkish glow. There were no tall buildings, no traffic, and the air was indeed like nectar. A gentle breeze ruffled the leaves. This sound of nature chattering was the sweetest music. It was heaven. Perfect, quiet and peaceful.

Gil frowned at his fiancée. 'What are you thinking?' he asked.

'Just how lucky I am.' She sipped her wine, leaning on the doorframe.

A loud woof came from the corridor; it seemed that Bob was disgruntled about something. She walked into the hallway. Her breath still caught in her throat at the sight of the towering Christmas tree, laden with red and gold baubles and other trinkets that filled the cathedral-like space with its grand presence. The numerous strings of fairy lights that she and Gil had spent a whole day draping meticulously over the sharp branches twinkled in the low evening light. The effect was stunning.

She stooped to chat to Bob, as Tessa nuzzled him in the side. Even though he'd been with her in Tutukaka for almost ten months now, fully microchipped and with his own passport, he was still a little wary of Tessa's funny foreign ways. 'Is she annoying you again, Bob? She loves you, that's the thing, fella and she just wants to snuggle. And I can't blame her, you are utterly gorgeous!' He placed his nose on his paws and ignored the compliment. 'Hang in there, Tess, you lovely girl. He'll come around.' She winked.

Vivienne loved this time of day. After many

hours spent working at her new cottage-industry business, spinning and dyeing the wool from which she made garments fit to be branded with the Aropari label, she looked forward to the evenings the most. This was when she and Gil took to the deck, watched the sun go down and sat arm in arm on the sofa, nattering about nothing much in particular. When it rained, they sat in the kitchen and watched the water splashing on the terrace; when cold, they retired to the sitting room and threw a couple of logs on the fire, toasting their bodies in front of the flames as they sprawled on the sofa. And when called for, Gil fetched her socks from the laundry room and popped them over her chilly toes.

Gil patted the space next to him on the sofa and she wandered over, slotted in and nestled next to him, with her feet curled under her.

'I can't believe my bestie's coming over and she's already in full planning mode.' She hunched her shoulders in excitement.

'God help us all,' Gil said. 'A lot's happened since she was last here.'

'It has.' She thought about that fateful trip twelve months earlier. And for the first time in a long time she thought about Ray and how he had appeared, as if magicked from thin air. She was grateful, however, for the speedy, no-nonsense divorce that had been granted. These days she rarely thought about him, apart from when Emma or Aaron mentioned their sporadic and ever dwindling contact with him. He had enquired as to whether Michael or Gil might like to invest in his business but they had declined to respond. She was hurt on their behalf – her two wonderful kids definitely deserved more – but it was no surprise.

It was hard for her to picture the person she had been, so shy in front of strangers and often too nervous to let the words that rumbled in her throat find their way out of her mouth. The best thing about her new life, apart from residing in such a beautiful setting with a man she loved and her beloved Bob by her side, was the feeling of contentment. Her dreams had come true; she was part of a happy family, and that was all she had ever wanted. She could live without fear for her future. It was bliss.

'I can't believe everyone's arriving tomorrow! This is our last peaceful evening for a while. We need to make the most of it.'

'You can't fool me – you actually can't wait, can you?' He hugged her tight.

'Oh, Gil, you're right, I can't! I'm so excited!'

He kissed her head.

Vivienne had posted the invitations a couple of months ago. When she dropped them off at the post office on a bright spring day, she'd pictured Ellen yawning, as she trod the stairs in her bathrobe and stooped low to gather the pale grey envelope from the coconut welcome mat. The postmark would reveal that it was from New Zealand and she could almost hear the squeal of her friend's excitement.

True to form, it was a mere twenty minutes after Ellen had ripped open the envelope that Vivienne's phone had rung in the kitchen at Tutukaka.

'One thousand, six hundred quid, plus a six-hour stopover in Hong Kong, what do you reckon?'

'I reckon book it, book it now!' She laughed.

'All right, give me a chance, haven't had my cuppa yet.' She tutted and put the phone down. There was no need to say goodbye, that wasn't their way, not when they would be chatting or seeing each other again so soon.

Gil had walked into the kitchen in his standard-issue jeans and denim shirt with the sleeves rolled above the elbow. 'Who was that on the phone, love?' he asked, after casually planting a kiss on her cheek as he passed by on the way to the study.

'Only Elle. She's booking tickets for her and Trev.' Vivienne returned to the task of uncorking the cold bottle of white wine.

'Ah, great.' He winked. 'We'd better get extra cake in.'

The time had flown and here they were: the house shone, food had been bought, flowers prepped, beds made and her frock was ready. All they needed were the guests.

'Are we mad, getting married on Christmas Day? Like we won't have enough to deal with.' He stroked her hair.

'I think it's a bit late to worry about it now,' she said. 'The key is not to stress about it. It'll all just happen and there'll be plenty of people around to do their bit. What can possibly go wrong?' She shook her head, thinking of the last wedding that had been organised on that very spot.

'I love you, Mrs McKinley.' They both liked the sound of that.

'Stop it! That's bad luck. I won't be Mrs

McKinley for another four days, and after that you can say it as much as you like.'

She lay back with her head resting on his arm and closed her eyes; a little nap about now was always good.

The sound of a horn beeping roused her. 'What's that?' She sat up, unsure of how long she'd drifted off for.

'Someone on the front drive, probably a delivery. I'll go.' He stood up.

'I'll come with you. We can't be storing things just any old where, and I don't want you messing up my plan.'

She took his hand and they walked across the lawn, into the kitchen and out the other side of the house. Gil had just touched his hand to the front door when Vivienne peeked through it. Her hand flew to her mouth and her tears sprang.

'Oh God! Oh, Gil!'

The two women ran towards each other, holding each other tight and not wanting to let go. It was some seconds before they spoke, easing their grip as they did so.

'Elle,' she breathed, 'you look lovely.'

'Primark.' Her friend sniffed on her shoulder, plucking at her frock. 'Seven ninety-nine.'

They moved apart and stared at each other, laughing.

'I missed you so much,' Vivienne said.

'That's funny, because I've barely given you a second thought.' Ellen sighed before they both erupted into giggles again. 'Actually, don't make me laugh, I haven't had a loo stop since Whangarei and I'm desperate.'

'You're a day early! We weren't expecting you until tomorrow.' She giggled.

'I got in a muddle. I can't be doing with all these time and date changes, it only confuses me.' Ellen waved her hand, dismissing this minor detail. 'Gil, you little best-friend stealer, this is my husband, Trev. Trev, this is the one I told you about, got us over here on false pretences and nicked my mate.'

'It's lovely to see you too, Elle.' He swept her up in a hug.

'Be nice to me.' She pointed at him. 'I am the chief bridesmaid, after all.'

'Are you?'

'You are?' Vivienne and Gil asked at the same time.

'Yes, I've decided.' Ellen gave a nod. 'I've bought those plastic flowers back out, thought I could finally put them to good use.'

Trevor stepped forward, a little overwhelmed by the incredible property he found himself in front of, and by the fact that the three of them were already well acquainted. He held out his hand. 'Hello, Gil. Good to meet you at last.'

'And you, Trev. You a fishing man?' he asked.

'I've been known to dabble, caught a decent pike once in the quarry not far from us.'

'Ah, you'll love a bit of sea fishing then. Maybe I can take you out?'

'I'd love that.' Trev rubbed his hands together.

'Great. Fancy a beer?'

'Do I ever! It's been a long journey.' He jerked his head towards his wife.

The two men sloped off to the kitchen. Finally, Vivienne knew what it felt like to be part of a foursome, to have her man larking around and joining in the banter. And it felt lovely.

'I have got so much to tell you!' Ellen roared, as comfortable as if it was twelve minutes ago that they'd last seen each rather than twelve months. 'You'll never believe what I found out.'

'What?' Vivienne leant forward.

'You'll have to wait; I really need that loo. Don't worry, I know where it is. Am I in my old room?' she yelled as she ran ahead.

'I hope you were sat on a towel in that hire car,' Vivienne called after her.

Ellen reappeared with her skirt bunched into her hand. 'You can talk, you're the one who had to wear Nicola Brown's gym knickers.' And she disappeared back inside the house.

'For the love of God, how many times? It was Ribena!' she called out, beaming and so, so happy to have her friend close.

With the arrival of the first guests, Aropari burst into life. Gil hit the music and there was a party-like atmosphere about the place. The four spent an unforgettable evening sitting on the deck, drinking in the view and catching up.

They were up bright and early the next day. Gil set off in a borrowed minibus and returned over six hours later with Aaron and Lizzie, and their baby daughter, Frankie and Emma and Shaun. For Vivienne, seeing her ever-growing brood piling out of the minibus was something very special. She clapped her hands and jumped up and down on the spot in excitement.

'Hello, hello!' She ran forward, kissing her kids and her daughter-in-law and Shaun Lewis, the boy who lived up the road and who had made Emma the happiest she had ever seen her. She was unable to stop herself from scooping baby Frankie into her arms and kissing her little face. The tiny girl reached up and tried to grab her grandma's hair.

'She's such a pretty girl! And she's grown, look at her!' It was one thing to have seen her weekly over Skype, and to receive Elle's updates, but to hold her grandchild in her arms was quite another. She held her close, inhaling the scent of her.

'This is some place, Mum.' Aaron turned a full circle, taking in the view.

'It is, my darling. And you know you are all welcome any time and for as long as you like – there's plenty of room! I can't believe you are all here; it's like a dream. I have missed you so much.' She cursed the tears that she couldn't prevent from falling. Frankie started to bawl.

'Oh God!' Lizzie sighed, running her hand through her dishevelled hair. Vivienne noticed the little pile of sick smudged on the shoulder of her blouse. 'Please don't cry, Frankie! I tried to comfort her on the plane. She's a little unsettled.' She and Lizzie had grown close via their weekly Skype chats and giving birth to the first grandchild, gave Lizzie a special place in the heart of the family that she relished.

Vivienne wrapped her free arm around her. 'Lizzie, you are the best mum, ever, look at this baby! She's perfect. You are doing a great job.'

She kissed her cheek. Aaron beamed.

Gil stepped forward and took the little girl into his arms. 'It's okay, Frankie, I've got you.' He cradled her close. 'There we go, little Frankie, Grandpa Gil's got you. There's no need to cry, life's too short for crying. Come and look at the view – if that doesn't make you feel good, nothing will. Reckon you've got farming hands there...' His soothing tone seemed to do the trick. Frankie stopped crying.

'He's a natural.' Emma smiled as she stepped into her mum's arms. They stood there, holding each other tight. 'It's so good to be back,' she murmured.

'I missed you.' Vivienne kissed her.

'I missed you, when I wasn't redecorating the house or working as Shaun's favourite receptionist at the garage.'

'Oi, firstly, I did most of the redecorating and secondly I'd like to sack her,' he informed Vivienne, 'she's rubbish at the job, but she won't let me, turns up day after day. I can't shake her off!' He was a cheeky boy that Shaun Lewis. Emma thumped him playfully on the arm.

Vivienne was glad that they were making the little house in Mendip Road their own. 'How's your mum, Shaun?' she asked.

'Sound. Sends you her best.'

Vivienne smiled. She had always liked Mrs Lewis.

'Shaun, come and grab a beer!' Gil called from the kitchen.

Vivienne watched him walk into the house.

'Are you all set then?' Emma asked.

'I think so.' She paused. 'This doesn't feel too weird?' Vivienne checked her child's expression, knowing she wouldn't be able to hide the truth.

'What, that my would be father-in-law is about to become my actual stepdad and my ex-fiancé, who will be my step-brother, is pitching up any day now to celebrate by my side on the exact spot where we were to be married, while I'm here with my new man?' She shook her head. 'Nah, it's fine, Mum.'

They both chuckled.

'When is Michael getting here, anyway?' Emma asked casually.

'Not until Christmas Day. He's working.'

'Of course he is.' She smiled. 'Do you see him much?'

'Maybe once a month.' She held her daughter's gaze.

'Can I ask you something?' Emma bit her nail.

'Of course!'

'Now you've got to know him, maybe better than I ever did, can you see me being married to him?'

She thought about how best to phrase her response. 'I *have* got to know him and I am fond of him, but as a life partner for you? Not in a million years.'

They both resumed their hug, thinking about what might so easily have been.

'I think he might have clipped your wings, Em.'

'I think I might need them clipping sometimes,' she whispered.

'Never.' Vivienne held her tight. 'Are you happy?'

'Oh, Mum, happier than I ever thought possible. I've found where I want to be.'

'Mendip Road, Bedminster?'

'No,' she shook her head. 'Next to Shaun.'

'He's a good man.'

'He is,' Emma smiled, 'and I'm hoping he's going to be a good dad, too.' She took her mum's hand and placed it on the slight swell of her stomach.

Vivienne placed her hand over her mouth, as she cried, 'Really?' It was the most wonderful news.

'Yes, really.' She beamed. 'I'm thirteen weeks pregnant.'

'Oh you clever, clever girl!'

It was a beautiful summer's day, Christmas Day. Ellen and Emma took turns styling Vivienne's hair and applying her minimal make-up. The wedding was to be a mainly family affair, but Nick and the team from Schnappa Rock, who were part catering the event, were all invited, as were Aropari's neighbours, whose land bordered theirs and whose friendship Vivienne and Gil had come to value over the last year.

They had agreed to exchange their Christmas gifts that evening. It was to be both a wedding and a Christmas celebration, with chilled sparkling Kiwi wine flowing freely, exquisite canapés served on round platters and, quite incongruously, carols on the stereo.

The vast wooden table had been positioned on the main terrace at the back of the house and was draped with starched white linen and white-cushioned garden chairs. At each place setting were a set of sparkling crystal glasses, a pale rose-coloured linen napkin and a shallow glass bud-vase filled with sprigs of gypsophila and a single frond of berried spruce in a nod to the season.

'There you are Michael! Happy Christmas, love.' Vivienne jumped up from in front of the mirror and gave her stepson a hug. He had made an effort and looked lovely in a cream linen shirt and dark trousers; he was still, however, in his jandals. 'You must be exhausted. Long shifts?'

'Yes, but I wouldn't have missed today, not for anything.' He shuffled his feet, a little nervous. 'I am so glad Dad is happy. And it's down to you.'

Vivienne patted his arm. His words were generous and heartfelt. 'Oh thank you, Michael. I think it's going to be a right old day for tears and if I start now, there'll be no stopping me.' She waved her hand in front of her face, trying to stop the slide of her make-up.

'Hey, Em.' He walked over to where Emma stood with a powder brush in her hand and the two exchanged a sincere, lingering hug.

'Hey, you.' She smiled.

'Are we good?' he asked, shyly.

'We were always good, Michael, good mates.'

'Yep.' He nodded.

Ellen and Vivienne exchanged a look and Ellen started singing under her breath. 'If you like pina colada...'

Michael gave Ellen a wary look. 'I better go see the old man.' He indicated with his thumb and left them to it.

'Elle!'

'What?' She laughed.

As the sun dipped in the late afternoon, Vivienne

slipped into her dress. The simple cream-linen shift skimmed her slim figure and over her arms she draped the pale pink, silk pashmina she'd picked up on that memorable day in Stanley Market.

'Oh! Look at you!' Ellen, the chief bridesmaid, was unable to contain herself. 'My beautiful best friend. I am so proud of you.'

'I'm proud of you too.' She managed with a catch in her throat.

Vivienne beamed at her, before taking Aaron's arm and walking slowly out into the garden, towards the deck where the registrar stood. The whole space was edged with vintage terracotta flowerpots tied with natural raffia, crowded with semi-dried blue and pink hydrangeas with fresh two-tone roses dotted throughout the display, a stunning variety with large creamy-coloured centres and delicate petals edged in dusky pink. Sprigs of eucalyptus, rosemary and thyme not only gave the centrepieces height and much needed splashes of green, but the scent was intoxicating. The whole effect was stunning.

Gil looked great in his pale suit and open-neck shirt, if a little nervous. His hands fidgeted, trying to find the right position.

He reached out and helped her climb onto the raised deck. As their hands joined, she felt it once again – the thunderbolt.

Standing on the deck with the sun shining overhead, casting its golden rays over Aropari, Vivienne took a deep lungful of Tutukaka air, in the magical place that she now called home. It was a world away from where her story had started on the sloping banks of the Malago River.

As she prepared to marry the man she loved, with all the people who loved her standing close by, Vivienne knew it was time to stop hiding from the world, time to stop being afraid. She had finally chosen to live a different life, one where she valued her own happiness.

The registrar's words rang around the garden.

'Will you love her and treasure her for the rest of your days?'

'I will, every day.' Gil squeezed her hands that sat neatly inside his own.

'And will you love him and treasure him for the rest of your days?'

'I will,' Vivienne managed with tears in her eyes, 'cross my heart.'

Author's Note

I Won't Be Home for Christmas is a work of fiction and I have taken the liberty of stretching (if not snapping!) the rules and laws when it comes to the length of stay that a visitor visa to the country would normally permit. For all visa and visitor entry requirements please visit: www.immigration.govt.nz before planning any trip.

Thank you x

Hello lovely reader,

Thank you for reading my novel – I hope you enjoyed it.

It's both nerve-racking and exciting for me when a new book is published. There's very little you can do, other than watch it drift out towards the horizon and wait to see how it is received. So, if you have time, please take a minute to write a review of this book or share it on social media @MrsAmandaProwse. Hearing your thoughts would make me very, very happy!

I write stories for a wide and varied audience and I sincerely hope that my characters are ones that you would like to take for a coffee and get to know. Some of these characters have terrible secrets, some of them have to face great adversity, some pull through, some don't, but each and every one of them is confronting challenges that people like us face every day.

I invite you to join my online community and sign up to my magazine at www.amandaprowse.org. Here you can put your feet up, grab a cuppa and enjoy exclusive stories, special offers, events, competitions and much more.

With love and thanks
Amanda x

The publishers hope that this book has given you enjoyable reading. Large Print Books are especially designed to be as easy to see and hold as possible. If you wish a complete list of our books please ask at your local library or write directly to:

Magna Large Print Books
Magna House, Long Preston,
Skipton, North Yorkshire.
BD23 4ND

This Large Print Book for the partially sighted, who cannot read normal print, is published under the auspices of

THE ULVERSCROFT FOUNDATION

THE ULVERSCROFT FOUNDATION

... we hope that you have enjoyed this Large Print Book. Please think for a moment about those people who have worse eyesight problems than you ... and are unable to even read or enjoy Large Print, without great difficulty.

You can help them by sending a donation, large or small to:

The Ulverscroft Foundation, 1, The Green, Bradgate Road, Anstey, Leicestershire, LE7 7FU, England.
or request a copy of our brochure for more details.

The Foundation will use all your help to assist those people who are handicapped by various sight problems and need special attention.

Thank you very much for your help.

(

- 9